A WEDDING

AND

A KILLING

A MAC FARADAY MYSTERY

BY
LAUREN CARR

A WEDDING AND A KILLING

Designed by Acorn Book Services

Publication Managed by Acorn Book Services
www.acornbookservices.com
acornbookservices@gmail.com
304-995-1295

Cover designed by Todd Aune
Spokane, Washington
www.projetoonline.com
Candle Cover Image provided by Halfpoint@fotolia.com

ISBN-10: 0989180441
ISBN-13: 978-0-9891804-4-3

Published in the United States of America

To My Brothers and Sisters in Christ

A WEDDING

AND

A KILLING

A MAC FARADAY MYSTERY

Cast of Characters

(in order of appearance)

Jason Fairbanks: Murder victim in New York.

Mrs. Tuyon Weber: Fairbanks' next door neighbor.

David O'Callaghan: Spencer police chief. Son of the late police chief, Patrick O'Callaghan. Mac Faraday's best friend and half-brother.

Chelsea Adams: Paralegal for Ben Fleming. First and current love of David O'Callaghan. Suffering from epilepsy, she has Molly, a service dog trained to sense and warn of seizures.

Molly: White German Shepherd. Chelsea Adams' service dog.

Ben Fleming: Garrett County prosecuting attorney. He's one of the good guys.

Senator Catherine Fleming: Ben Fleming's wife. United States Senator from Maryland.

Mac Faraday: Retired homicide detective. On the day his divorce became final, he inherited $270 million and an estate on Deep Creek Lake from his birth mother, Robin Spencer.

Archie Monday: Former editor and research assistant to world-famous mystery author Robin Spencer. She is now Mac Faraday's lady love.

Gnarly: German shepherd. One-hundred pounds of fur, claws, and teeth. The only K-9 dishonorably discharged from the United States Army. Don't ask them why. It's classified and they refuse to talk about it.

Robin Spencer: Mac Faraday's late birth mother and world-famous mystery author. As an unwed and pregnant teenager, she gave him up for adoption. Her ancestors founded Spencer, Maryland, located on the shore of Deep Creek Lake, a resort area in Western Maryland.

Police Chief Patrick O'Callaghan: David's late father. Spencer's legendary police chief. The love of Robin Spencer's life and Mac Faraday's birth father.

Deputy Chief Arthur Bogart (Bogie): Spencer's Deputy Police Chief. David's godfather. Don't let his gray hair and weathered face fool you.

Reverend Deborah Hess: Pastor at Spencer Church, located on the shore of Deep Creek Lake. Over a hundred years old, the church was started by the Mac Faraday's ancestors.

Eugene Newton: Chief Trustee at Spencer Church. Murder victim.

Ruth Buchanan: Caretaker for Spencer Church. Lives in caretaker's cottage next door.

Edna Parker: Office Manager at Spencer Church.

Chip Van Dorn: Murder suspect.

Helga Thorpe: Trustee at Spencer Church. Business manager at Thorpe Sporting Goods and Boat Rentals in McHenry, which has been in business for fifty years.

Officer Nathan Brewster: Spencer Police Officer.

Natalie Buchanan: Ruth's teenaged daughter.

Chase Hess: Deborah's daughter.

Sirrus Thorpe: Helga's husband. Owner of Thorpe Sporting Goods and Boat Rentals.

Carmine Romano: Trustee at Spencer Church. Owner of Carmine's Pizza.

Tonya: Desk Sergeant at Spencer Police Department.

Ed Willingham: Mac Faraday's lawyer.

Marilyn Newton: Eugene Newton's widow and murder suspect. She bought twenty gallons of gasoline, a pig, and booked a cruise to Hawaii the day after her husband's murder.

Bill Clark: Member of Spencer's town council. Marilyn Newton calls him Twerpie. He wants David O'Callaghan fired.

Reese Fairbanks: Jason Fairbanks' father.

Jenny Fairbanks: Jason Fairbanks' mother.

Winston Hawkins: County Prosecutor in upstate New York where Jason Fairbanks was murdered.

Sheriff Quinton Nichols: Sheriff who investigated Jason Fairbanks' murder in New York.

Sid Delaney: FBI Special Agent.

Portia Hagar: Jason Fairbanks' mistress.

Deputy Guy Stacey: Sheriff's Deputy in New York. Did things go too far when he decided to take the law into his own hands?

Fire and swords are slow engines of destruction, compared to the tongue of a Gossip.
Sir Richard Steele, Irish Writer and Politician

PROLOGUE

Catskill Mountains, New York: Seven Years Ago

"Dad's home!"

In most homes, such an announcement from a ten-year-old girl of her father's arrival would cause sounds of joy. The mother would smile in anticipation. The children would maybe squeal in delight.

In contrast, upon seeing her father's red Jaguar pull into the driveway and make its way to the garage, Holly Fairbanks shrieked and ran into the foyer to help her mother, who almost fell in her haste to carry a heavy suitcase down the stairs.

"What are we going to do?" Holly fought the tears that were making their way to her eyes.

Scarlett Fairbanks shoved the suitcase at her daughter. "Go out through the French doors and around the house. Make sure your father doesn't see you. Get in the car and don't come back in. No matter what happens." She thrust a cell phone into her daughter's hand. "If anything happens and

I don't make it out, call Madame X. Her phone number is the only contact on this phone. Tell her what happened and she'll help you."

They both turned to the kitchen door at the sound of the garage door opening on the other side.

"Hurry," Scarlett hissed while pushing her daughter toward the French doors leading to the spacious backyard at the foot of the Adirondack Mountains. "Go now. Go!"

Scurrying as fast as she could, Holly went outside and dragged the suitcase behind the shrubbery to the driveway where their SUV was parked.

Scarlett smoothed her long chestnut-colored hair with her hand and sucked in a deep breath to calm her frazzled nerves. *Calm. I must remain calm. It's almost over.*

Trying to appear as casual as possible, she made her way into the kitchen where her purse rested on the table in the breakfast nook. Reaching into the front compartment, she rested her hand on the thirty-two caliber semi-automatic that had been delivered to her home only five days before. The surge of confidence the touch of the cold metal gave her was surprising.

The kitchen door flew open.

"There you are." Jason Fairbanks slammed it shut.

For a split second, she wondered if he was even capable of closing a door without slamming it. But when she laid her eyes on him, her wonder gave way to another question.

Jason Fairbanks looked like he had taken a shower in his slacks and sports coat. His shirt stuck to his body. His hair was caked flat to his head and his face looked pained.

She opened her mouth to ask what had happened. Then, concluding that the reminder of what was obviously an unpleasant experience would only contribute to his bad mood, she opted to say nothing.

He tossed his valise onto the counter on his way to the refrigerator. As was his custom, he yanked open the door and took out a beer.

Glancing at the clock, she noted the time was three-thirty. Even if he was Reese Fairbanks' son, he was expected to at least make the appearance of working until five o'clock at the bank which the Fairbanks family owned. "You're home early. Something happen?"

Like a rattlesnake striking its prey, he whirled around and grabbed her by the throat. "Yes, something happened. You want to make something of it?"

She grasped her hand around the gun's grip. *He knows! How does he know? I've been so careful.* Her eyes wide, she fought to inhale air past his grip on her throat.

"You've been talking to Portia."

She tried to gasp out her denial.

"Having a good laugh?" His dark eyes, the whites yellowed from years of drinking, were rimmed in red. His breath reeked of whiskey and cigarettes. His body smelled of expensive men's cologne.

So that's it! Portia. His latest mistress—until she left him. He thought he had gotten his revenge. Obviously not.

Oh, how Scarlett yearned for when she had the courage to fight back. "No!" she forced out. "I haven't."

"Liar!" He released his grip on her throat and slapped her with the back of his hand.

She flew sideways against the wall. In spite of the force that sent her flying, she maintained her grip on the gun so that it went with her. When she bounced off the wall, fury built up over years of pain and humiliation came together. Instantly, she found her footing and the courage to grab the gun with both hands and aim it at her abuser.

"What's that?" Jason laughed at the sight of his wife standing before him on both feet with a gun aimed directly at his chest.

"It's called a gun." Swallowing the blood that she felt oozing into her mouth from the fat lip, she pulled back on the hammer. "You're never going to lay a hand on me or our daughter ever again."

"Really?" He stepped toward her. "And how are you going to stop me? Shoot me?"

Holly jerked in her seat at the sound of the two gun shots. *He killed her!* She yanked open the car door to run inside to her mother's aid. Then, just as abruptly, she stopped. *No, stick to the plan. I need to call Madame X.* Clutching the cell phone, she stared at the keypad. Fear paralyzed her. *He did it. He finally did it.* Her teeth clenched. *And Grandpa will make sure he gets away with it.*

"You okay, Miss Scarlett?" she heard Mrs. Weber, the kindly old woman who lived next door call out while trotting up the driveway. The tiny Vietnamese woman was clad in baggy jeans and an oversized work shirt. Her floppy gardening hat bounced on her head.

From the other direction, Holly saw her mother running toward the car from the house.

"I'm fine, Mrs. Weber," Scarlett gasped out while yanking open the driver's side door.

Holly was overwhelmed with joy to see her mother was safe. She had a welt across her cheek and a bloody mouth, but at least she was alive. Her elation disappeared when she saw the anxiety in her face.

"Want me call police?" Mrs. Weber asked with her thick Asian accent. Even though she had lived in America for several decades, her accent was still so thick that Holly had trouble understanding her.

"No!" Seeing the shocked look on the old woman's face, Scarlett stopped to take a deep breath. "I'm sorry, Mrs. Weber. Everything is going to be okay."

"Hope so, dear," Mrs. Weber said. "You go now. No worry. Things good here."

Scarlett paused to gaze into the kindly old woman's face.

"Mom, we should go," Holly insisted.

"Go now," Mrs. Weber said. "No time to waste." Tugging on her gardening gloves, she stepped back from the car.

Scarlett tossed her purse into the backseat, turned the key in the ignition, and gunned the engine when she tore around the circular drive and raced out onto the road to head south toward the main freeway.

"What happened, Mom?" Seeing the bloody lip, Holly asked, "Is Daddy coming after us? Is Grandpa going to send people to bring us back again?"

"No." Scarlett wiped the sweat from her forehead. Her voice shook when she told her, "Call Madame X, please, and hand me the phone."

Holly hit the button and listened for the phone to ring. When a woman answered, she handed the phone to her mother.

Keeping her eyes on the road while driving as fast as she dared, Scarlett propped the phone against her shoulder.

"Have you made your escape?" the voice on the other end of the phone asked.

"Yes," Scarlett said, "but something terrible has happened." She sobbed. "I don't know what I'm going to do."

"Don't worry, Scarlett," Madame X said. "Keep to the plan. Tell me everything that happened and I'll take care of it."

CHAPTER ONE

Deep Creek Lake, Maryland—Present Day

"I'm waiting." Police Chief David O'Callaghan bent over to breathe into Chelsea Adams' ear to distract her.

Keeping her pale blue eyes on the screen of her laptop, she giggled at the feel of his hot breath brushing through her wavy platinum locks to tickle her neck. "I'm almost ready. Why don't you go bother Molly and let me get my out-of-office replies set up for my email?"

David turned to where Molly, a white German shepherd, was curled up on her bed in the corner behind Chelsea's desk, which was located in the outer office of Garrett County's prosecuting attorney. Molly's bushy tail slapped her bed when she wagged it in response to his attention. Trained to detect oncoming epileptic seizures for her mistress, Molly was Chelsea's constant companion.

"Hey, Molly, how are you today?" he asked. She answered by getting up and nuzzling her snout in his lap where he sat on the corner of Chelsea's desk. He returned the greeting with scratches behind her ears.

"No uniform today, David?" Prosecutor Ben Fleming came out of his office to see that the police chief was dressed in khaki slacks and a blue short-sleeved shirt.

Looking like he had just stepped off the golf course, Ben was equally casual in a polo shirt, slacks, and loafers. Coming from a long line of old money and political connections, the prosecutor spent almost as much time at the Spencer Inn, the five-star resort at the top of Spencer Mountain, as he did in the courtroom. In keeping with his elegant upbringing, Ben Fleming was never caught with a blond hair out of place or a smudge on his tailored shirt.

"I am allowed to take a day off once in a while," David said before turning to Chelsea. "You did ask Ben to take this afternoon off, didn't you?"

"That's why I'm setting up my email." She slapped the lid down on her laptop and reached into the desk's bottom drawer for her purse.

"I just assumed you were at the station this morning, too," Ben said.

"I had errands to run." David slipped off the desk and attached Molly's leash to her collar.

Before they could leave, Ben's wife, Catherine, stepped through the door. With a deep sigh, she announced, "It's a gorgeous summer day out there." Seeing Chelsea and David, she grinned. "Going to lunch? If I were you, I'd hit one of the lakeside bistros and enjoy the breeze off the water."

"Chelsea is taking the whole afternoon off to spend with David," Ben said with a wink.

"The whole afternoon?" Catherine said with a naughty tone. "Well, you picked the perfect day for it. What are you planning?"

"Picnic," David quipped at the same time that Chelsea answered, "Shopping."

They exchanged chastising glares before David explained, "We're going on a picnic, but we'll have to go to the store first to shop for what we're going to eat."

The corners of Ben's lips curled up before he uttered in a low voice, "I see."

Catherine took note of Chelsea's long pink dress, which fit her tiny frame like a glove. Her high-heeled pumps were dyed the same hue as the dress. "We're kind of formal for a picnic, aren't we?"

Grasping Chelsea's hand, David threw open the door. "We have to go. We're going to be late. Come, Molly." The German shepherd trotted out ahead of them.

"Late?" Catherine asked. "For what?"

David had already closed the door.

She turned to her husband, who was openly chuckling. "I didn't mean to pry."

"Well, you did."

"What are they up to?" she asked. "It isn't like everyone doesn't know about them. What's with all the clandestine stuff?"

"Haven't you ever heard of being discrete?" Ben asked.

"Of course, I have." Catherine tossed her purse onto Chelsea's desk. "I'm a United States Senator now. I eat discretion for breakfast, lunch, and dinner. It's enough to make me throw up."

"Well, forget about politics for a little bit and think back to when we were young and in love and enjoying the first breath of spring fever."

She turned around to see her husband locking the outer office door.

A naughty grin filled his face. "Lucky for you, my dear, my calendar is clear this afternoon and all of the staff is out." He took her hand and kissed the inside of her palm. "Come into my office and I'll make you forget all about that slimy world you work in now."

She allowed him to lead her into his office. "As long as we're discreet about it."

"Does that mean no selfies allowed?" He closed the door.

"I get why we invited David and Chelsea," Mac Faraday told Archie while staring up into his Audi SUV's rear view mirror. "They're our witnesses. Molly is coming because she's Chelsea's service dog, so she has to be here. What I'm having trouble understanding is why we invited *him*."

A long whine came from the back seat of Mac's black SUV.

Archie Monday, the love of Mac's life, turned around in her seat to look back at Gnarly. His tall ears rested back flat against his head. The German shepherd focused his attention on the church building belonging to the parking lot where they were waiting. "Mac, Gnarly's a member of the family and I want him to be here. This is the most important day in our lives and we can't not include him. It'd be like leaving our son at home while we were joined in holy matrimony."

"I did not sire him," Mac said. "I inherited him from my birth mother, who had adopted him. So, if anything, he's my brother."

"Well, if you're going to look at it that way," Archie said, "if your half-brother David can be at our wedding, then your adopted brother should be allowed."

Once again, Gnarly uttered a low whine that grew in volume until it crescendoed into a loud bark. Turning away from the window, Gnarly climbed across the center console to get up into the front seats.

"Oh, yeah, this is going to be a nice little ceremony," Mac muttered while pushing against the hundred pounds of fur and claws depositing hair and drool on his new shirt and khaki slacks.

"Gnarly, what's wrong with you?" Archie grabbed Gnarly's collar to pull him back, but he was too strong. "You're getting dog hair all over my dress." Desperately, she tried to brush Gnarly's black and tan fur off her white outfit. Dark strands clung to the lacy overlay.

Refusing to back down, Gnarly wedged his body in between the steering wheel and Mac.

"Gnarly, I'm going to kill you!" To save the seat upholstery from Gnarly's sharp claws, Mac threw open the door. The German shepherd was in such a hurry to get out that he didn't give his master a chance to escape before plowing over Mac to send him out the door and flat on his back on the pavement. Landing on all fours at a full sprint, the dog charged across the parking lot.

"Oh, dear Lord!" Archie threw open her door and ran to the driver's side where Mac was sprawled spread-eagle on the ground.

Turning his police chief cruiser into the parking lot, David O'Callaghan slammed on the brakes to keep from hitting Gnarly as the dog darted up to the church's main entrance.

He was still catching his breath when Chelsea pointed to where Archie, clad in a white summer dress, was kneeling next to Mac. "Did he have a heart attack?" Without waiting for him to park, she unclipped her seatbelt and jumped out of the cruiser to run over to Archie and Mac. Molly leapt out after her.

Gnarly was running back and forth in front of the church.

"Mac, are you okay?" Archie begged while clutching his hand.

Concerned for the fallen man, Molly was sniffing Mac all over in search of some way she could offer her service.

Chelsea knelt next to him as well. "What happened?"

"Gnarly," Archie answered her before turning back to Mac, who was trying to sit up onto his elbows.

"What's going on?" David demanded of them. "Do I need to call for an ambulance?"

"I don't know. He's not saying anything." Chelsea urged Molly to stop sniffing and lie down. "Mac, did you hit your head? Why don't you say something?"

"Because," Mac shot Archie a glare, "the only thing I can think to say right now, I can't say in front of ladies and on church property." He accepted David's offer of his hand and rose to his feet.

"Maybe Gnarly's nervous because he thought you brought him here for an exorcism," David joked.

"Protestants don't do exorcisms," Chelsea responded.

"Actually, some do," a feminine voice countered from behind them. "The Church of England does as a matter of fact."

Archie rushed over to hug the woman parking her bicycle in the bike rack. During the melee, they had not noticed her enter the parking lot via the bike path along the lake. "So Archie Monday is finally getting married," she said. "I guess since I'm the one doing the ceremony, you should introduce me to the lucky guy."

"Of course." Beaming, Archie led her over to where Mac was waiting with David and Chelsea. "Mac, I'd like you to meet Reverend Deborah Hess. She's the pastor here at Spencer Church."

A few years older than Archie, Deborah Hess did not look like a church pastor. Having grown up a Catholic, Mac had expected a Protestant version of a nun—an older woman who avoided cosmetics or anything that would be considered glamourous. In comparison to the Catholic nuns he had known as a child, Deborah was slender with silky chestnut-colored hair that fell to her shoulders and was dressed in a vibrant turquoise pantsuit.

The reverend took Mac's hand into a firm grip and smiled at him. "Mac Faraday. Your mother was a dear friend of mine. It is a pleasure to meet you." She studied his face. "You have her smile."

"My mother came to church?" Mac asked her before jokingly adding, "I didn't know you let murder mystery writers in."

"I've read all of your mother's books," the pastor said. "Robin Spencer brought Archie here after hiring her as her research assistant and editor. The Spencer family has a long history with us. Your ancestors built our original chapel and started this church well over a hundred years ago. Your grandparents and most of your ancestors on the Spencer side were married here. They have always been big supporters."

"That's why I insisted on us getting married here," Archie said. "It's what Robin Spencer would have wanted." She turned to the pastor. "Since Mac only inherited his birth mother's estate a few years ago, he's still learning about his family history."

"I don't know if you heard about Robin's story," Mac said. "She had me when she was an unwed teenager. My adoptive parents had told me that I had been adopted, but I didn't know who my birth parents were until after Robin Spencer's death and she had left her estate to me."

"I can imagine what an adjustment a lifestyle change like that can be for a homicide detective," Deborah said, "to suddenly come into an unbelievable fortune from a world famous murder mystery writer."

"At least he now knows where his talent for solving mysteries come from," Archie said.

"What about your birth father?" Deborah asked. "Do you know about him?"

Mac and David exchanged a long glance. Their identical blue eyes, inherited from their father, met. If Deborah looked closely at them, she would have noticed that the two men had the same tall slender build and attractive features. Years older, Mac had dark hair, inherited from his birth mother, while David's hair matched that of his birth mother, the late Patrick O'Callaghan's wife.

"He passed away before I could meet him," Mac said.

"I'm so sorry," the pastor said.

"So am I."

"Well," Deborah said, "I knew your mother quite well, and I can tell you that she was a woman of strong faith. She always strove to be more committed to this church, and we could always count on her support when we needed it."

Archie went on to introduce Chelsea and David, who reminded Deborah that they had met a few times before at various community events.

"Let's go inside and I'll show you around," Deborah said. "Then we'll do the ceremony. I don't know if Archie told you, Mac, but it's my policy not to marry couples unless they have three counseling sessions with me beforehand. However, since you are Robin's son, and Archie assures me that you will have the formal ceremony in December, then I've agreed to do this on the condition that you have your three sessions before the big wedding."

Mac fired off a glare in Archie's direction. "No, she neglected to tell me that."

Taking a set of keys out of her pocket, Deborah turned around and then paused when she noticed a green sedan parked under a tree in the corner of the parking lot. "Eugene's here—" She gasped. "Oh, that's right. He told me."

"Someone's inside?" Mac asked. "I would have thought with all the barking that he would have come out to see what the ruckus was."

"Eugene is the head of our trustees," Deborah explained while leading them to the front door. "He's here to count the offering. Since this past Sunday was Memorial Day weekend, no one wanted to stick around and the banks were closed yesterday. Eugene told me that he was coming in today to get the bank deposit ready."

When she stuck the key in the lock, Gnarly tore around the corner of the building. As soon as she had opened the door a crack, he charged inside before anyone could step in. Barking and crying, he raced down the hallway of the office wing.

"What's gotten into him?" David asked.

"He must think Eugene is a burglar," Archie said.

"More likely Gnarly is wanting to steal the cash to buy a new bone for himself," Mac said.

"Molly isn't acting bonkers," David said.

"Rub it in," Mac muttered to him.

"Just saying," David replied. "If that trustee is counting money, that racket is surely going to throw his calculations off."

Gnarly was up on his hind legs digging at an office door.

"Get off the door!" Mac shouted at him while storming down the hallway to grasp Gnarly by the collar.

"Oh, that's not going to throw off his count," David said with sarcasm. "The guy's probably afraid to come out because he thinks Gnarly is going to eat his face."

"Eugene doesn't like dealing with the public." Deborah giggled. "The last time he answered the door, it was a church member who broke down into hysterics because she wanted a divorce. She got tears and snot all over his shirt. He had to throw it away and swore never again. When he's here, he doesn't answer the door or the phone."

Gnarly yanked and pulled away from Mac until he got out of his collar and went back to the door. Whimpering, he plopped down onto the floor while gazing from the door back to Mac and then back again.

"Maybe we should knock on the door and apologize to him," Chelsea said.

"Eugene is extremely focused on his tasks," Deborah said. "Best to leave him alone." She waved for them to follow her. "Let's go into the sanctuary. I'll show you around and we can get started."

Mac tossed Gnarly's collar down the hall to where he was lying in front of the door. The dog looked dejected.

"Come on, Gnarly," Archie called to him. "Don't you want to see your daddy and me get married?"

"That animal did not come from my loins," Mac said in a low voice.

Ignoring his comment, Archie took Mac's hand and led him across the fellowship hall to the double glass doors that opened into a spacious sanctuary with a cedar-paneled cathedral ceiling with log beams across the width. The wall behind the pulpit was made of stone at the base of which rested the baptismal pool.

"I always thought this was the prettiest church in Spencer," Chelsea said while squeezing David's hand.

"You should see it when the sanctuary is lit and the waterfall flowing down the rocks to the baptismal pool is turned on," Archie gushed to Mac. "It's going to be a lovely wedding." She told Deborah, "We're going to have an evening ceremony on New Year's Eve, and want to say our vows right before midnight."

Deborah sighed. "It will be lovely, but I'm afraid we won't be able to use the waterfall."

Archie's face fell. "Why not?"

"It's broken," the pastor explained. "Two years ago. The plumbing is thirty years old and has to be completely replaced and we don't have the funds to have it rebuilt."

"Oh, I really had my heart set on the waterfall and candles," Archie said.

Molly whimpered.

As if to voice Archie's disappointment, Gnarly howled from where he was still in the office wing.

Mac cringed.

"Do you want me to put Gnarly in the car?" David asked him in a low voice.

Mac was more concerned with the disappointment on his bride's face. "How much will it cost to replace the waterfall?" he asked Deborah.

"Several thousand dollars," she replied. "They'll have to take out the stone to get back to the pipes and—"

"I'll pay for it," Mac interrupted.

Archie's eyes lit up and she tightened her grip on his hand.

"Willingham says I need more tax deductions," Mac said with a shrug of his shoulders. "If you want a waterfall at our wedding, then we're going to have a waterfall. We're only getting married twice."

"Oh, we would be most grateful, Mr. Faraday." The smile on Deborah's face stretched from ear to ear.

"Call me Mac."

"Well, Mac," she said while trying to contain her excitement over the sudden donation, "let's get you two kids married, and then we can discuss the particulars of your formal wedding ceremony in December."

Archie turned serious. "Deborah, there is one thing that we need to make clear."

"What's that?" Deborah looked from her to Mac and then to David and Chelsea.

"No one is to know about us getting married." Archie grasped Mac's hand. "You haven't met my mother …"

"No, I haven't."

"Well," Archie paused, "if she found out that Mac and I eloped and got married six months before the wedding—without her being there … well, she'd—things could get ugly."

Deborah's eyebrows rose. "Ugly?"

"I'm the only girl out of seven kids and the youngest," Archie said. "I'm their only shot for a big, fancy wedding for their little girl. My mother will feel like I cheated her."

"Then why are you not waiting?"

"Because we want to get married," Mac squeezed Archie's hand. "We've been together for three years and we don't want to wait any longer to be husband and wife."

Deborah looked Archie up and down. She cocked an eyebrow at her. "Are you pregnant?" she finally asked in a whisper.

"No!" Archie's nostrils flared.

"Okay," Deborah said. "I understand. We'll do the ceremony and mum will be the word." She whirled around and gestured toward the pulpit. "Let's get this show on the road."

Mac and David followed her down the aisle.

When Chelsea stepped forward, Archie stopped her with a hand on her elbow. "Do I look pregnant?" she asked.

"Of course not." Chelsea grabbed her by the arm and ushered her to the front of the sanctuary.

The reverend was instructing them each where to stand when one of the double doors leading into the sanctuary opened. A tall slender woman dressed in faded jeans, sneakers, and an oversized t-shirt stepped inside. "Miss Deborah, there's a police cruiser out front. Is everything okay?"

"That's mine," David said. "It's okay. We're here for personal business."

"I was just wondering," she went on, "because there's a big ol' German shepherd sitting outside Eugene's office and he doesn't look happy. I offered him a dog biscuit from Edna's jar but he'd have none of it."

"What's with the jar of dog biscuits?" Mac asked.

"Our office manager has a dog biscuit jar for canine visitors," Deborah replied before turning her attention to the woman at the back of the sanctuary. "Thank you, Ruth. Everything is okay. I'll be through here in a little bit and they'll be taking Gnarly with them when they go."

"Gnarly turned down food?" Archie covered her mouth with her hand. "That's not like him at all." She grasped Mac's hand. "Something must be wrong."

"Maybe he doesn't approve of our getting married." Mac asked the pastor, "Are you sure you don't want me to leave him as payment for your services?"

"Stop it, Mac," Archie admonished him.

Ruth stepped out into the fellowship hall and craned her neck to look out the window. "Edna just pulled in," she called to them. "She's great with dogs. She'll be able to figure out why he's so upset and make him feel better real fast." She went off toward the foyer and business wing.

Seconds later, Gnarly's barks could be heard in the sanctuary.

"Let's just get this over with," Mac told Deborah.

"That sounds romantic," Archie retorted.

"I'm not the one who broke the mood," Mac argued. "You did by insisting that we bring that beast hog with us to the church to get married."

"Gnarly is not a beast hog."

"He's got a criminal record," Mac said. "Just ask David. That dog is a canine delinquent."

"Don't drag me into your squabble." David held up both hands in surrender.

Deborah interrupted, "This is why I insist on counseling before the marriage ceremony."

"Oh, shut up," Mac blurted out before he realized what he was saying.

There was an audible gasp in the sanctuary.

As if he feared getting caught in a cross-fire, David backed away from Mac. "Now you've done it."

Deborah leveled her eyes on the couple standing before her. "I think we need to reschedule this ceremony. It just doesn't seem right." The pastor's previously congenial tone had shifted to firm and commanding.

"Nothing about this is right," Mac said. "Nothing has been right since I pulled into your parking lot and that animal trampled me."

"Are you still mad about that?" Archie said.

"Yes."

"Mac, you really need to learn to let things go."

Gnarly's barking had stopped, but Mac and Archie were too involved in their argument to notice.

"I took the afternoon off work to be here," Chelsea said. "Are you two going to get married or aren't you?"

"I know that I don't want to get married to the sound of that in the background." Mac jerked his head in the direction of the business wing.

Noticing that Gnarly's barking and howling had stopped, David asked, "Sound of what?"

Abruptly, the double doors flew open and a woman came running in. Her face was stark white and her eyes were filled with shock. Once inside the sanctuary, she stopped. Her mouth hung open while she gazed wide-eyed at each of them.

"Edna?" Deborah asked. "What's wrong?"

Clutching both hands to her chest, Edna sucked in several deep breaths.

Wondering if the woman was having a heart attack, Mac and David exchanged glances filled with concern.

David took a step forward to suggest the stricken woman sit down. "Maybe—"

Before he could finish, she uttered an ear piercing scream that reached all the way up to the rafters to bounce and echo throughout the church. Unable to form the words to communicate the meaning behind her scream, she pointed toward the office wing.

David and Mac were the first out of the sanctuary. In the fellowship hall, they found Gnarly at the end of the hallway leading back to the offices. Seeing that he now had their full attention, he turned and led them down the hall.

Now, the office door was open.

David ran inside, halted, and held out his arm to stop Mac who was directly behind him.

At first, the office appeared like any other with a desk, computer, phone, and calculator. However, there was a big difference where this one was concerned.

This office had a man lying in a pool of blood behind his desk.

Chapter Two

"Mac, we need to contain this scene," David said.

Whirling around, Mac threw out his arms to block the doorway to keep Deborah and the other women from entering the office.

"Eugene!" Deborah cried out upon seeing her friend. "What—who?"

"You need to wait outside," Mac ordered while gently pushing the pastor back into the hallway.

Understanding the need to keep any possible evidence free of contamination, Archie took Deborah's arm to usher her down the hallway. "Let's go to the sanctuary, Reverend. The best thing we can do for Eugene right now is pray."

Leading Molly to the foyer with one hand, Chelsea held her cell phone to her ear with the other. "Spencer's chief of police is already on the scene," she told the emergency operator.

"The office door was locked," Edna was blubbering to them. "I didn't know anyone was in there and I was showing the dog because he wanted in—"

Because he knew someone needed help, Mac thought.

Now quiet, Gnarly sat at attention outside the office door. His tall pointy ears stood erect. His brown eyes bore into Mac's blue ones. The German shepherd cocked his head at his master.

Mac could almost read the thoughts Gnarly directed toward him. *When are you going to learn to listen to me, Dummy?*

"Mac," David called out from where he was checking the victim, "he's alive! I got a pulse! Chelsea, tell them that he's alive! We need EMTs ASAP. He's going to need airlifted. Get my medical kit out of the back of my cruiser!"

While running to help David, Mac called out to the women, "Seal all exits and entrances in the building! No one is allowed in or out except the emergency crews."

"Is there anyone else in the building?" Archie asked while leading the pastor and office manager back to the sanctuary.

She stopped to listen to the police and ambulance sirens growing nearer by the second. They sounded like they were driving right through the doors when Chelsea slammed them open in her rush to take David's emergency medical kit to him. In sync with her master's pace, Molly ran by her side. The kit only provided the essentials. Archie hoped the EMTs would arrive quickly.

"The only other person who should be here is Ruth," the pastor said. "She takes care of our building's maintenance." She was holding Edna, the church's office manager, who was fighting to keep from completely breaking down. A relatively young woman in her early forties, Edna had long lush dark hair and big brown eyes.

As if in response to her name, Ruth ran into the fellowship hall. She was carrying a filthy cleaning rag. "What's going on?"

"Someone has attacked Eugene," Deborah said.

Ruth stood motionless. Her face was blank while she appeared to be computing the information. "Are you serious? I mean … who? Why would …" she stuttered. "Was it robbery? How did they get in? The building was locked up when I came in this morning." She turned to look down the hallway leading to the classroom.

"Was Eugene already here when you came to work this morning?" Archie asked.

"I come in through the back door." Ruth covered her mouth with her hand. "I do leave it unlocked because I have to go in and out emptying trash." Tears came to her eyes. "Oh, dear."

"Ruth Buchanan and her daughter live in the caretaker's cottage on the other side of the church grounds," Deborah said. "She walks over on the path along the lake and comes in the back door. I live in the pastor's house on this side."

"I've been cleaning the Sunday school classrooms," Ruth said. "I was running the vacuum cleaner so someone could have come in without me noticing. I didn't even know Eugene was here until I heard the dog barking after I put the vacuum cleaner away. That was when I looked out the window. I saw his car over under the tree. He doesn't really come in that often during the week."

"No, he doesn't." Deborah nodded her head in agreement. "He only came in today because of the holiday weekend." She choked. "Who would do this?"

"Had to be robbery," Edna said.

Going to Ruth, Archie took her by the shoulder. "We need to go into the sanctuary."

"We need to pray for Eugene and the emergency crews," Deborah said. "That's the best thing we can do right now. They all need our prayers."

The church erupted into further chaos when the front doors at the entrance flew open and Chelsea escorted emergency crews inside and down the business wing to the office. As if to announce his role in the discovery of the crime, Gnarly bounced by the entrance and barked at each responder coming inside.

When the EMTs waded in to tend to the man lying in the pool of blood behind the desk, Mac and David backed out of the office, while still trying to stay in eyesight of the office's interior. Both tried to commit to memory the layout of the scene as best they could.

Saving Eugene's life was the emergency crew's priority. Not disturbing any possible evidence was secondary.

Lurking off to the side in the office doorway, Mac didn't notice that Spencer's deputy chief of police, Arthur Bogart, also known as Bogie, had arrived on the scene until he heard his deep voice ask for the details of what had happened.

Startled by a note of anxiety in Bogie's usually calm tone, Mac turned away from where the EMTs were lifting Eugene onto the gurney.

The tall, silver-haired deputy chief possessed the solid, muscular built of a wrestler. His muscles weren't simply for show. On more than one occasion, he had pinned law officers half his age who had mistaken his hair color for a sign of weakness to the mat.

Glancing up and down the hall, Bogie's eyes were wide. "Who would do a thing like this?" he asked before David could utter a run-down about the situation. "Who is it? Edna Parker? She's—"

"It's Eugene Newton," David said. "He was counting the church offering."

"Eugene?" Bogie rubbed his hand over the top of his gray head. "Oh, no, poor Eugene."

"Are you a member of this church, Bogie?" Mac asked him.

"Been for five years," Bogie said. "I started coming after Ol' Pat's funeral service was held here. Best, warmest folks you'd ever want to have as friends. This is ludicrous!" His question to David betrayed a hint of his anger over the crime. "What happened?"

"Three gunshot wounds," David reported to him. "One looks like it grazed his scalp. Another went through his right shoulder. Then there is a third right in the forehead between the eyebrows."

"And he's still alive?" Bogie's eyes were wet. He swallowed.

"The office door was locked," Mac reported. "I heard the woman who found the victim say that." He nodded toward a cartridge resting on the floor next to the victim's head. "The killer left the shell casings behind. The weapon must be a semi-automatic, which ejects the cartridges."

"Those will help ballistics to match it up to the gun," David said, "if we're lucky enough to locate it."

"Does Eugene have family?" Mac asked the deputy chief. "What do you know about him?"

"Eugene is a nice, stand-up guy. His wife, too. Marilyn. She's awesome." Bogie whacked his forehead with the palm of his hand. "Oh, man! His wife. We need to call Marilyn." He gazed back into the office.

"Robbery can't be the motive." Mac pointed through the crowd to the desk behind which the church trustee had been shot. Neat stacks of dollar bills and coins were organized along the desktop. A bank money bag rested next to the calculator.

"So someone came in, shot him, and then locked the door on their way out," David said, "and left hundreds of dollars laying behind."

In a low voice, Bogie said, "No one would want to hurt Eu—Chip!" His dark eyes sparked. His face grew hard.

"Who?" David asked.

"Chip Van Dorn," Bogie said. "Former church member. A year ago, he took a swing at Eugene out there in the parking lot—Sunday morning—right in front of me. I put a stop to it real fast. The church didn't want to press charges." He pointed at the man being wheeled out of the office. "Chip swore then that if he had a gun he'd blow Eugene's brains out."

"Why?" Mac asked. "What were they fighting about?"

Bogie shrugged. "Church didn't really want to talk about it. Chip and his wife never came back again. I remember she was one of those real quiet docile type of women—the type who usually end up marrying loud mouth idiots like Chip Van Dorn—he was moodier than a woman with PMS. He always seemed to be ranting and raving about one thing or another."

David started to tell Bogie to locate their first suspect, but found that the deputy chief was already writing down the name in his notepad.

"There's one suspect," Mac said.

"One is all we need," Bogie said. "It takes only one homicidal psychopath to ruin the lives of a lot of good people."

"I don't believe this," Archie whispered to Chelsea while watching the reverend and the two members of her staff huddled together—praying for the trustee who was fighting for his life.

"Neither do I." Chelsea stroked the top of Molly's head.

While the three women comforted each other, Chelsea and Archie sat on the steps leading up to the pulpit where less than an hour before they were preparing for a wedding ceremony. Laying down between them, Gnarly licked Molly's ears. When she didn't seem to properly appreciate his affection, he would whine and paw at the white German shepherd clad in her service dog vest.

"Actually, I guess I should believe it," Archie said. "I mean, with the life Mac and I lead, how could there not be a murder at our wedding?" She sighed. "I feel terrible."

"He's not dead yet," Chelsea said. "Miracles do happen. He could survive. When I was in that car accident years ago, I was in a coma for days. At one point, they didn't think I would make it."

"No," Archie said, "that's not what I meant. But it's what I should have meant." She looked up at the distraught women. "There's a man fighting for his life. He has friends and family, and here I am upset because of a stupid marriage ceremony. At least Mac is safe. We'll be together tonight. That man's family may not have him. I can be so selfish sometimes."

Realizing she had misunderstood Archie's meaning, Chelsea's lips formed a pout. She reached across the dogs to squeeze Archie's hand. "That's completely understandable. You've been waiting for this day for a long time. And don't worry. You two are going to get married. It's going to happen. Maybe not today, but certainly—I mean, this church is booked for your wedding on New Year's Eve."

"We want to get married now," Archie said.

"Why?" Chelsea's eyes grew big. She covered her mouth with her hand. "You aren't preg—"

"No," Archie said more harshly than she wanted. Standing up, she smoothed her white dress over her flat stomach. "Do I look pregnant?"

Through the double doors, she saw Mac, David, and Bogie enter the fellowship hall from the business wing.

Exhausted from their prayer vigil, the three women separated. Sobbing, Edna sat in one of the cushioned pews. Glancing at the police on the other side of the glass doors, Deborah ushered Ruth to the other side of the sanctuary and spoke to her in low tones.

"What's that about?" Archie asked.

"What's what about?" Chelsea asked her, but Archie was already on the move.

"Hey, Ruth," Archie called to her while approaching the two women, "what time did you come in this morning?"

"I was just asking her," the pastor replied. "Ten o'clock."

"You heard Gnarly barking, but you heard no gunshots?" Archie asked her.

Ruth was nodding her head. "I was putting the vacuum cleaner back in the supply closet when I heard the barking and came to this side of the building to see what was going on."

"Normally, the church's front doors would be open and the building unlocked and open for business," Deborah said, "but Edna's sister and mother were visiting from out of town, and she took this morning off. That's why she came in so late."

"So if business had been as usual today," Archie turned to where the church's office manager was sobbing in her seat, "Edna would have been here …"

"And Eugene shouldn't have been here at all."

As far as Bogie was concerned, Chip Van Dorn was a prime person of interest in the shooting of Eugene Newton. Before Mac and David had left the business wing to go interview the pastor and other possible witnesses, the deputy chief was on his radio requesting a background check on the former church member who had threatened the trustee.

Lagging behind them, Bogie nabbed one of Spencer's uniformed officers in the fellowship hall. "Fletcher, I want you to do something for me."

"Yes, sir," the young officer replied.

"Go to Deep Creek Books and Beans in McHenry," the deputy chief ordered. "The manager is Chip Van Dorn. I want you to get eyes on him and don't let him out of your sight until I get a chance to question him."

"Do you want me to bring him in for questioning about this shooting?"

"No, just get eyes on him," Bogie added in a low voice. "Once I get everything I can on the slimy little cretin, I'll question him myself."

"What have you told me about taking cases personally?" David reminded Bogie when he rejoined them outside the sanctuary.

"This guy shot a church trustee in God's house," Bogie said. "If that's not low, I don't know what is."

"We'll get him." Mac gave Bogie's muscular arm a squeeze.

"By the way, what were you two doing here?" Bogie asked them. Not only was his question out of personal curiosity, but he needed the information for the case file.

Stopping in the center of the fellowship hall with the sanctuary directly on the other side of the glass double doors, Mac and David exchanged glances. "We were meeting with the church's pastor to discuss the wedding," Mac answered while hoping Bogie didn't notice the pause before his response.

"The wedding isn't for six months," Bogie pointed out.

"So far the guest list is up to four hundred," Mac said. "We needed to see if the sanctuary would be big enough."

Bogie nodded his head. His bushy gray mustache twitched, which was a sign that there was something puzzling him. Abruptly, he turned to David. "What were you and Chelsea doing here?"

"They wanted our input," David said as smooth as if it were the truth. "It's a beautiful summer day. Chelsea and I decided to take the day off to spend together. When they found out that we were available, Mac and Archie asked us to come with them to get our opinion."

"Your opinion on whether the sanctuary is big enough for four hundred?" Bogie asked.

"On the ceremony," David said. "Decorating the sanctuary for the wedding. Chelsea has a good eye about that kind of stuff."

"I didn't know that," Bogie said.

"She does," David said in a firm tone that dared the deputy chief to ask any more questions about it. "After we were through here, Chelsea and I were going to go have a picnic together down by the lake."

"Nice day for it, too." Bogie stepped between them to go on into the sanctuary. "Too bad murder ruined your plans."

CHAPTER THREE

Upon entering the sanctuary, Bogie greeted Deborah, Edna, and Ruth with a bear hug big enough to envelope all of them into his massive chest.

"It appears to me that every one of you knew the victim," Mac noted.

"No one would want to kill Eugene," Deborah said. "He was the most upstanding guy you'd ever want to meet."

Edna agreed. "He had integrity coming out of his ears."

While David expressed his sympathy, Mac went over to where Archie was sitting on the altar steps with Gnarly's head in her lap. The sadness in her face reminded him of why they were at the church in the first place. He bent over to take her hand into his and kissed her fingers. When she lifted her face to his, he kissed her softly on the mouth. "I'm sorry," he whispered before brushing his lips across her cheek.

"I'm not the one you should be apologizing to," she said in a low voice.

He followed her eyes to Gnarly, who, while keeping his head down in her lap, peered up at him with his big brown eyes. They were pleading for the apology Mac owed to him. "Sorry, Gnarly."

The German shepherd raised his head. The bronze spots that practically served as eye brows arched and moved toward each other. A rumble formed in his throat.

"That's it?" Archie replied. "Gnarly tried to tell you, and all of us, that there was an emergency and we all ignored him. You're his partner. You should have listened."

As if in agreement, Gnarly sat up and uttered a low bark.

"I said I was sorry," Mac replied. "What more do you want from me?"

Lowering his head, Gnarly eyed him.

"A little more respect," Archie answered for the canine.

"Maybe I'd respect him more if he'd stop drinking out of my toilet." Deciding that now was not the time for this conversation, Mac turned to rejoin David where he was interviewing the reverend.

"Maybe Gnarly would respect you more if you stopped peeing in his porcelain water dish," Archie quipped.

Mac stopped, shook off the insult, and pushed the situation out of his mind to refocus on the attempted murder.

"Who worked the closest with Eugene?" David was asking.

"That would be me and Deborah," Edna said. "We talked almost daily."

"Was he an actual church employee?" Mac asked.

"The only employees this church has are myself," Deborah said, "Edna, who works part-time managing the office; and Ruth, the building caretaker. She lives rent-free in the cottage and gets a small salary."

"Tell them what you told me," Archie instructed Deborah from where she had stood up to join them. When David turned in her direction, she explained, "No one knew Eugene was going to be here this morning. Normally, Edna would work in the morning, but she came in late today. Get it? If this was a regular day, it would have been Edna, not Eugene, here."

The church's office manager was gazing down at her feet.

Mac asked, "Can you think of anyone who would have wanted to hurt you, Edna?"

Saying nothing, Edna shook her head.

"I don't believe this," Deborah said. "It can't be a member of our church. It has to be someone from the outside who came in to steal the offering."

"There are piles of cash on the desk where Eugene was shot," Mac said. "If robbery was the motive, it'd be gone." He glanced at Edna. "Does anyone know how much money was in the offering?"

Edna shook her head so fast that her thick dark locks swayed with the movement. "It hadn't been counted yet."

"That's why Eugene came in," the reverend said, "to put together the bank deposit." Tears came to her eyes. "Everyone in our congregation is a good person. We care about each other and our community. How could one of them do this to one of their own?"

"We'll find whoever did this to Eugene." Bogie hugged her. "You have my personal promise about that, Deborah."

"Thank you, Bogie," Deborah murmured into his chest.

Casting a glance in Mac's direction, David clinched his jaw.

His stomach turning in a knot, Mac slowly shook his head at the vow that he hoped Bogie would be able to keep. A career officer, Bogie surely knew better than to make such assurances.

"What about Chip Van Dorn?" Bogie asked. "Last year, I saved Eugene from a punch in the face right out here in the church parking lot."

Gasping, Edna covered her mouth with her hand. "I forgot all about that."

"What was that fight about?" David asked them.

"It was really nothing," Deborah said.

"Nothing?" Bogie replied. "The guy threatened to blow Eugene's brains out and then stormed inside the church, grabbed his wife by the arm, and dragged her out screaming and crying."

"I had forgotten what a drama queen Chip was," Deborah said, "but that was a year ago."

"And Chip has hated all of us ever since," Edna told the reverend. "You've seen the anti-Christian stuff he has posted on the social media sites." She turned in her seat to tell the detectives, "Chip Van Dorn did a complete one-eighty after that blow up. Now he hates all church people and everything we stand for."

Mac repeated their previous question. "What was the blow up about?"

"A bake sale," Deborah said with a heavy sigh.

"Bake sale?" Archie asked. "Do you mean bake sale as in cakes and cupcakes on a table to sell for a couple of bucks a pop?"

"And cookies for a quarter a piece," Edna answered.

"Yeah," the pastor replied with a roll of her eyes. "Our church is always in dire need of money, but last year it got really bad. Decisions had to be made to cut costs and raise more funds. The trustees and I decided to tell our members how serious things were. That was when Chip suggested we do fundraisers—specifically a bake sale—and he volunteered to coordinate it. The trustees decided against it."

"Why?" Chelsea asked.

"One," Deborah held up a finger, "in the couple of years that Chip had been a member of Spencer Church, he had proven to be …" She paused to search for the right word.

"Nuts," Bogie offered.

"Offensive," Edna said.

"Chip was a control freak," Deborah said. "Anytime he was placed in a position of even a tiny bit of power, it would go to his head. He would demean people he considered beneath him. You can't do that to volunteers who are giving their time to help out. So, we would consciously keep him out of leadership positions and he resented that."

"Resented it enough to physically attack and threaten Eugene," Bogie noted.

"You said one," Mac reminded the pastor. "Where there's a one, there's usually a two."

"Generally, bake sales do not bring in a lot of money," Deborah said. "The reward is not worth the investment in time and money. As chief trustee, Eugene was tasked with breaking the news to Chip. You know what they say about shooting the messenger. That was what happened. Chip blew up and directed his anger at Eugene."

"We have copies of the emails," Edna said.

"Emails?" David asked. "I thought this happened in person in the church parking lot."

"Eugene told Chip about the trustees' decision in an email," Deborah explained. "He completely over-reacted. Eugene blind copied the trustees in his replies to make them aware of what was going on and how he was handling it. Eugene wanted all of the trustees to be aware of the level of Chip's spiritual immaturity for future consideration when it came to leadership positions."

"Eugene was covering his butt," Mac said.

"That's another way of putting it," Deborah confessed. "He was making sure the right hand knew what was happening on the left."

"Then, someone decided to tell Chip about the blind copied emails," Edna said, "and that was when things got ugly and he attacked Eugene."

"But Chip left the church and has never come back since then," Deborah said. "None of us have seen or heard hide or hair of Chip since then."

"Well ..." Edna said, "not exactly."

"What exactly?" Mac asked.

"About a month ago, I got a call from Chip's wife, Tina, asking for an anonymous prayer request from our members," Edna said. "She suspected Chip was having an affair and she noticed that he had been acting erratic lately."

"What do you mean by erratic?" David asked.

"Tina said he was acting paranoid and every time she tried to talk to him about it, he'd fly off the handle."

"More than usual?" Deborah replied before telling David and Mac, "Chip gave new meaning to 'flying off the handle.'"

"We need to talk to Chip Van Dorn," David said.

"Chip Van Dorn?"

When David turned around, he came face to face with a short, stern-faced woman wearing a purple hat with a red bird perched on the rim. She made her entrance into the sanctuary by throwing open both glass doors. After stepping through, she released the doors and placed her hands on her broad hips. "Are you in charge here?" she demanded to know in a shrill voice.

Spotting the bird, Gnarly sat up at attention and trained his eyes on the prey bobbing on top of the intruder's head.

"No, Gnarly," Archie ordered him.

With a low growl, Gnarly laid down. Still, he refused to let the feathered tidbit out of his sight.

When Officer Nathan Brewster grabbed her elbow in an effort to usher the formidable woman out, she shook him off. "What the hell is going on here?"

"Sorry, Chief," Officer Brewster said. "This woman just barged in. I'll take her back outside." A retired Marine, Spencer Police Officer Nathan Brewster was not the type of man to be easily thwarted. With his broad shoulders and barrel chest, and years of combat training, he could be counted on to handle any assailant … unless she was welding a big fat purse.

"Back off!" She struck him about the head and shoulders until he backed away—covering his head with both of his arms.

When he lowered them to peer back at her, she threw her hand up over her head with her purse—daring the officer to try again. A wickedly triumphant grin crossed her bloated and wrinkled face.

Brewster's eye narrowed with determination. His thick, curly, salt-and-pepper hair stood up on end where it had been beaten to form what appeared to be a spiky, punk hair-do. His mustache curled as a sneer came to his lips. He reached for his gun.

"Stand down, Brewster!" Bogie charged directly into the line of fire.

"Oh, can't you let him shoot her?" Edna asked in a low voice. When she saw the pastor fire off a stern glance in her direction, she cleared her throat. "Did I say that out loud?" Blushing, she covered her mouth. "I'm so sorry," she said through her fingers.

After dismissing Brewster to return to his post, Bogie told David in a low tone, "There's always one in every crowd."

"Extra grace required," the church pastor said with a nod of her head.

Spotting the gold badge that David had clipped to his belt, the intruder made a beeline for the chief of police. "I'm Helga Thorpe. I am a trustee of this church and I demand to know what's going on. Did I hear you mention Chip Van Dorn as a suspect for some crime committed here?" With a glare in her eyes, Helga demanded answers.

Clearing his throat, David stood up to his full height to meet the challenge of the woman who fell several inches shorter than he. "I'm not at liberty to discuss an open police investigation."

"I heard Eugene Newton had gotten shot and that you need to question Chip Van Dorn," Helga said. "Well, if he's a suspect, then I have some information that can help you."

"Information or gossip?" Deborah asked in a displeased tone.

"I heard it from a friend of Tina's mother," Helga told the pastor before redirecting her attention to the police chief. "Tina Van Dorn left her husband just last week after confirming that he was having an affair and he didn't take it well at all."

"Are you sure about that?" Edna asked.

"Positive," Helga said. "She moved in with her mother who lives up the mountain on the McHenry side of the lake. Since then, he's been taking up residence at The Blue Mermaid bar and closing the bar every night."

"Why would he shoot a church trustee for his wife leaving him because she caught him cheating?" Chelsea asked.

"Maybe Eugene wasn't the intended target," Archie said. "He wasn't supposed to be here this morning. Edna was."

"I could have been the target." The pastor's face went paler than it had been before. "I was counseling Tina when they were members. Chip may have blamed me …"

David ordered Bogie, "Put out a BOLO on Chip Van Dorn. Let's find out if he even owns a gun."

"Already on it, Chief." Bogie stepped away to speak into his radio.

"I can't believe anyone from our church would do this," Deborah said.

"Especially to Eugene of all people," Edna said. "Granted, Eugene wasn't the warmest and fuzziest of people—"

"That's why we have Edna," Deborah said. "She provides the warm and fuzzy."

"Can you think of anyone else who has objected to Eugene's less than warm and fuzzy personality?" Mac asked the pastor.

He did not miss Edna's glance in Helga Thorpe's direction.

Ignoring the office manager's expression, Helga ordered the pastor, "You should tell them about Alan."

"Alan who?" David asked.

"Someone else you need to talk to." Helga Thorpe shook a finger in all of their directions. "Alan Bennett."

While Deborah Hess and Edna shook their heads, David asked Helga, "Who's Alan Bennett and why would he shoot Eugene?"

"He's the moron who should have been counting with me on Sunday, except Eugene fired him last week," Helga said.

"Fired him?" Bogie asked. "But he's not a church employee."

"From the counters," Helga said. "Alan gambled away all of his money and made one bad investment after another. He's come to the church to bail him out time and again. It got so bad that we were afraid he would get sticky fingers counting the offering, so Eugene fired him."

When David and Mac turned to the pastor and office manager, they saw them hanging their heads in shame while nodding in agreement.

"It wasn't that we didn't trust him," Deborah said. "We just felt like—for the sake of appearances, if something was to happen." She added, "And it wasn't Eugene's decision. The board of trustees made the decision—" She fired off a glare in Helga's direction, "a unanimous decision. So it wasn't Eugene who decided alone to fire Alan. However, as the chief of the trustees, Eugene has the dirty job of passing bad news to members and some will often blame Eugene when it's not his fault."

"Bearer of bad news," Bogie said. "It's a tough job, but someone has to do it."

"Can be a fatal job sometimes," David said.

"How did Alan take the news of being fired from the counters?" Mac asked the pastor.

"He was fine," Deborah replied.

"Or so he said," Helga interjected. "He didn't come to church service on Sunday."

"It was a holiday weekend," Edna pointed out. "A lot of people didn't come this past Sunday. They didn't all shoot Eugene."

"Hey, Chief," David's radio crackled.

The police chief pressed the button on his radio. "Yes, Brewster …"

"We've got a couple of young people here at the front door insisting that they need to come in," Brewster reported. "They claim their mothers are inside … and the girl is extremely upset." He added in a whisper, "She's crying, sir. I'm not good with sobbing girls. I can handle flying bullets and blood and even dead bodies, but this …"

"That's probably my daughter," Ruth said.

The reverend added, "And Chase, my son."

With a sigh, David instructed Brewster to escort them into the sanctuary.

Seconds later, a teenaged boy and girl rushed inside. The girl ran to hug Ruth while the boy rushed to Deborah. "Mom, what's going on?" the boy asked. "I heard one of the officers saying there's been a shooting. Has anyone been hurt?"

"It was Eugene," Deborah said. "Someone shot him." She hugged the teenager tightly.

"Eugene!" the girl gasped. "Who would want to hurt Eugene?" She turned to Ruth. "Do they know who did it?"

Deborah ordered her son, "Chase, you need to take Natalie back to the house. Stay with her. Pray for Eugene and the police and doctors—"

From where he observed the girl hugging the caretaker, Mac recognized the terror in Natalie's face when she asked, "Was it—"

"No," Ruth shushed her daughter. "It was someone trying to steal money from the offering or the church office."

"Are you sure—" There was a desperate tone in the girl's queries.

With a quick glance in Mac's direction, Deborah pulled Natalie from Ruth's grasp. "Dear, we have a lot of questions to answer for these police officers. You really can't be here right now." She grasped her son's hand and placed Natalie's hand in his. "Go home with Chase and stay there." She ushered both of them in the direction of the door. "We'll be back home as soon as possible."

In spite of their desire to stay, Chase led Natalie out of the sanctuary at the same time that Brewster arrived with a man dressed in worn shorts, sandals, and a fishing hat. "He says he's with the woman in the hat," the officer said with a shrug of his shoulders.

David replied in a low voice, "Go back to your post and tell everyone else that no more sightseers are allowed inside."

Brewster rushed back out the door.

"Sirrus," Helga grasped the man's arm, "you would never believe what has happened here! Someone shot Eugene."

"That's awful." Sirrus took off his fishing hat to reveal a dark brown toupee plastered on top of his head. Greasy gray strands hung below the toupee, sticking to the side of his sweaty face. Beads of perspiration hung from his flabby jowls. He went over to where the three women from the church were comforting each other. "Edna, are you okay?"

"I'm fine, Sirrus," Edna assured him. "Thank you for asking."

"Is there anything that I can do for you … any of you?"

"Right now we need to go to the hospital," Deborah said.

"Hospital?" Sirrus repeated the word before grinning. "Does that mean Eugene is going to be okay? Thank the Lord."

"It's really bad," Deborah said. "We're praying for a miracle right now."

"Sirrus," Helga's voice snapped. "Come," she ordered as if she were calling a dog. "These officers have work to do and I need to call together the trustees to let them know what's going on. We need to appoint a new chief to be in charge—no telling how long Eugene will be out of commission—if he survives."

"No," the pastor said in a sharp tone.

"You seem to be moving awfully fast to take over the board of trustees, Helga," Edna said.

"Really fast," Deborah said. "Too fast, if you ask me."

Mac's voice echoed the reverend's tone. "Right now we need to keep a lid on what information is made public. I recommend that any statement made about the shooting be cleared through Chief O'Callaghan beforehand."

Helga's hands were back on her hips. "I am on the board of the trustees. I expect to be kept informed during every step of this investigation."

His own hands on his hips, David stepped up to the difficult woman, who met his gaze with a glare. "I am in charge of this investigation, Mrs. Thorpe, not you. I will decide who receives what information when, not you. Do you understand me?"

"Did Eugene say who shot him?" Sirrus asked.

"Hopefully, he'll get through this and be able to answer all of our questions," Ruth said.

Nodding her head, Helga shook her finger in Deborah's direction. "If you had listened to me, none of this would have happened."

"None of this is anyone's fault except the evil person who shot Eugene," Deborah said.

Gesturing for Bogie to remove Helga from the sanctuary, David said, "Ms. Thorpe—"

"Misses," she corrected him. "Call me Misses. I am Mrs. Helga Thorpe." She gestured at her husband, who was eying her with narrowed eyes. "My husband, Sirrus, and I own Thorpe Sporting Goods and Boat Rentals." Beaming with pride, she announced, "We've been here on the lake for thirty-five years and are close friends with every member of the town council, including Bill Clark."

Chuckling when he saw David's lips purse at the name of the chief of the town council being dropped, Mac swallowed a scoff that fought its way to his lips.

Oblivious to Bogie gesturing from the open sanctuary doors for Brewster to come remove the unwanted witness, Helga continued, "I manage all of our store's business matters, which is why the church asked me to take charge of the counters. When we were last audited, they found the church to be only seventy-five cents off in our favor."

"That's very impressive, Mrs. Thorpe." As soon as he saw his officer, David gestured for Brewster to get her and her husband out of his sight.

"I am very detail oriented." Helga pulled away from Brewster's grasp while raising her handbag to strike if need be. "Nothing ever gets past me. Before I was in charge—"

Cutting her off, David ordered, "Get her out of here."

"How rude!" Throwing back her shoulders and thrusting her nose up into the air, Helga marched out of the sanctuary and toward the church foyer.

Snapping Sirrus' attention away from where he was staring at the pastor, office manager, and Ruth, Mac ushered him toward the door as well.

When his radio crackled, Bogie turned around to speak into it in a low voice.

David ordered Officer Brewster before he returned to his post, "Tell forensics to bring in the fingerprinting kit. We need to get prints for everyone on the church staff and all of the trustees."

"Fingerprints!" Ruth clasped her hand over her face.

Deborah stepped forward. "What are you going to do with these prints?"

"We're going to need to compare them to the prints we collect in the crime scene," Mac explained as gently as possible. "That way, we can eliminate those fingerprints that belong on the scene from anyone who doesn't belong in there." He gestured at Ruth. "Since you clean the church and take care of the building, then we can expect to find your prints on the scene. But the only way we can identify them are by taking your prints."

"Are you going to be running background checks on everyone whose prints you take?" Deborah asked. "Like putting them in the national database?"

"Is there a problem with that?" Mac asked.

Her eyes wide, Deborah gazed at him.

"If there's a problem," Mac said, "it would be more advantageous for everyone if we talked about it now."

They all waited while Deborah stared at Mac. She then turned to where the portrait of Jesus Christ hung on the wall to look down onto the sanctuary. "No," she said in a strong tone, "there's nothing we can't handle."

"We've got a lead," Bogie turned from where he had been making and receiving calls on his radio. "As of this morning, Chip Van Dorn owned a gun. Tonya just radioed that he applied for a permit last week and records showed that he picked up a nine-millimeter Colt semi-automatic at a store in Oakland this morning. I just called Fletcher to tell him that Chip Van Dorn was armed. He reported that he's not at his bookstore and the assistant manager said Van Dorn and one of his employees were supposed to open up this morning but, when she got there at one o'clock for her shift, the store was locked up tight and had never been opened."

"He applied for the gun permit last week," Mac asked, "the same week that his wife left him? My guess is that his wife would be the intended target."

"Eugene could have been collateral damage when Chip came to the church to take out Deborah for counseling Tina to leave him," Chelsea said.

"We don't have time to hash this out right now," David said. "We need to make sure Tina Van Dorn is safe and locate her husband."

Edna was rushing for the sanctuary doors. "I have her mother's address in our database."

CHAPTER FOUR

Once he was armed with the home address for Tina Van Dorn's mother, David directed Officer Brewster to take Reverend Deborah Hess and Edna Parker to the hospital. "Be sure to pay close attention to how Newton's wife behaves."

"Do you want me to try to get a statement from her?" Brewster asked.

"Just a preliminary," David said. "Let her know that I'll be coming to the hospital as soon as possible. We need to track down this lead on Van Dorn first. Hopefully, he hasn't left the area."

Across the parking lot, Mac was saying good-bye to Archie, who was driving Chelsea and Molly home in his SUV. He would be riding with David to meet the county sheriff in McHenry to question Chip Van Dorn's estranged wife. When backing out of the parking space, Archie almost plowed the vehicle into Sirrus Thorpe, who was darting across the parking lot toward Officer Brewster's cruiser.

"Ms. Edna, where are they taking you?" He ran up to the rear door and grabbed the car handle. "Are they arresting you? They don't think you shot Eugene, do they?"

He turned around to the police chief. "Miss Edna would never hurt anyone."

"They're taking her and the reverend to the hospital to check on Eugene and be with his wife," David assured him. "We're still taking statements and interviewing witnesses."

"It's okay, Sirrus." Deborah rolled down the front passenger seat window to assure him. "Officer Brewster needs to talk to Marilyn, so he's driving us since he's going there anyway." She gestured for him to move on.

David ushered the old man out of the cruiser's path. "I understand how extremely upsetting a violent crime like this can be, especially when it happens to someone you know. The best way you and your wife can help us is to go home. We'll call you if we have any questions."

Wordlessly, Sirrus peered after the cruiser that had pulled out of the parking lot onto the lake shore road before shuffling back to his old pick-up truck.

"Ready to go, Chief?" Bogie came up to him to ask.

"Just about," David replied. "I have a question for you. What do you think you're doing? You promised Reverend Hess that we'd catch whoever shot Eugene Newton. I remember a time you would have kicked my butt from here to Morgantown if I had said something like that. Don't make promises to a victim's friends and family because you don't know that you can keep them, and it only makes things worse if you can't. That's what you and Dad used to drill into my head from the time I got my first badge and now you're doing exactly the same thing."

Bogie's thick silver mustache twitched. "I know what I've told you. I also know what I said in there." He jerked a thumb in the direction of the church building. "I'm not senile … yet."

"Then why—"

Bogie hitched his thumbs inside his utility belt. Before David's eyes, the powerfully built deputy chief appeared to age several years. "Your daddy was sick for a very long time before he died," he said in a gentle tone. "He was like a brother to me. Watching someone that you're really close to—slipping away the way he did—it makes a man think about things, especially a man like me who was always the one in control of everything."

David uttered a deep sigh. "I know exactly what you're talking about, Bogie. I was there. I never felt so helpless—"

"Then you know what that does to a man," Bogie said. "How it makes him ask questions … about why. Why are we here? Who would let a good man like Patrick O'Callaghan get so sick and suffer the way he did for so long? Why do bad things happen to good people like Patrick and now Eugene and other good people who I have seen hurt throughout the years?" He turned around to face the church. "This is where your daddy's funeral was held. It was standing room only. Folks came from all over to pay him their respect."

Unable to think about that awful day, David refused to look at the building. He concentrated on a pebble near the toe of his loafer. "I remember."

"But I was here before that," Bogie said. "One day, when your dad was in a whole lot of pain, so much that I couldn't watch it anymore, I came in looking for answers. Deborah was here. We prayed together and when I left, I didn't have all the answers, but I had a few. I left this place with a whole lot of peace, and I think your daddy got some, too, thanks to our prayers."

Turning back to David, Bogie captured his attention. "These are my people and something evil came in to hurt them today," the deputy chief said in a low voice. "Yeah, I promised Deborah to find the slime ball who shot Eugene, and I intend to keep that promise."

The intense glare in Bogie's eyes made David back up a step. "Just don't go off the reservation, Bogie."

"I won't," he said. "I know how to handle myself."

"Go meet Sheriff Turow in McHenry. Mac and I will catch up with you there." David glanced around the parking lot. "Did you see where Mac went?" At the same time Bogie was about to answer, the police chief's cell phone vibrated on his hip. Grabbing the phone, David turned away.

Bogie tossed his head in the direction of the church building. "Mac went back inside. I think he wanted to take another look at the crime scene."

Thanking the caller, David disconnected the call. "I'm afraid it's not a shooting anymore."

Bogie's jaw dropped.

"Eugene just died." David laid his hand on Bogie's shoulder.

Sniffing, the deputy chief hung his head.

"It's gone from a shooting to a murder," David said. "I'm sorry, Bogie."

Inside the church building, Mac stared into the small office which was still being searched by the forensics team for clues. Not permitted inside the office until they had completed their work, he had to satisfy himself with committing the scene to memory in order to get a jump start on the case.

Out of the corner of his eye, he sensed David's approach from the other end of the business wing. When the police chief stepped up to him, Mac refused to tear his eyes from the mini laptop resting next to the ledger sheet. Eugene appeared to be entering the amounts after totaling the money on the calculator.

"It is now a murder case," David whispered as if he did not want to disturb Eugene's spirit inside his office.

"I'd be surprised if it wasn't," Mac said. "Shot in the head, right between the eyes. It was a miracle he lived as long as he did." He glanced over at David. "Did he regain consciousness to say anything?"

"Nope."

"I didn't think so." With a heavy sigh, Mac turned back to the scene.

David joined him in staring into the office. "Brewster is taking the reverend and office manager to the hospital to meet with the widow. He'll try to get a preliminary statement from her about who may have done this. Bogie is on his way to McHenry. Sheriff Turow is already on the way with a couple of his deputies to make sure Van Dorn's wife is safe. One of my officers is rounding up Gnarly, who is stalking Helga Thorpe's hat. We need to get going." He gestured at the blood soaked carpet. "Any inspiration?"

"How did Chip Van Dorn get in here?" Mac asked.

"He could have gone in through the back door after Ruth came in to start cleaning," David said. "She says she started work at ten o'clock, and she did leave the back door unlocked."

"Why would Van Dorn come to this church to kill Eugene Newton?"

"He was in the wrong place at the wrong time," David said. "Van Dorn blamed the reverend for breaking up his marriage because she was counseling his wife to leave him."

"Last week," Mac said. "She left him last week. They stopped coming to church a year ago. Deborah hasn't seen Tina Van Dorn since then. As a matter of fact, she wasn't even aware that Tina had left her husband. Why would Van Dorn blame the reverend or the church for his marriage breaking up?"

"Because he was incapable of taking responsibility for his own mistakes," David said. "Come on, Mac. We see it all the time. He had to blame someone, so he blamed the church that first planted the seed in his wife's mind to leave him. Edna said he's been posting anti-Christian stuff all over the social media since threatening to blow Newton's brains out for saying no to a bake sale."

Mac said, "When you say it, it makes sense. But something isn't adding up." He shook his head. "Nope. Eugene, this nice upstanding man, who gave his time to his church and his community, was sitting in here, the place where he prayed and served his Lord, and someone just walked in and blew him away. Why?"

"He wasn't supposed to be here," David said. "Remember what Archie told us? Deborah confirmed it. The office manager comes in at ten o'clock in the morning. This morning, she was late. Eugene came in to count the offering because there weren't enough counters on Sunday. There are supposed to be two people counting the offering to deter anyone with sticky fingers from stealing money out of the plate. Since only Helga came on Sunday, Eugene decided to count it himself this morning. Otherwise, he wouldn't have been here and he'd still be alive."

"It isn't a case of him surprising the killer." Mac gestured toward the laptop, calculator, ledger, and stacks of bills. "He was in the middle of counting. He had time to unlock the door, come in, set up, and it looks like he had sorted the money and checks before he was shot. The murderer must have come in after he did."

"Why did the shooter come in?" David asked. "To kill Edna?"

"Why would Van Dorn want to shoot Edna?" Mac asked.

"Because she represented the church he hated," David said. "Maybe he's on a killing spree, in which case we need to get going to pick him up." He grasped Mac's elbow to urge him down the hallway to the front door.

"If the murderer intended to shoot Edna ..." Mac allowed David to lead him down the hallway to the church's main office. Through the glass door, he could see the desk behind a welcome counter. "The door to this office was closed when we got here. The light was off."

"Edna stated that her office was locked when she arrived. She unlocked it and went in to put her purse away, turned on the light, and then went down the hall to see what Gnarly was fussing about." The police chief added, "Plus, the front door to the church building was locked when we got here. Remember? We both saw Deborah unlock it."

"That's right," Mac recalled. "Gnarly was trying to get into the building until Deborah arrived. As soon as she unlocked and opened the door, he tore in. Did Eugene have a key to the church office?"

"Yes, but the money was in the safe in the back office where he was shot," David said.

"Think about it," Mac said. "Ruth was on the other side of the building."

"Running the vacuum, which is loud."

"Eugene was counting money in the office down the hallway with the door shut. So if someone walked in—"

"They couldn't have come in unless they came in the back door," David reminded him. "Eugene wouldn't have left that door unlocked because he didn't want people walking in from off the street. He didn't like dealing with the public. Remember what Deborah told us about the woman who came in wanting a divorce and she got snot all over his shirt."

"He said never again." Mac nodded his head. "Whoever murdered Eugene either had a key or—"

"Or they came in the back door," David said.

"Most people leave as soon as they try the front door and find it locked," Mac said. "They wouldn't go all the way around to the back unless they really wanted in."

"Like an enraged former church member who blamed the church for breaking up his marriage." David pressed through the front door.

"Let's get a list from Deborah of everyone who has keys to the building." Mac followed him into the parking lot.

Outside, they encountered a robust man in a chef's jacket and a red and green ballcap with Carmine's Pizza emblazoned across the front. Upon seeing the police chief badge, he scurried around the crime scene tape and up to the front door.

"Chief O'Callaghan …" He took off his cap to reveal a head of thick dark hair. His Roman nose would have appeared larger if it weren't for his chubby cheeks that gave his face the appearance of being as round as a pizza pie. "I'm sorry to bother you, sir. I'm Carmine Romano, one of the church's trustees. I just got a call from one of our members …"

"Carmine." Seeing the chubby restaurateur brought an involuntary smile to David's face.

"That's my name."

David stuck out his hand. "You own Carmine's Pizza in McHenry. My friends and I used to hang out at your restaurant when I was in school."

The always happy grin flashed across Carmine's face. "A lot of kids have hung out at my place throughout the years."

"Carmine only has the best pizza in the area," David told Mac. "Friday night was never Friday night without one of his pizzas."

Reminded by the police cars of their reason for meeting, Carmine swallowed. "I heard something happened to Eugene, our head trustee."

David gently nodded his head. "I'm sorry, Carmine."

Instantly, tears came to the pizza man's eyes. "No … not Eugene." His lips quivering, he shook his head. "He can't be … dead? He and Marilyn came into my restaurant for lunch only yesterday."

"They did everything they could—" Mac said.

"How?" Carmine clutched his chest. "What happened? How did he die? Tell me he didn't suffer?"

65

"Someone shot him," David said while being careful to be vague. By keeping the details to himself, the killer might unwittingly reveal himself.

Carmine hung his head to his chest. "Poor ... Marilyn? Does she know?"

Concerned that he was about to collapse with a heart attack, David and Mac grasped his arms and ushered him to a bench next to the front door.

"Your pastor is going to the hospital to meet her," Mac said while helping the older man to sit down.

"Is Bogie on the case?"

"Yes," David said. "Do you know Bogie?"

"Sure do." A small grin came to Carmine's lips. "He'll get the evil monster who did this and I want to be there when he does." He paused. "Maybe not. I'll strangle the creep with my own bare hands." He gazed down at his thick fingers.

Mac sat down beside him. "Carmine, do you have any immediate thoughts about who would want to hurt Eugene?"

"He has been one of my closest friends," Carmine said. "I've known him for nearly twenty years. He and Marilyn ... everyone here ..." Abruptly, he jumped to his feet. "Ruth? Where's Ruth? Was she hurt? Did they hurt her?" His dark eyes were round with fear when he grabbed both of Mac's arms. "Ruth was cleaning the church today. Tell me that the maniac who killed Eugene didn't hurt her."

"Ruth is fine," Mac assured him. "They took her to the police station to get her statement."

"What about Natalie? Ruth's daughter. Is she okay?"

"She's with the pastor's son Chase," David said. "They're right next door."

The big Italian checked the time on his watch. "They're all going to be hungry when they get back. I wonder if Deborah has anything in her kitchen. That woman doesn't ever have anything except lettuce and salmon." He continued muttering, "Lucky for them I was at the grocery store when I got the call. There's nothing like a nice robust lasagna, fresh Italian bread, and a hearty Chianti after a police interrogation."

With a shake of his finger in Mac's direction, Carmine turned to leave, only to have the detective circle around to cut him off. "Wait a minute. What about Eugene?"

"Oh," Carmine gasped. "That's right, you wanted to know who would want to kill him."

"That would be good to know," Mac said. "It would give us an edge in our murder investigation."

"Have you talked to Helga Thorpe?" Carmine asked.

"We've met her," David said. "Yes."

"She's one of our trustees," Carmine said, "but you wouldn't know it by the way she bad mouths Deborah and the way Eugene managed the trustees and the church. It all started a couple of years ago. Eugene has been on the board for twenty years. He's been chief of the trustees and in charge of the church finances for almost that long. Well, Helga got it in her head that she wanted to be chief of the trustees and started a campaign to have Eugene voted out. She failed—miserably."

"Why?" David asked, even though he suspected.

The corners of Carmine's thick lips curled. "The chief trustee is virtually the middle man between the pastor and the members of the church's congregation. He has to work closely with the clergy. Deborah and Eugene are close friends. He was there for her when her husband died. He helped her get on her feet financially and adjust to being a single mother."

"Helga Thorpe didn't have what it took to be chief trustee?" Mac asked.

"It would have been a disaster," Carmine said. "You met her."

"Yes, I did."

"If Helga was made chief trustee, Deborah would have killed her. We would have had to cover it up on account of there being a scandal. There would have been a major police investigation. Our pastor would have gone to jail, Chase would have been without a mother as well as a father, and we all would have gone to hell for an eternity." Carmine peered into Mac's eyes. "Do you know how long an eternity is?"

Feeling drawn to answer, Mac replied, "A really long time?"

"Seems even longer when you're in hell with a bunch of stupid atheists. After five minutes of saying, 'I told you so,' then what are you going to do?" With a shake of his head, Carmine shrugged his shoulders. "No way Helga could have been chief trustee."

"Did she take losing the chief trustee spot poorly?" David asked.

"Very," Carmine said. "She's been undermining everything Eugene does ever since. She'd revealed to one of our former church members that Eugene was blind-copying the board in his emails to him. It was totally above board, but Helga made like it was something else and this guy wasn't wrapped too tight to begin with. He ended up attacking Eugene."

"So we heard," David said. "Do you think Chip Van Dorn was capable of killing Eugene?"

Carmine's dark eyes narrowed in deep thought. "Not a year later. Van Dorn has a short fuse all right, but he lives too much in the moment. If you're looking for someone who's diabolical, look at Helga Thorpe." He leaned in to whisper, "She even started rumors accusing Eugene and Edna …" He arched his thick dark eyebrows.

With thoughts of the attractive office manager having a secret affair with the married trustee, David asked with all seriousness. "Were they?"

"No way!" Carmine said with force. "Obviously you haven't met Marilyn Newton!" He shook a thick index finger at the police chief by way of chastising him for thinking such a thing. "Edna is a good woman! Get your mind out of the gutter, Chief."

"You were the one who brought it up," David said in his defense. Seeing Mac snickering behind the restaurateur's back, he fired off a glare in his direction.

"Helga only started those rumors after the ones about Eugene embezzling from the church funds got laughed out of the building," Carmine said. "We have an audit every year, at Eugene's insistence. He always comes out clean."

David had to ask, "Why would Helga continue coming to this church if she thinks so poorly of it?"

"To torture all of us?" Carmine replied. "Deborah was taking action to have Helga fired from the board of trustees and kicked out of the church, which has never happened in all of our church history." He nodded his head. "Yep, that's why Helga was the first one who came to my mind just now when you told me Eugene was dead."

A shriek came from across the parking lot.

With a purple hat in his mouth, Gnarly raced from around the corner of the church building. He made a beeline for David's cruiser.

David's radio crackled. "Code K!" an officer shouted. "We have a Code K in process."

David tapped the button. "Evacuate the canine. Repeat, evacuate the canine—ASAP."

Seeing the dog galloping toward the police cruiser, Mac threw open the rear door to allow Gnarly to jump into the back. Then, he casually opened the passenger door to climb in. Equally casual, David slipped into the driver's seat and started the engine.

"Has anybody seen my hat?" Helga Thorpe raced into the parking lot from the bike path through the pine grove that separated the church grounds from the parsonage next door. "There was a gust of wind from off the lake and I turned around to catch my hat and suddenly—it has to be here someplace!"

While stomping across the parking lot, she continued ranting to anyone who would listen. "Someone must have picked it up. I'll bet it was the pastor's kid. I wouldn't be surprised if Chase Hess stole it right off my head somehow. It couldn't have blown completely away. He's evil, I tell you! He absolutely refused to let me in the house just now. Says Natalie is too upset!" She scoffed. "Upset, my eye! Those two are having sex, I tell you! S-E-X! Right now. I'll bet you money! They're having sex while laughing about stealing my hat!"

"Ma'am," one of David's officers suggested gently while pointing out onto the water, "I think I just saw your hat out on the lake. A pelican had it."

While Helga followed the direction of the officer's finger, behind him, David turned his cruiser, in which Gnarly was crouched in the back seat with his ill-gotten good, onto the lake shore road.

"What does a *pelican* need with a hat?" Spinning on her high-heels, Helga slammed the uniformed officer on top of his head with her handbag.

"Sirrus! We're leaving!" Upon seeing the empty space where her husband's truck had been parked earlier, she refocused her fury. "Sirrus, where are you, you twit!"

CHAPTER FIVE

McHenry was located on the opposite end of Deep Creek Lake, the man-made body of water that was the center of the resort area in western Maryland. The small town consisted of the lakeshore and a mountain, at the top of which rested The Wisp Resort.

Homes spotted the landscape all the way up the mountaintop. Some were luxurious with fabulous views of the lake and countryside. Others were cozy, tranquil, and secluded among the heavily wooded area.

Abby Harmon's home fit in with the latter. Tina Van Dorn's mother lived in a small, three bedroom home that was tucked deep into the woods off a side road halfway up the mountain. It barely afforded a view of lake.

During the short drive to the other end of the lake, Mac wrestled with Gnarly to keep him from swallowing the styrofoam bird he had captured at the church. While Mac won that battle, Helga's hat was a casualty of the war. Gnarly had managed to shred it into a hundred pieces. Holding up the mangled bird to show David, Mac announced, "Yet another police cover-up thanks to Gnarly."

"We'll frame the seagulls," David said. "It'll be easy. We'll wait until it gets dark, and plant the feathers along the lakeshore. Helga will never know … unless one of us breaks down and confesses during interrogation."

Eying Gnarly, who was still tearing into the hat, Mac said, "My money's on Gnarly for being the weak link."

In the rearview mirror, David glanced at the huge German shepherd growling and digging at the purple hat with both front claws. "Nah, Gnarly's tough. He won't break." With a wicked grin, he added, "I think you'll be the first to cut a deal."

Seeing the emergency vehicles lined up along the mountain road, the police chief said, "Looks like a full house." He continued past the cruisers until he came upon a sheriff's deputy he knew. Stopping, he rolled down the driver's side window and held up his police chief's badge. Since he was still dressed in plain clothes, David didn't want to take a chance on being mistaken for a "civilian," as if the cruiser he was driving was not enough of a clue that he was on official business.

After the deputy indicated with a nod of his head that he recognized the police shield, David clipped it back on his belt. "What's the situation inside?"

"We got here to find a bunch of cars filling the driveway," the deputy said. "The sheriff went in to check it out and he hasn't come out yet. Deputy Chief Bogart is inside, too."

"Guess that means it's safe," Mac told David. "We might as well join the party." He turned around to Gnarly. "Guard the car … and don't steal anymore hats."

Inside the Harmon home, they found Abby Harmon's living room filled with a dozen women taking up every available chair. They all sat with their fingers and toes gingerly extended while freshly applied nail polish dried. Some of the lucky ladies held their hands under one of the two driers set up in the kitchen to speed things along.

Two of the women were soaking their feet in plastic tubs filled with sudsy water.

Flustered to have her party interrupted by a team of uniformed officers, the beauty consultant, a busty redhead with big hair and heavy make-up clad in a white linen robe, offered a bowl of fruit on ice. "Grapes, gentlemen? I do have products for men, if you're interested in a manicure." She flashed a nervous grin.

While Mac shook his head, David accepted a handful of the fruit. "We're looking for Tina Van Dorn," he said before popping a grape into his mouth.

Instead of answering, she grabbed David's hand. "You have great hands." She squeezed. "Strong, and such long, elegant fingers." An eyebrow arched. "You know what they say about men with long fingers, don't you?" She wet her full lips.

Mac stepped forward. "Tina Van Dorn, please?"

She pointed toward the kitchen. "In there with her mother, talking to the sheriff."

After they brushed past her, she thrust a business card into David's hand. "Call me to make an appointment. I would love to give your hands a massage."

"I don't think she'll stop with your hands," Mac muttered while dragging David through the crowd of women, being careful not to mess up any of their freshly polished nails.

In the tiny kitchen, they found a teary eyed young woman holding out her hands flat on the table. Her fingernails were painted bright purple. She sat with cotton balls wedged between her toes to protect the wet polish that matched her fingernails.

Unable to move for fear of messing up the beauty treatment, Tina Van Dorn relied on her mother to dab the tears that seeped from her eyes.

"I take it Chip Van Dorn isn't here," David whispered to Sheriff Christopher Turow, a middle-aged man with a military haircut.

Bogie had taken a position near the kitchen window. Regularly, he would peer out the window to check in case Chip Van Dorn was planning to make a surprise visit.

"She spoke to him first thing this morning," the sheriff said.

"He sounded really strange," Tina sobbed. "I should have called the police, but … I guess I've been in denial about his sanity."

"What did he say when you spoke to him?" Mac asked.

"He said that he was calling to say good-bye," she answered.

"I told her that he was leaving town," Tina's mother said. "I knew he was a jerk, but I didn't think he was—"

"Oh, Chip has a horrible temper," Tina said. "It was scary sometimes. That's why I was always glad that we didn't have a gun. I mean, Chip was the type that if he had a weapon, he would just grab it and shoot someone without thinking about it."

Mac, David, Bogie, and the sheriff exchanged grim expressions.

Tina stopped sobbing and looked up at their faces. Her mother stopped mopping her daughter's tears.

Silence fell over the room.

"Don't tell me Chip has a gun," Tina said.

"A man was shot at Spencer Church this afternoon," David said.

"The church?" Stunned by the news, Tina stopped sobbing. "Why would he go shoot someone at the *church*?"

"He was angry with them for nixing his bake sale," Mac said. "He had threatened Eugene Newton in front of witnesses."

"Yeah, but Chip has been mad and threatened at least a dozen other people since then," she said.

"Chip is always threatening someone for something," Abby said.

"If my husband got his hands on a gun, he wouldn't be going after the church. He'd go after—" Tina stopped. Her face turned white.

"Who?" Sheriff Turow asked. "Who would Chip be mad at enough today to kill?"

Tina swallow. "I am so humiliated." A fresh flow of tears came to her eyes.

Abby mopped them away. "Tell them, dear. Tell them about Heather." She told the officers, "He'd go after Heather. The bartender at the bar where he hangs out. He's been having an affair with her and she called Tina last week to tell her about it. It's been going on for over six months and she wanted Chip for herself. Tina said she could have him and left. Chip was furious with Heather for calling Tina. He wanted the best of both worlds—a devoted wife and a sex slave on the side."

Sheriff Turow was writing down the name. "Heather— What's her last name?"

Tina choked out a gut wrenching sob. "No!"

"We have to tell them, dear." Abby patted her daughter's shoulders. "Even if she was sleeping with your husband, we can't let him—"

"No!" Tina covered her face with her hands. "You don't understand."

"We do understand," Abby said before adding, "Be careful of your nails, dear. They're still wet."

"No." Tina shook her head firmly. "It wasn't Heather who called me."

"Who told you about Heather?" David asked.

"You don't understand," Tina said. "Chip wasn't having an affair with Heather. I just said it was her. She had nothing to do with it. Chip was cheating on me with …" She took in a deep shuddering breath before choking out, "Frank-Frankie!"

Sheriff Turow crossed out the name on his notepad. "Frankie. What's her last name?"

"*His* last name is Sandler," Tina sobbed. "My husband cheated on me with a man!"

"Frankie Sandler," Abby said with a gasp. "That creepy clerk at the bookstore who always wears long dangly earrings and—" She stopped to shudder.

Grabbing a handful of tissue, Tina rattled on while mopping the tears that flowed freely from her face. Clearly, she cared no longer about disturbing the wet nail polish. "Frankie called me last week and told me that he and Chip were in love and, if I cared for Chip, I'd let him go. Of course, I confronted Chip and he didn't deny that he was having sex with Frankie, but he said he didn't want to come out of the closet. Frankie had been insisting that if Chip loved him, he'd go public with their relationship. Chip said he loved me and didn't want me to leave him." She clenched both hands into tight fists.

"He wanted you to be his cover," Abby said with disgust.

Tina nodded her head. "So I left and Chip was furious with Frankie for breaking up our marriage." Her voice cracked when she continued, "This morning, when Chip called, he said that he was sorry for embarrassing me and that he was going to end it today."

"Did you say Frankie was a clerk at the bookstore?" Bogie tapped David on the shoulder after she nodded her head. "The assistant manager at the bookstore said Chip and one of his clerks was supposed to open this morning. Neither of them showed."

"Chip ended it by taking out Frankie," Mac said. "We need Frankie's address."

In Friendsville, Sheriff Christopher Turow found telling evidence that Chip Van Dorn was on the scene. His van with the bookstore logo on the side was parked out front.

"He's here." Sheriff Turow told David and Mac before trotting up the steps into the apartment house.

The apartment manager was both annoyed and pleased to see them. She had been receiving complaints all day about the music blaring in the ground floor apartment and was about to go check on her strange tenant when the sheriff demanded that she let them inside.

Upon following David through the door, Mac felt as if ice water had been poured down his back. It was late afternoon but the apartment was dark with the blinds drawn. A musty smell hung in the air.

Even though there was no physical person coming after him, Mac felt an intense, heavy presence lurking in the shadows.

After turning off the computer that was blaring offensive curse-filled lyrics from the Internet radio, David eased open the bedroom door and, with his gun drawn, went inside.

An eerie silence fell over the apartment that was cluttered with sex toys catering to sadomasochism, including chains, leather, handcuffs, and whips.

"Feel that?" the sheriff asked with a shudder. "I felt it overseas, usually in places that had been taken over by terrorists. It's the presence of evil."

"That's what it is." Mac nodded his head. "I've felt it before, too. More times than I like to remember."

David came out of the bedroom. "Wait until you see this."

Bracing themselves, Mac and the sheriff stepped into the apartment's only bedroom. Reeking of sex and violence, the room looked like a den of depravity with magazines, pictures, and toys focused on male on male sex scattered about the room.

They found two naked men in the bed. A slightly built man was handcuffed spread-eagle to the bed, face down and blind-folded. The back of his head was blown off.

The naked man on top of him still clutched the gun that he had stuck into his mouth before pulling the trigger and blowing the top of his head off to propel him backwards. The bloody pulp that was left of his head and upper torso hung over the foot of the bed.

Mac bent over to study the gun that Chip Van Dorn clutched in a death grip. "Nine-millimeter Colt-semi-automatic."

David read the driver's license he found in the wallet on the floor next to a pair of trousers. "Chip Van Dorn. He certainly fell a long way since walking away from the church last year."

"Unfortunately, that's how it happens," Mac said.

CHAPTER SIX

With a sigh of pleasure, Archie dropped her head onto Mac's shoulder. Slipping her arms around his moist shoulders, she took in the scent of citrus left over from the steam shower where she had ambushed him. "That'll teach you to try to take a shower without me."

She had launched the attack by sneaking uninvited into the master bath's steam shower. Engrossed in washing off the discovery of three violent deaths in one afternoon, Mac didn't realize he had company until she wrapped her arms around him and planted a kiss on his naked back.

He finished what she started by carrying her into the bedroom, placing her in the bed, and making love to her the way he had planned after taking their wedding vows … the vows that had been so rudely interrupted by murder.

Hugging her tight, Mac pulled the comforter up around her shoulders. "I'm going to need a lot of showers to wash the smut from Van Dorn's lover's apartment off me." He sighed. "Yep, what we have, compared to what I saw there, brings the difference between love and depravity all home."

"Oh, the way I feel about you can only be called love, my darling." She reached up to stroke his face before kissing him.

79

He held her gaze to admire the striking hue of her emerald eyes. Her face resembled that of a pixie with her short blonde hair. "I'm sorry things didn't work out today."

She brushed her fingertips down his bare chest. "You already told me you were sorry."

"Now I'm using words." He kissed her on the tip of her nose.

"That was action, not words."

His breath feathered her face while he resisted the urge to kiss her again on the mouth. "Do you have any idea how much I love you?"

"Tell me."

"I want to marry you, Archie Monday. I'm done with this rolling around in the hay stuff. I want you by my side for the rest of our lives, through thick and thin, better or worse, richer or poorer."

She held up her hand to admire the engagement ring he had put on her finger. "It's going to happen. It's just a matter of when."

"It would probably be bad form to go back to Deborah to ask her to marry us tomorrow after one of her best friends was murdered," Mac said. "How about if we go to the justice of the peace in the morning?"

"No." Sitting up, she confirmed her answer with a shake of her head.

"Why not?"

"Marriage is more than a legal contract," she said.

"Try telling that to my lawyer," Mac said.

"Marriage is a moral and spiritual commitment," she said. "Yes, there's a legal part, but the real commitment—the exchanging of vows where they really count—is between those two people and the big guy who brought them together in the first place—God. And that has to be in His House, in church.

As far as I'm concerned, it doesn't count unless it's in church. And I want Deborah to be the one to marry us."

He took her hand and pressed it against his chest. "I never knew this was so important to you."

"Neither did I." She sighed. "Going into that church today brought back so many memories. Robin had a very strong faith about her. She used to beat herself up for not being more committed to that church that her parents went to every Sunday. She said her mother, your grandmother, was a big church lady. Robin was always very generous and contributed a lot of money, but ..." Her voice trailing off, she held his gaze.

"Maybe we've seen so many bad things that we've become blinded to all the good things that God has blessed us with." Mac stroked her bare shoulder. "My adoptive parents were devout Catholics. I grew up surrounded by priests and sisters. To me, believing in God was never a question. I only stopped attending Mass after I became a cop. Usually, I was too busy and my schedule didn't work out. Other times, I felt like what's the use—especially after a particularly brutal case." He sighed. "That scene in that apartment today was as far from God as you can get."

He lifted his eyes to hers. "I guess we need to solve this murder so that we won't feel like such heels asking Deborah to marry us—if she'll marry us after I told her to shut up."

"But the murder is solved," she replied. "We just need to give Deborah a couple of days—"

Mac was shaking his head.

"You don't think Chip Van Dorn did it? But he bought a gun. He was a hot head."

"With a short fuse and a short attention span to go with it," Mac said. "One of the trustees said so and, based on what witnesses said about him, he would have gone to the last guy who ticked him off, this male lover who blasted him out of the closet, before going all the way back to the church to blame them for things going wrong." He concluded, "They're going to find out he didn't do it."

Mac's cell phone rang from where it rested on the night stand. "I'm not going to answer that."

Archie reached across him to grab the phone. "Why do they all have to be complicated?"

Playfully, Mac swatted her bare rump. "I'm going to remind you of this next time you accuse me of ruining a moment."

"David," Archie gasped into the phone, "what's up?"

"Are you okay?"

"Sure," she replied, "why are you asking?"

"You sound out of breath," David said.

Ignoring his comment, Archie put the phone on speaker. "Mac's here."

"Hey, Mac," David said, "I've got good news and bad news."

"The bad news is Chip Van Dorn did not kill Eugene Newton," Mac said.

"Give the man a cigar," David said. "Doc Washington puts Chip's and Frankie's time of death between ten and eleven o'clock—before Eugene's murder. Plus, Van Dorn's gun is a nine-millimeter. The slugs they took out of Eugene are forty-five caliber."

"What's the good news?" Archie asked.

"Carmine Romano, one of the trustees, stopped by the church after you left, Archie," David began.

"He makes the best pizza in Deep Creek Lake," Mac interjected.

"I never ate it," Archie said.

"All these years that you've lived here and you never ate Carmine's Pizza?" David asked her.

"That's what I just said."

"Carmine's is only one of the best Italian restaurants in the area. It's where all the young kids hang out," David said. "They aren't fancy enough for snobby socialites like you, Archie."

"Hey!"

David plunged on, "If you're under thirty and like loud music, cheap beer, and good pizza for a reasonable price, you go to Carmine's."

"Carmine never serves fish with their heads still attached." After dodging Archie's elbow to his ribs, Mac asked, "What's the lead, David? We need to get this case solved so Archie and I can make it legal."

"You were there, Mac," David said. "Do you remember Carmine saying how Helga Thorpe has been a real bad sport about not being chief trustee and she was in danger of being removed from the board, as well as the church?"

"That's a motive," Mac said. "Does she own a gun?"

"We're running a check on that as we speak," David said. "Bogie went to the hospital. Everyone there is extremely distraught—"

"Of course," Archie said.

"But he found out something extremely interesting from the ladies," David resumed, "and Ruth confirmed it during her statement. Eugene was shot in the little office down the hall from the church's main office."

"We know that," Mac said.

"That office is used by Eugene and the trustees for various business operations," David said. "Because of the safe in that office, it's always locked—unless someone is using it—usually a trustee. Now follow me. Ruth cleaned the whole church on Saturday, including that room. She dusted the furniture and ran the sweeper. She closed and locked up afterwards. That room remained unused until the murder.

The church has two Sunday services. Immediately after the offering, two ushers will carry the money into that office, which Deborah unlocks before the service. They put the offering into a money bag and drop it into the safe, which is like the safes they have at convenient stores. You can drop the money in but, unless you have the combination, you can't open the safe and take money out. After the second service, Deborah locked the office. Allegedly, no one else was in that office until this morning when Eugene went in to take the money out of the safe to prepare the deposit. Are you following me, Mac?"

Mac was nodding his head. "That means the only fingerprints that should be in that crime scene belong to Ruth, Deborah, Eugene, and the four ushers who put the money in the safe."

"Unless one of them's our killer," David said, "we'll be able to nail him."

"Unless our murderer wore gloves and didn't leave fingerprints," Archie said.

"No," Mac said firmly, "this is going to be an easy case. Our killer is not one of those ushers, did not wear gloves and is going to confess to the murder, and Archie and I are going to get married before the end of the week."

"Yeah, right," Archie said with a sigh, "and Gnarly is going to be your best man." With a roll of her eyes, she threw back the comforter and climbed out of bed.

"No, really," Mac called after her while she went to the bedroom door and threw it open. "Tomorrow. I can feel it. We're going to get a confession by noon."

Without bothering to dress, she made her exit from the room—upon which Gnarly made his entrance. From halfway across the room, the German shepherd jumped to land next to Mac on the bed. After plopping down and burying his face in the cushions, the dog uttered a deep sigh.

A Wedding and a Killing

"This isn't how I envisioned the day ending when I got up this morning," Mac said.

CHAPTER SEVEN

Located along the shore of Deep Creek Lake, Spencer's small police department sported a dock with a dozen jet skis and four speed boats. For patrolling the deep woods and up the mountains trails, they had eight ATVs. Their fleet of SUV cruisers was painted black with gold lettering on the side that read "SPENCER POLICE."

The next morning, David handed Mac a mug of hot coffee while reporting where the case now stood. "We've managed to narrow down the kill zone to a surprisingly small window. Eugene Newton was shot at twelve twenty-eight—almost an hour and a half after Chip Van Dorn killed his lover and committed suicide."

After setting the coffee mug on the corner of an empty desk in the squad room, Mac took his time examining each photograph of the crime scene from the previous day's murder. "Twelve twenty-eight? How did you manage to get it down to the minute?" With a grin, he asked, "Did Eugene's watch stop working when he got shot?"

"Something like that." David pressed a fingertip on a picture of the laptop next to the stacks of bills and coins. "According to Edna Parker, the church's office manager,

Eugene kept count on his mini-laptop with an accounting program. He had entered the dollar bills and coins, but not the checks, which, she says, are entered individually. The checks were in a neat pile. But none of them were entered. According to forensics, the last keystroke Eugene had made on his laptop was at twelve twenty-eight. It's a safe assumption that he was shot before he could enter the checks."

"Twelve twenty-eight was less than twenty minutes before we got there," Mac said.

"His wife told Bogie that Eugene had left home at eleven thirty," David said. "He got a burger and coffee at McDonald's. We found the bag and wrapper in the trash. Here's the interesting thing."

"Something more interesting?"

"Eugene had made a phone call on his cell phone at twelve minutes after noon," David said. "Four minutes after his laptop was turned on and two minutes before he started entering his count."

"So he made that call while he was at the church," Mac said.

"Exactly what I'm thinking," David said. "And he most likely told the person he called where he was. Want to know who he called?"

"Tell me."

"Helga Thorpe's business phone at Thorpe Sporting Goods and Boat Rental," David said.

"Eugene calls the woman who is itching to replace him as chief of the trustees," Mac said, "and sixteen minutes later he's shot."

"He spoke to her for one minute and forty-two seconds," David said.

"Too long to have been a voice mail," Mac said. "He certainly spoke to someone."

"Funny that Helga didn't mention that phone call yester-day when she was pointing the finger at Chip Van Dorn while ordering us to keep her informed about our investigation." He eyed Mac while taking a cautious sip of his hot coffee.

"Any idea why Eugene called her?" Mac asked.

"The check that was on the top of the pile was from Helga Thorpe," David said. "It was made out to the church for one hundred dollars, but it wasn't signed. A yellow stickie on the check read, 'call Helga.' The office manager confirms that it was Eugene's handwriting. He was meticulous about keeping notes."

"Bank wouldn't take her unsigned check. He called her to ask that she come in to sign it. Seems innocent enough." A slow grin came to Mac's lips. "Didn't she say yesterday that she was supposed to count the offering on Sunday?"

"Yes, she did," David said.

"But the person who was on schedule to count with her had been fired," Mac recalled.

"That's right."

"And it was a holiday weekend," Mac noted. "Helga Thorpe has been a trustee for several years, so she would know the routine. With this other counter gone, and a holiday weekend, she could probably bank on Eugene counting the offering Tuesday morning. If she's as devious as Carmine Romano claims, maybe she didn't sign that check on purpose."

"Forcing Eugene to call her to let her know when he was at the church," David said. "But how would she know Edna wasn't going to be there to witness the shooting?"

"If she was a trustee and a church busy-body, she could have easily found that out," Mac said. "She may have planned the murder when Eugene said he was going to count the of-fering Tuesday morning and maybe Edna mentioned that she would be late because she had family visiting from out of town."

"At which point," David said, "it became a murder of opportunity."

"You need to bring her in," Mac said.

"I'm way ahead of you," the police chief said. "I called her last night when I got the report from forensics about the phone call and the unsigned check. Helga Thorpe is scheduled to come in for an interview at ten o'clock."

"That gives you two hours to beat a confession out of her by noon to satisfy Archie."

Over the top of his coffee mug, David asked, "Why the sudden hurry to get married?"

Mac uttered a heavy sigh. "I'm through playing house."

"But you can't tell Archie's mother that you're married," David said. "You have to keep it a secret. So while you're really married, you're pretending to play house. I don't get it."

Unable to come up with a response, Mac said, "You have to be there."

Across the squad room, Tonya, the desk sergeant, yanked a sheet of paper from the printer. "Sirrus Thorpe has a forty-five caliber Smith and Wesson, semi-automatic, registered to him. He bought it back in two-thousand and two. Eugene Newton was shot with a forty-five caliber." She handed the report to David.

"Should be enough to get a search warrant for the gun," David said. "I'll call Fleming. Maybe we can have one by the time Helga Thorpe comes in."

Mac rubbed his hands together. "I can feel a confession coming our way already."

"And your bachelorhood going out the window," Tonya said.

The front door opened. Carrying two white pastry boxes, Carmine Romano stepped inside and sauntered to the reception desk.

Tonya rushed back to her chair. "May I help you?"

Like he was acting as her assistant, Gnarly leapt from where he had curled up on the sofa and jumped up to place his front paws on top of the counter.

Unfazed by the hundred pounds of fur and teeth, Carmine grinned at Gnarly. "Well hello there, handsome. You must be the clever canine who found Eugene yesterday." He patted Gnarly on top of the head. "You're as good looking as you are smart."

When Gnarly leaned across the counter to sniff the larger of the pastry boxes, Carmine slid it out of his reach. "Sorry, dude, these aren't good enough for someone as regal as you are. These are for the lowly humans you're forced to work with." He moved the smaller of the boxes toward the German shepherd. Gnarly's tall ears stood at attention. His nose twitched while he focused on the box. "I made you something much better." Carmine opened the box. "Dog biscuits made from a special family recipe."

In a low voice, David explained, "Carmine doesn't know the meaning of processed food."

A devoted dog lover with three dogs of her own, as well as grown children and grandchildren roosting in her home, Tonya gasped when she saw the box filled with what appeared to be freshly baked double chocolate cookies with chocolate drizzled across the top. "Those are dog biscuits? I hope that's not chocolate. It'll kill him."

"Oh, no." Carmine held up one of the dog treats. "They only look like chocolate. These are actually carob chips."

Gnarly was prancing in place.

"If you don't hand that over to him," Mac warned, "he make take off your hand."

"Can you sit?" Carmine asked the dog.

Gnarly plopped his butt down on the floor.

"Of course you can sit." Carmine handed him the cookie.

As if he feared it would be taken from him, Gnarly whirled around and raced back up onto the sofa to enjoy the treat.

Inspecting the contents of the box, Tonya said, "These are still warm. Did you just bake them?"

"Hot out of the oven." Carmine slid the other box down the counter to her. "And these are for Gnarly's human co-workers. I hope I made enough for all of you."

After opening the box, Tonya turned to show David and Mac. "Cannolis! Oh, they look delicious." She took one out. "These are still warm."

"Are those homemade?" Mac asked.

"Humans aren't good enough for homemade," Carmine said with a mocking frown, before breaking into a jolly grin. "Of course. Only the best for our men in blue." Noticing David's black slacks and white shirt, he corrected himself. "I mean black and white."

Holding up a cannoli with a bite taken out of it, Tonya squealed. "Oh, this is heavenly!" She rushed back to her desk to retrieve her coffee mug. "This calls for fresh coffee and gourmet creamer."

While she hurried down the hallway to the break room, Gnarly trotted back to the counter, jumped up, and managed to take another dog cookie from the box. He then returned to the sofa.

Mac went over to close the lid to the box. "If we don't want Gnarly to eat all of these in one sitting, I suggest we put this box in the cupboard in the break room."

"Good idea," David said.

Seeing his treat box being taken away, Gnarly fell in behind Mac to go to the break room.

Once he was alone with the police chief, Carmine turned serious. "If you don't mind, sir, may I have a word with you?"

When his smile fell from his usually jolly face, the hearty Italian appeared to have aged no less than ten years.

"Carmine," David asked, "have you come in because you remembered something that might help us solve Eugene Newton's murder?"

"Gnarly is now sitting at attention, staring at the cupboard, trying to will that box of treats to come to him," Mac said when he came back down the hall. He stopped when he saw the two men's serious expressions.

"Yes," Carmine said to David. "I did remember something about the murder and I wanted to come in right away to tell you so that we can get this all wrapped up and close this case—How you say? ASAP?"

"What did you remember?" Mac asked.

"Who the killer is," Carmine said.

"That's great, Carmine. Can you tell us?" Trying to maintain his professional demeanor, David swallowed and sucked in a deep breath to contain his excitement.

"Most definitely." Seeing a notepad on one of the officer's desks, Carmine picked it up and handed it to David. "You're going to want to write this down." He then took a pen from his shirt pocket and handed it to the police chief. "Here. You can use my pen."

"Give us the murderer's name," David said.

"Carmine Sergio Romano," Carmine said. "I have his address, too, if you need that."

David was halfway through writing down the name when he stopped. "That's you."

Carmine grinned. "That's right. I'm your killer." He held out both of his hands. "Slap the cuffs on and take me away."

"Are you serious?" Mac asked. "You're confessing?"

"Of course, I am," Carmine said. "I'm a cold-blooded killer. If you don't cuff me, I might hurt one of you. So you better slap them on me right now."

"If you think this is funny…" David tossed the notepad down onto the desk.

The Italian placed his hands on his fat-padded hips. "I'm serious." Carmine's voice went up an octave.

"You told me only yesterday that Eugene was one of your closest friends," David said. "You were seriously distraught."

"He was my best friend and that's why I was upset. It's not easy killing your best friend." Carmine shook his finger at the police chief. "Now I know my rights. I've seen *Law and Order*. If you don't Mirandize me then my confession won't be worth spit. So you better read it to me now." He looked around the squad room. "Where's your interrogation room?" He gestured down the hall at the end of which were the stairs leading to the cells down below. "Is it down that hall?"

Receiving no answer from the stunned men, Carmine marched with purpose down the hallway. "Don't worry, I'll find it. Get the swabs to collect a sample of my DNA and call the county prosecutor to tell him that you've wrapped up this case. Meanwhile, I'll be making myself comfortable."

Carmine went inside the break room.

"Have you ever seen anything like this?" David asked Mac.

"Nope."

Carrying a cannoli, Carmine stepped back out into the hallway and announced, "Confessing to murder can make a guy hungry." He took a bite from the cannoli before making his way down the hallway in search of an interrogation room. Finding one, he threw open the door. "Hey, Chief O'Callaghan, does your interrogation room have one of those set ups where it starts recording as soon as I go inside? If so, then we can get this show on the road and I can start telling you my confession while you're doing the paperwork."

David and Mac were too busy exchanging glances to respond.

"Whatever." Carmine took a bite from the cannoli and then continued speaking around it. "Just tell me what I need to do to make your job easier. I'll be waiting." After entering the interrogation room, he slammed the door behind him.

"You did want a confession," David whispered to Mac.

"Somehow, I'm not buying this."

The door to the interrogation room flew open. "Hey," Carmine yelled down the hall, "I need some handcuffs in here and don't forget to Mirandize me. I'd hate for you to go to all the work of cracking this case only for me to get off on a technicality." He went back inside and closed the door.

"I'm calling Reverend Deborah," Mac told David.

"You do that," David said. "Meanwhile, I'll go read our cold-blooded killer his rights."

At Tonya's desk, Mac was looking up Reverend Deborah Hess's phone number when Bogie came in. "You're here early," the deputy chief said. "I'm assuming you saw Doc's autopsy report on Eugene?"

"Shot three times with a forty-five caliber semi-automatic." Mac paused in writing down the phone number. "We may or may not have a break in the case."

"Oh?"

"We have a suspect in the interrogation room giving David his confession," Mac said.

Bogie's eyes lit up. When he grinned, his thick mustache stretched across his face. "Who?"

"Carmine Sergio Romano. He's the owner of Carmine's Pizza."

Bogie's smile dropped. "That's not funny, Mac." He pounded the welcome counter with his fist. "Carmine was one of Eugene and Marilyn's closest friends."

Mac shrugged. "He came in on his own, brought us cannoli and Gnarly dog biscuits, and then marched into the interrogation room and started confessing. He may lock himself in a cell before we can figure out what's going on."

"Well, I'm going to go get to the bottom of this right now." Bogie was halfway across the squad room before he stopped and turned back to Mac. "Where's the cannoli?"

"Break room."

"Thanks," Bogie huffed. "I should maybe go check that out first. We can't be too careful."

"We do need to examine all of the evidence." Mac grinned when he saw Bogie turn into the break room. He picked up the phone to punch in Reverend Deborah Hess's phone number when the door opened again and Chase Hess, the reverend's teenage son, stepped up to the reception desk.

"Detective Faraday …" Chase said in a formal manner. "I don't know if you remember me from yesterday …"

"You're Reverend Hess's son." Mac put the receiver back on the phone's base.

"Chase," he replied with a nod of his head. "We live next door to the church building in the parsonage … my mom and me."

"Yes, I remember," Mac said. "What can I do for you?"

"Well," Chase glanced around, "if you're busy …"

"No, I have time," Mac said. "I was just calling your mother as a matter of fact."

The color drained from the teenager's face. His eyes widened with fear. "Why were you calling her? Did you find out something?"

"We had some questions for her." Cocking his head, Mac studied the concern that filled the young man's face. He reminded Mac of his own son Tristan, a college student studying natural science at George Washington University.

Chase appeared equally serious and well-mannered. "How can I help you?"

Chase sucked in a deep breath before rattling off his announcement. "Sir, I've come to turn myself in."

Mac blinked. "Turn yourself in? For what?"

"Murdering Eugene Newton."

"Really?"

Chase nodded his head. "Yes, I decided that it was best for everyone if I do that." Looking around the police department, he asked, "You know this police station is much smaller than the ones you see on television. Where're are all the cops?"

"They're all out protecting our citizens from bad guys."

Holding a cannoli in her hand, Tonya stepped out into the hallway and called out to the reception area, "Hey, Mac, if you and David want any of these cannoli you better get in here. Bogie's going to eat them all."

Mac hung his head. "Chase, why did you kill Eugene Newton?"

"Because I'm crazy." Chase's eyes grew wide. "That's right. I'm criminally insane. I'm a danger to all of society and need to be locked up right away."

What in the world?

Seeing Mac's stunned silence, Chase said, "If this isn't a convenient time for you to lock me up to protect society, I can wait until after you eat your cannoli."

Mac cocked his head at him. "You're criminally insane?"

"Sure. I'll prove it to you. Give me a psyche exam and I'll flunk it."

In the interrogation room, David asked the oversized restaurant-owner why he killed Eugene Newton, a man who by all accounts was one of his closest friends.

"The mob hired me to do it," Carmine said in a loud whisper.

"The mob?" David repeated. "Eugene's murder was a mob hit?" A doubtful as he was about the truth of Carmine's confession, the police chief was intrigue enough to want to hear it.

Gesturing with his hands for David to keep his voice down, Carmine continued in a low voice, "Eugene had a plumbing business here on the lake for like thirty years until he sold the business and retired about eight years ago or so. Marilyn had inherited a boatload of money from her folks and they moved into a house on the lake." He asked the police chief, "Well, have you ever heard of the Italian mob?"

"I have seen *The Godfather*," David replied.

"The mob laundered their illegally obtained money through Eugene's business—"

"Which was plumbing … here on Deep Creak Lake?"

Carmine nodded his head. "And so Eugene learned a lot of their secrets."

David squinted at Carmine in an effort to make sense of how a savvy organized crime family could effectively launder its dirty money through a small-time plumber in a rural lakeside resort area.

Carmine plunged forward. "Eugene knew where all the bodies were buried. He was a dangerous liability. So they decided—" He made a slashing gesture across his throat. "They called me to whack him. I spent a lot of time getting close to him so that he could trust me and I could get close enough to kill him."

"Twenty years according to what you told me yesterday," David said.

"You can't rush these things," Carmine said. "I'm an artist."

David was doubtful. "Why did the mob call you?"

"Because I'm one of their top assassins. Like I said. I'm an artist."

Unsuccessfully, David fought the smile and laughter that came to his face.

"What?" Carmine sat up in his seat. "You don't believe me? You think just because I'm not a tall, slender, dark, handsome Italian with six-pack abs that I can't be a lethal, highly paid hit man?"

Literally wiping the grin from his face, David asked him, "How many hits have you done for the mob, Carmine?"

"I lost count," Carmine said.

"Tell me about your first hit," David asked.

"Have you ever heard of Jimmy Hoffa?"

David stood up and headed for the door.

"You don't believe me?" Carmine called out with a plea in his tone.

David whirled back to him. "Carmine, how old are you?"

"Fifty."

"Jimmy Hoffa disappeared in the nineteen-seventies," David said. "You would have been ten years old when you killed him."

"Would you believe I was a child prodigy?"

David stepped out into the corridor to find Mac coming toward him. "We're running out of interrogation rooms." With a jerk of his thumb, Mac gestured at the door on the other end of the hallway. "Chase Hess is in the next room insisting he killed Eugene Newton."

"Why?" David asked.

"Because he's insane," Mac replied. "He wants to take a psyche exam to prove it. What excuse is Carmine using?"

"Because he's a highly trained assassin sent by the mob to kill Eugene in order to protect their secrets," David said.

"Which goes to prove that the younger generations lack imagination and creativity," Mac said.

"I don't believe either one," the police chief said.

"They're protecting someone," Mac said.

Tonya stepped into the end of the corridor. "You two must be running a special on confessions." She tossed her head in the direction of the reception area behind her. "We have a young lady at the front desk wanting to make a confession to murder. Her name is Natalie Buchanan."

"That does it." Mac turned to David. "I know who they're protecting." He turned back to Tonya. "Have we gotten the results back on the fingerprints that forensics collected from the church staff?"

"Not yet," Tonya said.

"Have Natalie take a seat in the waiting room," Mac said. "Then use the phone in Bogie's office to call the crime lab to ask them to put a rush on Ruth Buchanan's prints."

"Why Ruth's?" David said. "I would think they would be protecting Deborah. Chase is her son."

"But he's sweet on Natalie," Mac said. "Ruth was upset when you ordered that everyone be fingerprinted. Deborah was upset, but out of concern for her friend."

Tonya came back down the hallway. "Call was coming in when I went back to the desk," she said in a low tone. "Ruth Buchanan's prints brought up a flag all right. She's wanted for a murder in New York."

Chapter Eight

"Will I ever get to the point where nothing will surprise me?" David glanced across the front compartment of his cruiser to Mac, who was engaged in sending a text message. He searched for a sign that the seasoned homicide detective had been surprised by the discovery that the mild-mannered cleaning woman was a killer. Unable to detect any, he re-directed his focus back to the twisting lakeshore road.

"We don't know her story yet." Mac pressed the send button before setting the phone back in his lap. "All we know is what was on the outstanding warrant. Those fingerprints belong to a Scarlett Fairbanks, who is wanted for the murder of her husband, Jason Fairbanks, seven years ago." He scanned the contents of the report that they had printed up from the police database. "It says here that her prints were in the system from when she had abducted her daughter before in a custody dispute while she and her husband were separated. Those charges were dropped after she and her husband reconciled."

"So that she could kill him."

"And run away to live her dream of cleaning toilets," Mac said while checking a text that came in on his phone. "Three people came into the police department to confess to murder to protect this woman. That tells me that she's not your average gold-digger."

"She's a church lady." David spun the steering wheel to turn into the church parking lot. "They can be worse."

"My adoptive mother was a church lady," Mac said with a warning in his tone. "I grew up with church ladies and nuns and all that. Yes, there were a few like Helga Thorpe but, truthfully, church ladies like her are the exception to the rule."

"That may be your experience, but not mine." David put the cruiser into park.

"What's your experience? Did you get ruler-whipped by a nun?"

David leaned across the console to say in a firm tone. "Repeatedly slapped in the back of the head by a big-ole church woman in a flower dress."

"Why'd she head-slap you?"

Silently, David glared at him.

Not receiving an answer, Mac said, "I'm waiting."

"I gave her son a bloody nose." David opened the car door and slid out.

"Why?" Curious to learn more, Mac jumped out of the cruiser to follow David up to the main entrance.

"He deserved it," David said. "It was the one and only time I did Vacation Bible School." His eyes widened when he recalled, "Robin Spencer signed me up for it." As if to take out his pent up frustration, he turned around to poke Mac in the chest. "Your mother."

Clutching the spot where David had poked him, Mac laughed. "I had nothing to do with that. I wasn't even here then."

"Anyway this little jerk, Robbie Collins, provoked me, so I punched him in the nose," David said. "Then, his big-ole church-lady mother came swooping in a like a grizzly bear and head slapped me." He added in a low voice, "Ever since then, church ladies scare the hell out of me."

With a chuckle, Mac asked, "What did the jerk do to deserve a bloody nose?"

"Can't remember." David shot over his shoulder before throwing open the front door to step inside the church.

"That one time that you went to Vacation Bible School," Mac asked, "did they cover the topic of forgiveness?"

Inside the foyer, David whirled around to reply, "I forgave the old biddie."

Wiping tears from her face with a tissue, Edna came out of her office to meet them. She was wearing a phone earpiece. "Hello, Mac … Chief O'Callaghan." She cast her teary eyes in Mac's direction. The corners of her lips curled in a weak attempt at a smile. "I just got off the phone with Archie."

David turned to Mac. "Archie?"

"Are they in the sanctuary?" Mac asked Edna.

"Yes." She gestured across the fellowship hall. "You can go on in."

Mac led the way to the sanctuary.

"You're up to something," David told him.

Mac fought the grin working its way to his lips. "Yeah, I'm setting you up to be ambushed by a herd of church ladies gone wild."

Through the glass doors, they saw Reverend Deborah Hess stand up from where she was sitting next to Ruth in the front row. Ruth had a cell phone pressed to her ear.

Her long summer dress flowing behind her, the pastor hurried up the aisle to meet Mac and David when they came in. "Good morning, gentlemen."

"Good morning, Reverend," David said. "I'm sorry for our reason for meeting again today."

Deborah sucked in a deep breath. "So am I."

"I wish Ms. Buchanan, or rather Fairbanks, had told us about her circumstance yesterday," David said. "It'd be less unpleasant."

Up in the front row, Mac saw that Ruth was speaking quietly on her cell phone.

"I have always been an advocate for the truth, Chief O'Callaghan," Deborah said. "We didn't hide anything from you, I assure you. We just prayed that this tragedy would have ended with Eugene's murder—which I assure you has nothing to do with Ruth's situation—"

"Are you sure of that?" David said. "Maybe Eugene found out that she was wanted for murder and threatened—"

"Eugene had no idea," Deborah said. "None of us did. I only just now found out about the arrest warrant."

"You're Ruth Buchanan's employer," David said. "Are you telling me that you had no idea that her identity was phony?"

Deborah narrowed her eyes.

"Chief O'Callaghan is not the enemy here," Mac said. "He's got a job that he has to do and sometimes his duties end up putting him in the middle. If Ruth had told us about her situation yesterday, Chief O'Callaghan could have taken action then to—"

"There's a warrant out for her arrest for killing her husband," the reverend said. "He would have arrested her yesterday if she told him."

"True," David said. "But it would have looked better for her."

"What Chief O'Callaghan is saying," Mac said in a firm tone, "is that as the chief of police, he is obligated by his sworn duty to respect the arrest warrant and take Ruth into custody."

"Just like I have my duties as a church pastor," Deborah said, "and I answer to a higher authority than you two men do."

"You're playing the God card?" David chuckled.

"Yes," Deborah answered. "Chief O'Callaghan, you are in a place of sanctuary and, as pastor of this church, I'm granting Ruth Buchanan, aka Scarlett Fairbanks, safe haven. You cannot arrest her as long as she is here in this church."

David's brows furrowed when he turned to Mac. Behind him, he noticed that Edna had slipped into the sanctuary. She held the door open for him to leave.

In the front row of seats, Ruth turned around to face them. She still clutched the cell phone in her hand. "Mac, Ed Willingham wants to talk to you."

"Sanctuary? Safe haven?" David murmured before turning to Mac. "You did this. You called Archie before we left the station so that she could warn them to get Ruth here in the sanctuary so that we can't arrest her." His voice grew louder. "Then you got them in touch with your lawyer to defend her? Whose side are you on?"

"You asked me if I have ever run into a case like this before," Mac said. "My answer is no. I'm curious to learn the facts before we take her into custody."

While Mac went down the aisle to retrieve Ruth's cell phone, David told Deborah, "Ms. Buchanan can't seek safe haven in this church forever. She has to leave eventually and when she does, my officers will be waiting and she will be taken into custody. By doing this, she is only delaying the inevitable and it won't look good at her trial."

Deborah's voice was calm. "I know that, Chief. But in the meantime, she will be safe and we will get the time we need for Mr. Faraday and his lawyer to find out the truth. Ruth is a devoted Christian—a loving mother who will do anything to protect her child. She deserves justice."

"And what about the man she's accused of killing?" David asked. "Doesn't he deserve justice? He was Natalie's father."

"He was also a wife and child beater," Deborah said. "They ran away because they feared for their lives."

"Ruth could have called the police."

"She *did* and they did *nothing*." Gradually, the calm slipped from Deborah's tone. "She even pressed charges and insisted on testifying and her husband never saw a day in court. When Ruth ran away the first time, she was arrested." Forcibly, she told him, "Take a look at the case, Chief O'Callaghan. Read between the lines. Ruth killed her husband to protect herself and her child. She's a good woman."

With his options exhausted, David brushed past Edna and through the glass doors to leave. On his way out of the church building, he radioed in to have two of his officers come to the church to keep watch for when Ruth Buchanan left the building so they could take her into custody. She had to leave eventually. In the meantime, he would have Ben Fleming, the county prosecutor work in the courts to order her arrest.

"Ed, you're on speaker phone," Mac said. "David has left the building. He's going to be calling his officers to stake out the church for when Ruth leaves. I guarantee they'll arrest her as soon as she sets foot outside."

Quickly, he said a silent prayer that David would forgive him for what had to look like a betrayal.

The smooth voice of the high-powered lawyer came out of the speaker to instruct Mac, Ruth, Edna, and Deborah. "That's okay, Mac. We're not planning to camp out in the sanctuary for the long haul. We're just looking to buy some time for me to get the details on this case so that we can proceed as painlessly as possible. Archie is doing her thing to get as much background and evidence that we can use to our advantage about the Fairbanks family in New York."

"The Fairbanks owned that whole county," Ruth said, "including the sheriff and prosecutor. I mean literally. My father-in-law owned them. He used to brag about how many mortgages he had bought of the homes and businesses of some of the most influential people in the area. If they ticked him off, he could foreclose on their home." She choked on a sob. "I was in the hospital nine times during our marriage due to Jason's beating on me. He broke Natalie—I mean Holly's arm—twisted it until it broke. Her ER doctor filed a report against Jason and was going to testify against him. Reese bought the mortgage on that doctor's parents' house, which they were only a year from paying off, and threatened to throw them out on the street if he testified." Tears ran down her cheeks. "That's what we're up against."

"Did you kill your husband?" Mac asked her.

Wordlessly, Ruth hung her head. Deborah and Edna sat on either side of her and wrapped their arms around her into a group hug.

"But it had to be self-defense," Edna said.

"Yes," Ruth said. "I still, to this day, can't believe I killed him."

"Tell us what happened," Mac said.

"Wait a minute, Mac," Willingham's voice broke through the phone, "you're working for the police. For her to tell you what happened, you could be accused of conflict of interest."

"Willingham," Mac said, "I had Archie call you. I can't help you if I don't know the facts."

"You can't help us if you are ordered by a judge to testify as a hostile witness," the lawyer countered.

"What if I work for you?" Mac asked. "Don't you need a private investigator to work on this case? I work for the police department on contract. Case by case basis. Suppose you hired me for this case? Then, can I be ordered to testify for the prosecution?"

While the women sitting in front of Mac held their breath, they listened to silence from the cell phone until Willingham replied, "That might work. How much will you charge me to work on contract?"

"Does one dollar a day plus expenses sound fair?"

Ruth's, Deborah's, and Edna's heads jerked up.

"A dollar?" Willingham replied with a sigh. "I guess I can swing that." Considering that Edward Willingham was one of the highest paid attorneys in the country, it was a safe bet that he could afford to pay Mac Faraday a dollar a day.

"I'm sure you can. I'll take it out of next month's retainer." Sitting down on the steps leading up to the pulpit, Mac nodded his head at Ruth. "Tell us what happened."

Chapter Nine

"What do you mean you're not arresting me?" Carmine raged at Bogie after coming out of the interrogation room to find that the police chief and Mac Faraday had left to go to the church. He shook his finger at the deputy chief. "You're making a big mistake, mister!" With his jaw jutted out, Carmine took in a deep breath and pulled his pants up over his tubby tummy. "I know people—important people. I'll sue! That's what I'll do. By the time I'm through with you, you're going to wish you had thrown me in jail and thrown away the key."

Carmine's rant drew Chase and Natalie out of their respective interview rooms where they had been told to wait.

"Carmine!" Chase's eye were wide. "What are you doing here?"

"Getting ripped off, that's what," Carmine said. "What kind of country is this? I pay my taxes." He shook his finger first at Bogie and then Tonya, who was watching with a stunned expression on her face. "I pay your salaries! I'll go to the media. Good law abiding people are going to hear about how you let a notorious hit man back out on the streets after he killed a nice, decent, gentle, loving husband who never hurt anyone!"

"Carmine!" Natalie gasped. "You didn't kill Eugene!" She grabbed Bogie by the arm. "No, he's lying to protect me. I killed Eugene! Arrest me. Mom and Carmine didn't do anything."

"No, Natalie!" Chase grabbed Bogie's other arm to turn him away from her. "They're both lying. I'm the crazy one. I killed Eugene. Can't you see? Look at my eyes." He opened his eyes so wide that it looked like his eyeballs could pop out. "I'm insane. Lock me up in a rubber room. Do it now and you can close the case."

"Don't listen to them!" Carmine yelled to be heard over everyone. "They're all lying to protect me. I'm the cold-blooded assassin who's a risk to anyone and everyone. You can't trust me out on the streets." He took his cell phone from the pouch on his belt. "Do you want to know how many puppies I kicked just last week?"

Doubtful, Bogie folded his arms across his chest. "How many?"

"I'm sorry. Could you please excuse me for just a moment?" Carmine held up his finger in an order for Bogie to wait while he read a text. "Sorry, kids, we got to go. Soup kitchen is running low on sweet tea and Edna has run out of humane mouse traps for the church. All she's got left are nasty things that break those poor little critters' necks."

"Oh, I hate those things," Natalie said with a shudder.

"Me, too," Carmine said. "Good thing I picked up a nice big case on special at the discount club last week." He ushered her to the door. "Don't you fret, honey. I'll take care of you and your mother."

"They didn't even listen to my confession," she whined.

"I'll listen to your confession, Natalie." After shooting a glare in Bogie's direction, Chase fell in next to her.

They were in such a hurry to leave that Carmine collided with David, who was coming through the open door at the same time that they were exiting.

"Oh, I am so very sorry, Chief O'Callaghan." Once he was assured David was fine, Carmine took Natalie by the arm. "Watch your step, my dear."

Noting their displeased expressions, David waited for them to leave before stepping into the police station. "I take it our band of merry killers are unhappy about not getting locked up."

"Not happy at all." Bogie stuck his thumbs inside his utility belt. "I thought you went to arrest Ruth Buchannan."

"Reverend Hess is offering her safe haven in the church sanctuary." David noted the upward turn of Bogie's mustache at that news. "Mac has hired Willingham to defend her."

Bogie laughed.

"You don't think she did it."

"I know she didn't kill anyone," Bogie said. "Ruth is the gentlest of gentle women."

"Maybe she is now," David said, "but the fact is that there's a warrant out for her arrest and if we don't arrest her—"

Gnarly's bark sounded like a lion rudely awakened in the break room.

Both of them carrying a handful of dog biscuits, Officers Brewster and Fletcher ran down the hallway. Nipping at their heels, Gnarly was right behind them. Once they got into the squad room, Gnarly slid to a stop and continued to bark at both officers who held him at bay with chairs placed between them.

"What got into Gnarly?" Fletcher asked with biscuit crumbs spilling from his mouth.

"You're eating his dog biscuits," Tonya said.

"No!" Officer Brewster climbed up onto his desk when Gnarly charged toward him. Seeing that the German shepherd was coming after the biscuit he was clutching, the officer threw it at Gnarly, who jumped to catch it in mid-air. "It's Fletcher's doing!" He pointed at his partner. "He said they were for us."

"They looked like cookies," Officer Fletcher claimed when Gnarly turned to cross back to the other officer. "Tasted like them, too."

With a huff, Gnarly sat in front of Officer Fletcher. His unblinking gaze was trained on the officer.

"I never would have touched them if I knew they were yours."

Gnarly's snout twisted.

"All gone." Fletcher held up his hands to show they were empty.

The dog's lips curled to show his fangs.

"I don't think he believes you," David said.

"Are you sure you gave them all back?" Tonya asked Officer Fletcher.

"Okay, here! Take them all." Officer Fletcher reached into his pants pocket and tossed two more cookies onto the floor in front of Gnarly.

Satisfied, Gnarly snatched up both cookies into his mouth and, without chewing them, trotted back to the break room to save them for later.

"No respect," Fletcher called after him before telling David, "The county's K-9 doesn't act like that."

"The county's K-9 doesn't get homemade cookies baked special for him," Tonya said.

Brewster grumbled. "Last time I'll take a cookie from the break-room without asking first." He started to return to the room for his lunch before deciding to go into town.

Since they were leaving, David gave them orders to go to Spencer Church to keep tabs on Ruth Buchanan.

"What do you want us to do if she leaves?" Officer Fletcher asked. "Arrest her or follow her until the New York guys get here?"

"She's not going to try to leave," David said. "Mac got Ed Willingham to defend her. He'll be flying in today to meet with her. Just keep tabs on her."

"Why the special treatment?" Officer Brewster asked. "Because she's Mac's friend or Willingham's client?"

"Both," David said. "Mac wouldn't be doing this if he didn't have good reason to. Not only that, but I know Ed Willingham. He plays fair. Once he gets here, he'll advise her to turn herself in. Let's give her the chance to do that."

"And when she does, we'll treat her with respect," Bogie ordered.

The deputy chief waited until they had left before thanking David for ordering them to hold off on arresting Ruth. "You'll see. She had nothing to do with what happened to Eugene."

"Unless Eugene found out she was wanted for murder," David said. "Ruth is an employee of the church. Eugene handled their administrative affairs. He could have uncovered the outstanding warrant."

"As the church's business manager, Eugene could have run into problems with a lot of different people," Bogie said. "Like Alan Bennett. Eugene was forced to fire him from the counter's schedule because he had to keep borrowing money because of his drinking and gambling."

"Alan Bennett's wife committed him Saturday night," Tonya said, "after he went on a giant binge. She had him picked up by ambulance and taken to Pennsylvania. He was in detox at the time of the murder."

"That's why he wasn't in church on Sunday," Bogie said.

"Sounds like he's got an airtight alibi," David said.

She sighed, "I did find another possible suspect a little while ago while checking into Eugene's finances."

"Who's that?" Bogie asked.

"His wife," Tonya said. "While David was out, Marilyn Newton booked a ten-day Hawaiian cruise—mini-suite with balcony and double occupancy—for next month."

"Her husband's body isn't even cold yet..." David turned to Bogie. "Bring the grieving widow in. I want to know who she's running off to Hawaii with."

"Jason and I had been married thirteen years," Ruth began. "We had been dating a few weeks when he hit me the first time. I should have known better, but he was so apologetic afterwards. He insisted it was a fluke and ..." Clinging to Deborah and Edna, she sobbed. "He was so handsome and classy and rich. I was completely blinded by all this glitz that I realize now was just a façade that hid the real man—the one I saw very soon after we were married."

"Things only continued to get worse," Mac said.

"I can't tell you how many times I've heard women say that," Deborah said.

"I thought I could put up with it," Ruth said, "live with it and pray that Jason would die first and leave me a rich widow ... until he broke Natalie's arm. She was only eight years old. A child. And the doctor reported it and Jason was arrested. Then, the doctor recanted his statement and the prosecutor said they didn't have enough for a case, even though Natalie was going to testify against her father—oh, how she hated Jason. She's closer to Carmine than she has ever been to any man."

Thinking about Carmine's confession, Mac asked, "I guess Carmine is nothing like her father."

"Not at all." A soft smile came to her lips. "He is such a gentle and loving man. He always brings me flowers … just because they reminded him of me."

"Really?"

"For years," Ruth said. "Even in three feet of snow, he manages to get through in his catering van to come to the house to check on Natalie and me. He'll always have an arm-load of flowers for both of us—"

"And food," Edna interjected.

"Something homemade from a secret family recipe." Ruth giggled. "Oh, yeah, Carmine Romano is no Jason Fairbanks."

While the three women grinned at each other, Mac wondered if he should tell them about Carmine, Chase, and Natalie being down at the police station, each of them con-fessing to Eugene Newton's murder. Opting to get the details of the murder that Ruth was accused of, he decided to hold off on divulging that information.

"After charges against Jason were dismissed for breaking Natalie's arm," Ruth said, "we left. While Jason was at work, I packed a bag, went to the school and picked up Natalie, and we ran. Three months later, my father-in-law's private investi-gator caught up with us in Montana and I was arrested." With a hollow laugh, she shook her head. "Those charges stuck. My lawyer, who was under Reese's thumb, rolled over and played dead, and I was facing jail time for child abduction. The prosecutor, this pig by the name of Winston Hawkins, made me an offer I couldn't refuse. Withdraw my petition for divorce, which I had filed while Jason was facing charges for child abuse, and move back into his home to be his wife, and they would withdraw their charges against me for abduction. If I didn't, I would go to jail and Jason would end up with Natalie anyway. I thought as long as I wasn't in jail, I could defend her … as best I could." She looked down at her hands in her lap. "I had no choice."

"Your father-in-law had that much power?" Mac asked.

"Believe it or not."

"I believe it," he said. "I've come up against people like that before." He paused. "So you went back to your husband."

"It was terrible," Ruth said. "Worse than before. Jason was so pleased with himself. He was actually cocky—believed there was nothing that he couldn't get away with. He told me that he could kill me and no one would ever do a thing—they would never find my body—and he wouldn't spend a day in jail for it. Natalie would forget about me. I went from wife to his possession and slave as far as he was concerned." She paused to bite her bottom lip. "Then, about a month after I made that deal with the devil, the doorbell rang, and that was when God answered my prayers."

"How?" Edna asked.

"Jason was at work," Ruth said. "Natalie was at school. When I answered the door, there was a big, thick, brown padded envelope on the welcome mat. It was addressed to me and marked personal. After I took it in and looked inside ... I couldn't believe what I found."

"What did you find?" Deborah asked in a breathless voice.

"A Maryland driver's license, with my picture, in the name of Ruth Buchanan. The address was here in Maryland. It was for an apartment in Oakland. Two social security cards. One in the name of Ruth Buchanan, the other in the name of Natalie Buchanan. A check book and debit card for a bank account with a balance of fifty thousand dollars."

Mac felt his mouth drop open. He saw an identical reaction from the church reverend. Her eyes grew wide until she blinked.

"How much?" Willingham's voice reminded them that he was listening on the cell phone.

"Fifty thousand dollars," Ruth said. "There was also a flip cell phone, one of those—I guess you call them burner phones, with a note taped to it that said, 'Call Me.' I opened it up and there was one contact on it. The name listed was Madame X. So I hit the call button and she answered."

"I take it her name was not really Madame X," Mac said.

Ruth shook her head. "I didn't want to know her real name. If the Fairbanks ever found out that she was helping me—there's no telling what would happen to her."

"Why was she helping you?" Edna asked. "Did she tell you how she found out about you and where she got all that money?"

"She simply told me that she knew about my situation. The money was to help me and Natalie start over with our new lives and to get on our feet. She said if I needed more than that, to call her on the burner phone and she would make a deposit to the account. Her exact words were 'whatever it takes.'"

Pulling away, Deborah sat up straight. "That's awfully generous."

"Very," Mac said.

"I know," Ruth said. "But it was the miracle that Natalie and I needed. Over the next week, I worked out with her exactly how to make our escape without leaving a paper trail. She had suggestions on what to do. She became my life-line. For the first time, there was someone I really felt like I could trust and talk to about what was happening and she completely understood." She sucked in a shuddering breath. "I think she was an abused wife, too. I had a feeling. She so understood exactly what I was going through." She added, "Madame X could not have come at a better time."

Mac returned to the day of Jason Fairbanks' murder. "What happened on the day you left?"

"The week before, Jason accused me of talking to his mistress, which I hadn't," Ruth said. "I had never even spoken to her. She had broken it off with him and somehow it was my fault. I thought he was going to break my neck. I had bruises around my throat for a week. The day after I told Madame X about it, a gun was delivered to the house by Fed-Ex. She had a note inside to keep it with me and not to be afraid to use it if Jason ever laid another hand on me. On D-day, as Madame X and I had come to call it, Natalie went off to school like usual. Jason was at work. He was supposed to be there until five, but on that day he came home early—at three-thirty. When we saw him coming into the driveway, I sent Natalie out the back door and around to the car to wait for me. Jason was drunk, as always when he came in. He was furious and accused me of talking to Portia again. When I denied it, he grabbed me by the throat and was choking me. Then he hit me. When I caught my balance, I realized I had the gun in my hand. He saw it and laughed at me. He didn't think I would have the guts to pull the trigger but I did."

"You shot him?" Mac asked, though it was more of a statement.

"I had never fired a gun before," Ruth said. "I was surprised I even hit him. I shot him in the shoulder. He was surprised, too. Then, he was mad. So he came running at me. I said a prayer and pulled the trigger again. This time, I didn't even try to aim. I just wanted to stop him. That shot hit him in the leg and he went down. Then he was cussing a blue streak. I grabbed my purse and ran. I peeled the car out of the driveway. Natalie called Madame X. She told me to keep on going. Don't look back. She would take care of everything. So I did. I drove straight here to Deep Creek Lake. Madame X had given me Deborah's name as a contact." She added, "But I never told Deborah about shooting Jason. She never even knew my real name."

Mac turned his attention to the pastor. "But you knew Ruth was running away from an abusive situation."

Deborah's eyes met his.

"Was this all part of the underground railroad?" Mac asked.

Deborah's expression softened.

"I was a detective in Washington, D.C., for twenty years," he said. "I had a colleague who had helped abused spouses and children escape horrible situations. The only way I knew about it was because I ended up catching a case in which he had helped a woman fake her death in order to escape her husband."

"Then you know that the best way to protect these women and children is for the left hand to not know what the right hand is doing," Deborah said. "That way, if the left hand gets caught in the cookie jar, it can't give away the right hand. That's why Ruth was instructed to never tell anyone here her real name. As far as anyone was concerned, Scarlett Fairbanks was no more."

"Then you have no idea who Madame X is?" Mac asked her. "How did Ruth end up with your contact information here?"

Deborah answered, "I was contacted by someone who knew that the church was in need of a custodian. The job included a caretaker's cottage. He asked if we would be willing to take a mother and child. I said yes, if the woman and her child were Christians who would be willing to become members of our congregation." She offered a soft smile. "It wouldn't exactly look good to have someone taking care of our building who was a Satan worshipper having wild parties. Everything worked out lovely. We all became best friends."

"Is it customary to set up these women with fifty thousand dollars to start out?" Willingham asked. "Where would that money come from? It had to come from somewhere."

Deborah shook her head. "I have no idea. This is the first I've heard of this." She turned to Ruth. "The whole underground railroad is made up of volunteers. After years of standing by wringing our hands, a bunch of us from across the country banded together and decided that it was time for us to do something—on our own. Believe it or not, we have been more effective than any government agency could be. Some of our volunteers work for the government. Some in law enforcement, some doctors and nurses, and even some lawyers. You would not believe the number of women, children, and even abused men we have helped to set up new, and safe, lives." She added with a shake of her head. "But giving a woman and child fifty thousand dollars? I've never heard of that. We're all volunteers who make things happen with what we have. If a woman or child or children need money, we usually will give it out of our own pockets. I've paid for hotels and security deposits for rundown apartments in out of the way places, but …" She looked at Ruth again. "Fifty thousand is a lot of money."

"Call me cynical," Mac said, "but I have found that people aren't usually that generous with so much money unless they have a personal stake in the situation."

"Ruth? You're talking about Ruth Buchanan?"

David could practically hear Prosecutor Ben Fleming scratching his head. Gritting his teeth, he swiveled his chair around to take in the tranquil beauty of the lake off the docks behind the police station. The office that was home to the chief of police occupied the shady corner of the upper floor. Its breathtaking view of the lake was supposed to aid in reducing the daily stress that came with the job.

David afforded himself a beat to remind himself to stop and enjoy nature's beauty more often before turning his back on it in order to answer Garrett County's prosecutor. "Yes, Ruth Buchanan. Her real name is Scarlett Fairbanks. After killing her husband, she's been hiding out at Spencer Church, right here under our noses."

"Your father's funeral was held at that church," Ben said.

"Yeah," David said. "She must have had quite a laugh cleaning up the sanctuary after it had been attended by over seven hundred cops from all across the country."

"I know Ruth," Ben said. "Reverend Hess is a very dear friend of mine. She, her husband, and I all went to college together. The only reason they didn't officiate my wedding to Catherine is because she's Catholic and her family insisted on my converting."

"What are you saying, Ben?" David suspected he knew the answer. *Back off.* He rubbed his aching head.

"Deborah is not a fool," Ben said. "She wouldn't be offering safe haven to Ruth unless she was one hundred percent sure that she was innocent."

"The reverend claims Ruth killed her husband in self-defense," David argued. "Neither of them have said anything like Ruth didn't do it. If it was self-defense, then this woman should turn herself in and go back to New York and defend herself." He added with a growl in his tone, "Ben, her guilt or innocence is not my concern. The fact of the matter is that there's an outstanding arrest warrant in New York for this woman. There are detectives coming down from New York as we speak. We are going to look like a bunch of idiots if we let that rogue woman pastor hold us at bay with a cross in one hand and a Bible in the other."

There was silence from the other end of the line before Ben asked, "What does Mac say?"

"I'm the chief of police," David said. "Mac's thoughts are irrelevant."

"So he agrees that something doesn't add up," Ben said. "He sees that Ruth is not a cold-blooded gold-digger."

"He got Willingham to defend her." David sighed while rubbing the back of his neck.

"Good," Ben said. "I can work with Willingham. I'll call him and we'll decide the best way to proceed. In the meantime, you have a couple of officers sitting outside looking like they're staking the place out."

"Looking like?" A smile crept to David's lips.

"Tell them not to make any move to arrest Ruth until Willingham, Mac, and I can figure out what to do," Ben said. "When the guys from New York show up, put on your best 'I've got my hands tied behind my back' expression. You know that look, right?"

"Law enforcement one-oh-one." Thinking about how he had already given that order to Brewster and Fletcher, David grinned. *If Fleming knew how well I knew him.*

"If those New York detectives want to whine to someone, send them my way," Ben said. "Right now, I want you to concentrate on finding Eugene Newton's killer. Where are you on that, by the way?"

The reminder of the shooting that had started the whole stand-off prompted David to check the time on his phone. It was twenty minutes after ten. Either Tonya had forgotten to buzz him that Helga Thorpe had arrived, or she had stood them up.

"Eugene was shot with a forty-five caliber semi-automatic," David said. "We have a suspect whose husband has a forty-five registered in his name. She's supposed to be here for questioning, but it looks like she didn't show."

"That's bad for her."

"Really bad," David said.

After hanging up the phone, David cradled his head in his hands while hoping Helga Thorpe would be disarmed of any handbags when he went to pick her up for questioning.

"Oh, how I hate church ladies," he moaned while shaking his aching head.

Chapter Ten

"Something is very wrong with Ruth's situation," Deborah confided to Mac while escorting him outside, where he was planning for Archie to pick him up. When David had stormed out, he had left Mac without a ride home.

Edna remained in the sanctuary to comfort Ruth.

"You're only now just figuring that out?" Mac replied.

After checking to ensure their privacy, the pastor closed the front door once they were outside. "How much do you know about the underground railroad and how it works—at least the group I work with?"

"Not much," Mac replied. "When I was working on that case I told you about, my colleague was very strict about only letting me know what I needed to know to close the case." He held his breath at the memory of turning a blind eye to a few details in order to close the case as an accidental death of a woman who was really still alive. The body involved in the case had been a cadaver obtained from a medical school.

"That's how we protect the women and children." Folding her arms across her chest, Deborah dropped her gaze to her feet. "Those we help are strongly encouraged not to talk about where they are from or the people and lives they have left behind. That way, there's less chance of them getting tracked down." She looked up at him. "Another way we ensure that their husbands don't find them is by moving them three, four, or maybe even more times before they reach their final destination. The volunteers at stop number one have no idea where the runaways they have helped end up." With an arched eyebrow, she studied Mac's face. "Ruth only made one stop."

"Are you saying she didn't come here through the underground railroad?"

Deborah's auburn hair brushed her shoulders when she shook her head. "She couldn't have."

"But she and her daughter had phony IDs and—" Mac stopped himself. "But anyone with connections to the right people could have that done up."

"Those types of identification, good ones like what we supply in the underground, don't come cheap," the pastor said. "We've been blessed with volunteers who have connections to supply them."

"Plus, Madame X gave her fifty-thousand dollars to get her on her feet," Mac said. "Obviously, this woman who helped her had deep pockets and connections to supply phony IDs. The question is if she was working alone or—could Ruth have been helped by a different underground railroad?"

"It's … possible," Deborah replied. "There are groups of people who help abused women and children—they don't need to be organized. I've even read of some men or women who have single-handedly helped women to escape bad situations." With a gasp, she clutched Mac's arm. "I just had a thought. Back when Ruth came to me, I was looking for a live-in caretaker here at the church. I advertised through an online employment service that was nationwide. I said in the ad that we were a church. Maybe Madame X—or her associate, since it was a man who called—found me through that listing, and I just assumed because of things he said that Ruth was coming through the underground."

"You mean that it was simply a coincidence that you work for the underground of abused women and Ruth ended up being an abused woman, too?"

"God knew she needed us, and so He sent her to us," Deborah said with a coy grin. "I've seen it happen more than once."

"Well, if Madame X was not part of the underground, she still had to be another part of Ruth's past," Mac said. "Why was it so important to her that she invested fifty thousand dollars to help her escape? Was she helping Ruth, or setting her up? I need to see the case file for Ruth's husband's murder. Archie should be able to get her hands on it."

"Archie?" Deborah asked. "What about Willingham? He's Ruth's lawyer now."

"Most likely the prosecutors in New York will refuse to turn the case file over until Ruth is taken into custody and arraigned."

"But if what Ruth says is true about her father-in-law running things up there …" The pastor clutched her throat.

Mac was nodding his head. "Everything is digital nowadays. If the notes for the case and the autopsy report are in the police system up in New York, Archie should be able to get access to it."

"Should I ask how she can do that?"

"No." Seeing Archie pull her SUV into the parking lot, Mac told Deborah good-bye and climbed into the front seat.

"Where's Gnarly?" she asked Mac after he gave her a quick kiss.

"Keeping a box of dog cookies under surveillance." Mac strapped himself in while she drove away. "What did you find out?"

"The autopsy report makes for some very interesting reading," she replied. "From the looks of it, Jason Fairbanks was already having a bad day before he got killed."

"What can be worse than getting shot to death?" Mac asked.

"Getting drenched in water and then getting shot in the groin multiple times with a stun gun." She turned her eyes off the road long enough to wink at him.

Cringing, Mac involuntarily clamped his knees together. "Are you sure about that?"

While keeping one hand on the steering wheel, she held up the finger to her other hand. "His clothes and body were moist when his mother found his body." She held up a second finger. "The medical examiner found several electrical burn marks in his groin area that are consistent with being shot with a stun gun at a very high setting. If he had survived, it's questionable whether he would ever have been able to father children again."

"Ruth said nothing about shooting him with a stun gun."

"She didn't need a stun gun," she replied. "She had the real thing. But wait. There's more."

"More?"

She grinned at him. "Wait until we get home. You're going to love what I have to show you."

Thorpe Sporting Goods and Boat Rental was located in McHenry, on the other end of Deep Creek Lake. Over fifty years in business, it was a staple on the lake and had expanded into a big operation. Additions had been attached to the main store to display sportswear, including wet suits and footwear. Another wing showed off kayaks, canoes, and other water craft. The original store was devoted to Sirrus Thorpe's first love: fishing equipment.

David found the business owner where he could usually be located—perched on a stool behind the scarred up counter in the main section—constructing a fishing fly.

All of the modern day glitz and glamour of Thorpe Sporting Goods and Boat Rentals was thanks to the driving ambition of his wife. Helga had a business office in the very back of the store. From his only encounter with Helga, David sensed that she was the motivating force behind every expansion of the family business that Sirrus had inherited from his father. Devoted to his fishing, Sirrus showed no interest in the goings-on of his employees or expanding the family business.

"Good morning, Mr. Thorpe." David leaned across the counter to draw Sirrus Thorpe's attention from his fishing fly.

"Sure is a good morning indeed," Sirrus replied in his usual monotone. "Caught me a twelve pound largemouth bass this morning."

"Twelve pounds?" David inhaled to keep the gasp out of his voice. The fisherman's calm made it seem inappropriate to show how impressed he was. Reeling in a twelve pound largemouth bass was no small feat. "I guess the rest of the day is all downhill from here on out."

"Only looking up since sunrise," Sirrus said without taking his eyes off the lure. "Dropped it off at the taxidermist on the way in. Be sure to check out my latest trophy next month. He'll be mounted right over my new line of fishing lures."

"I'll be sure to do that," David said. "Mr. Thorpe, is your wife here?"

"Nope." The old fisherman held up the lure to admire it.

David waited for him to elaborate.

Sirrus picked up his fishing tackle box and carefully placed his new lure among his collection. He then closed the lid and placed the box back on the floor under the counter. When he stood back up, surprise crossed his face when his eyes, framed with deep crow's feet, met David's blue eyes.

Did he think I had left? David asked him, "Did your wife tell you that I called her last night?"

"She never tells me anything."

"She had an appointment to come into the station for an interview about Eugene Newton's murder."

Sirrus set more fishing supplies on the counter in preparation for making another fly. After a long moment of silence, he responded to the police chief's comment. "And?"

"She didn't come in," David said.

Sirrus lifted his gaze from his fishing materials. The two men stared at each other.

"Do you know where Helga is?" David finally asked.

The old fisherman returned to sorting the fishing line. "Nope."

"When did you see her last?"

"Morning," Sirrus replied.

"Where did you see her?" David asked.

"Our house."

After not receiving any additional details, David sighed. "What was she doing at your house?"

"Packing."

David waited a long beat before making a rotating motion with his finger. "Packing to go where?"

"Someplace."

"Where someplace?"

Sirrus shrugged. "Don't know."

The police chief's voice rose loud enough to attract the attention of the employees in the kayak department. "Your wife was packing to go away and you didn't ask her where she was going?"

"Nope."

"Why not?"

"Don't care," Sirrus replied.

David found it impossible to keep the frustration out of his groan. He dropped his head and grasped the counter with both hands. After sucking in a deep breath, he lifted his head to meet the old man's eyes.

In contrast, Sirrus Thorpe appeared calm.

The police chief asked, "Did Helga take her car when she left?"

"Yep."

"Did she say where she was going?"

"Nope."

"You saw her packing a suitcase?"

"Yep."

"What time did she leave?"

To this question, Sirrus hesitated before answering. "Don't rightly know. She left while I was out fishing. Reeled in a twelve-pound largemouth bass." He flashed the police chief a wide smile that filled his wrinkled face. "It's been a great day all the way around."

David fought to keep his tone professional. "Mr. Thorpe, according to our records, you have a Smith and Wesson semi-automatic registered in your name."

One of the old man's thick gray brows, which starkly contrasted the dark brown of the toupee taped to the scalp above it, arched. "Really?" He added in a drawl, "How about that? I forgot all about that old thing. Got it years ago when some businesses here on the lake got broken into." He smacked his thick wrinkled lips. "I wonder where that got to."

"Eugene Newton was shot with a gun just like it."

Sirrus' eyes grew wide. "Really?"

David extracted a search warrant from his jacket pocket. "I have a search warrant for that gun."

Sirrus shrugged his bony shoulders. "If you can find it, you can have it."

"Mr. Thorpe, your wife is a person of interest in Eugene Newton's murder and she's left," David said. "Aren't you worried?"

"Only that she'll come back."

"Your wife was the business manager," David noted. "Where's her office and laptop?"

With a jerk of his head, Sirrus indicated a hallway leading to the back of the store. "Back there. Ask Becky to let you in."

"Who's Becky?"

"Helga's assistant." Sirrus went back to admiring his fishing flies. "Tell her I said to give you Helga's laptop."

David went down a short corridor which housed restrooms on either side of the hallway. The swinging doors at the end opened to a storage room filled with shelving that went up to the ceiling. The shelving contained every type of sports item from clothing to safety vests to gear. To his left, the police chief spotted a corner office sectioned off with thin scarred up walls.

A young woman clad in khaki slacks and a tank top sat at a small desk confined behind a cubicle outside the office door. With wide eyes that held more than a hint of fright, she watched the uniformed police chief approach her.

"Are you Becky?" he asked.

Swallowing, she nodded her head.

"Mr. Thorpe told me to speak to you." He offered her his hand to shake. "I'm David O'Callaghan. The chief of police in Spencer. I'm investigating the murder that happened yesterday and we have a warrant to search this store and that includes Helga Thorpe's office.

"You think she killed that man in the church yesterday?"

"I'm not able to answer any questions about the case it-self." David gestured at the office door. "Can you let me in, please?"

"It's already unlocked."

While going around her desk, David asked in a casual tone, "Did you work yesterday?"

"Yes." She turned in her seat to follow his movements. "I came in at nine o'clock and left at six o'clock."

"Was Helga Thorpe here the whole day?" David opened the office door and peered inside.

"She was in and out, like always. I know she went to the church in the afternoon after someone called to tell her about the murder." She followed him into the office.

He was surprised to see Helga's laptop resting on the desk. He had expected her to take it with her if she had left town. Most people he knew, especially those who worked in a type of career that depended heavily on the Internet or computer-ized data, would not leave their laptop behind.

Unless there's nothing helpful on this? Wonder if she deleted the hard drive and her emails?

After slipping on a pair of evidence gloves, David fingered the top of the laptop. "What about before the phone call? Around noon?"

"I wouldn't know," Becky said. "I go to lunch at twelve. She was here when I left. She came in about five minutes after me." She grinned. "I know because I was three minutes late getting back from lunch. She makes a big point of looking at the clock to make note if I'm late and since I was, I was really glad that I got back before her."

"Which made it eight minutes after one o'clock." David opened the lid to the laptop and pressed the button to power it up. "What was her manner when she came in?"

She shrugged. "She was breathless and her face was flushed." She nodded her head as if to confirm her own assessment. "And she looked sweaty, too."

"Like she was rattled?"

Becky continued to nod her head. "Exactly. Do you think she killed that man?"

"Did she say anything to you about where she'd been?" David asked.

She switched gears to shaking her head. "A couple of minutes after she came in, she got a phone call on her cell to tell her about the murder and she went flying out of here."

The login screen came up on the laptop. So far, so good. *Doesn't look like she wiped the hard drive.* While shutting it down, he asked her, "So you don't know where she was while you were at lunch?"

"She never said. I know she ran a lot of errands to the church. It's only like ten minutes away."

Noting how easily it would have been for Helga to run over to the church, shoot Eugene, and then get back to her office, David unplugged the laptop and placed it and the power cord in the laptop case resting against the desk. The laptop wasn't included in the warrant, but since Sirrus had voluntarily offered it, the police chief was not about to leave it behind.

"Do you know where Helga Thorpe is now?" he asked the assistant.

Becky's eyes were wide. "Actually," she swallowed, "when I saw you coming in, I thought you were coming to tell me that something had happened to Mrs. Thorpe—like that she was dead."

"Why did you expect that?" David asked her.

"Because I don't know where she is," Becky said. "She never misses work. She always makes sure I know how to get in touch with her, but she wasn't here when I came in today. When I asked Mr. Thorpe, he shrugged his shoulders and said she was gone and not coming back, which is really weird. Don't you think that's really weird, Chief O'Callaghan?"

"Yes, I do, Becky."

"It doesn't seem right us coming home and leaving Gnarly at the police station," Archie said while tapping away on her laptop's keyboard to bring up the reports for Mac to read her discoveries. "I feel like a mother foisting her child on another mother."

Mac sniffed to take in the scent of the rosy perfume on her shoulders. "Believe me, when it comes to Gnarly, there is no foisting him on Tonya. She loves animals more than people." He draped his arm across the top of the kitchen chair where she was sitting.

Even though Spencer Manor was a luxurious stone and cedar home at the very tip of Spencer Point, the most expensive piece of real estate in Spencer, Mac and Archie spent much of their time in the kitchen or on the deck. The mansion he had inherited from Robin Spencer had a massive study and library where the author had penned her world famous mystery novels.

While most men with Mac's bank account would spend their time smoking cigars in the parlor while sipping expensive cognac, Mac Faraday found that he spent most of his time chatting with Archie while sipping coffee at the kitchen table—the way his adoptive parents used to do.

Archie brought up the autopsy report. "How many times did Ruth say she shot Jason?"

"Twice," Mac reported. "Which didn't make sense because she said the first shot was to the shoulder and the second was to his leg. Unless she hit a main artery or vein—"

"She didn't mention the shot between the eyes?"

"Do you mean like the way Eugene was shot?" Mac asked in a somber tone.

"Exactly." She turned to Mac. "The one between the eyes was the kill shot. The ME says he would have survived the other two shots." She turned the laptop for him to see one of

the crime scene pictures. "His mother found him sitting up in a chair and look at what's in his lap."

Mac studied the picture. Jason Fairbanks' body was sprawled upright in a chair at what appeared to be a table. His face was bloody, with the center of the blood being between his eyes. Clearly evident in the photograph was a bloody towel in his lap. "Either the victim got or someone gave him a towel to help stop the bleeding—which means time had passed between the first two shots and the fatal one. Ruth says she ran right after shooting him in the leg."

"Considering that he had time to get a towel and sit down at the kitchen table," Archie said, "I believe we have evidence that someone coming in after Ruth finished the job she started."

"Ruth called Madame X to tell her what had happened," Mac said. "If she set Ruth up, then she had the golden opportunity to kill Jason and frame Ruth. Do you think you can find her?"

"Well, the forensics report does contain a clue to someone else being on the scene after Ruth left. That someone may or may not be our Madame X." Archie pointed to the report she brought up on the laptop monitor. "Chicken poop."

Mac forgot about the sweet rosy scent he was sniffing on her shoulder. "What did you say?"

"Chicken poop." She turned her head to grin at him. "The crime scene investigators picked up footprints in the kitchen that had dirt particles containing a variety of different types of substances, including chicken poop."

Rubbing the side of his face with his hand, Mac sat back in his seat. Trying to find where this piece of information fit into this case, he asked, "Did the Fairbanks live in a rural area?"

Archie was already shaking her head. "Upper-class suburbia."

"But certainly our killer came from or at least had some contact with farming or farm animals to have picked up chicken poop on his shoes."

"Maybe he worked at a petting zoo," Archie suggested. "Not only was it on his feet, but his hands, too. Traces of the same substances were found on the grip of the murder weapon."

"Fingerprints?" Mac asked with a hopeful tone in his voice.

"Not that lucky." She shook her head. "Sorry."

"That's okay. I still love you." Mac kissed her softly on the lips. "As a matter of fact, I may even marry you."

With a contented sigh, she pressed her forehead against his and closed her eyes. "Promises, promises."

CHAPTER ELEVEN

"County and state police have Helga Thorpe's plates and the description of her tan, four-door sedan," Bogie told David when the police chief returned to the station. "We've issued a BOLO to bring her in for questioning. What did you find out about Thorpe's gun?"

"He claims he hasn't seen it in years." Having noticed a red convertible sports car in the parking lot, David glanced around the squad room for the vehicle's owner while unpacking Helga Thorpe's laptop. It was wrapped and sealed in an evidence bag. "I've got four officers searching the store, house, and garage for it." He handed the laptop to his deputy chief. "This is Helga's laptop. If she's got as big of a mouth as I think, then maybe we'll find some evidence to use against her on here—like maybe she blabbed her intentions to one of her church lady friends."

"I'll get this to the forensics people." Bogie went to Tonya's desk to open up the evidence log book to check in the laptop.

"Any word from Mac?" David asked him.

"He called to see if it was safe for him to come in." With a sly grin, Tonya asked, "Is it?"

Spotting Gnarly stretched out on his back on the sofa, with his head straight back to reveal the underside of his chin, David replied, "He has to face me sometime." He turned his attention back to the car outside. Jerking a thumb over his shoulder, he asked, "Who does the car belong to?"

"Marilyn Newton," Bogie said. "She's waiting in the interview room."

"Did you interview her already?"

"I talked to her at the hospital last night," Bogie said. "She has no idea who would want to kill Eugene, but then, she was in total shock. Maybe she thought of someone since then."

"Other than herself?" David asked. "Her husband was dead for less than twenty-four hours before she booked a cruise for two to Hawaii. She's looking very good to me right now."

"And you haven't even seen her yet," Tonya muttered under her breath.

Not hearing what she had said, David replied, "Excuse me?"

"Nothing." The desk sergeant turned her attention to logging the laptop into the police system's evidence database.

"Marilyn Newton doesn't have access to a forty-five caliber semi-automatic that happens to be missing and she didn't skip town," Bogie said. "Look, David, I know this woman. She adored her husband and in spite of how things look, she didn't have anything to do with killing Eugene." He gestured down the hallway. "Have a go-around with her and see what you think."

"I will." Taking the case file from Bogie, David spun on his heels and went toward the interrogation room.

After winking at Tonya, Bogie fell in behind the police chief.

Years of working in law enforcement had put David in contact with different people from various walks of life.

During that time, he believed that he had developed the ability to anticipate what type of people are attracted to each other. "Birds of a feather flock together." Thugs usually hung out with criminal-types. Debutants socialized with other members of high society. After seeing a victim of a crime, David could make an educated guess about how that victim lived and what type of friends he or she had.

Eugene Newton was a middle-aged man who had devoted his life to his church. His volunteer work as the chief trustee was a time consuming job for which he did not receive any money. It was a meticulous job. The office where he worked was orderly. He had a precisely organized routine—like refusing to answer the door or phone while he was counting the offering—lest he make an error in his duty. Such men married women who could be equally disciplined.

Like her husband, a church elder, Eugene Newton's wife would be middle-aged, simply and conservatively dressed, and mild-mannered. She would wear a plain looking dress with a high neckline, flat shoes, and her make-up under-stated—or maybe no makeup at all.

Marilyn Newton could only be a first-class church lady. Hopefully, Bogie thought to disarm her of her heavy hand-bag upon entering the police station.

I hate church ladies. David was in the middle of this thought when he threw open the door to enter the interview room to find a strikingly attractive, blonde-haired woman with big blue eyes.

Marilyn Newton was clad in white Capri pants and a sapphire blue tank top that plunged down to reveal an abundant bosom. While waiting for her interrogation, she had removed a manicure kit from her purse and proceeded to touch up her long fingernails, which were painted blue with gold sparkles to match her toenails and earrings.

"Mrs. Newton ..." David turned around to see Bogie grinning when he came in behind him.

Fighting the chuckle working its way up his throat, Bogie backed David into the room and closed the door behind them.

With a wide grin that filled her face, their suspect jumped up out of her seat and offered her hand. "Are you the chief of police that Bogie told me about?"

David reached for her hand. Abruptly recalling that the top coat she had just applied was still wet, she retracted her hand and blew on her nails. "I'm sorry. Wet nails."

What is it with church ladies and their fingernails? Recalling the manicure and pedicure party he had walked into the day before, David muttered, "That's been going around a lot lately."

"It is such *an honor* to meet you, Chief O'Callaghan," she said with genuine enthusiasm before blowing on her fingernails. "Bogie has nothing but praise about how brilliant you are. Thank you so much for inviting me down here to talk about my Eugene. It makes me feel so good to know that his murder is a top priority and that you are working so hard on his case. I have no doubt about you finding the horrible person who took him from me."

She giggled when she saw David looking at the manicure kit spread out on the table. "Excuse me," she apologized while gathering up the bottle of clear polish and other materials. "I'd been waiting for so long and I needed to do something with my hands. I tried to get ahold of Doc Washington. Bogie said she would call to let me know when they'll be able to release my Eugene's body. I need to arrange to have him cremated." She continued to alternate between blowing on her fingertips to dry them and putting away the manicure kit into a leather case.

"I am so glad my Eugene and I talked about what we wanted," she said with a weak grin. "I can imagine what wives who have things like this happen must go through. It's shocking enough that someone shot him—at the church of all places. But if I didn't know what my Eugene wanted done …" She stopped and swallowed. "Pardon me, please. I talk a lot when I get nervous." She stuffed the case into her handbag.

"Mrs. Newton," David said, "I am so very sorry for your loss."

"Thank you, Chief O'Callaghan." She blinked back tears from her eyes. "I really appreciate how kind you and Bogie and all of your people have been. Do you know who killed my Eugene yet?"

At first glance, David had estimated that she was much younger than her husband. But upon closer inspection, he saw that her slender, fit figure and youthful manner were what gave that impression. Her skin was naturally youthful in appearance. Deep smile lines around her mouth and eyes gave away the hint to what had to be her age of early fifties.

"That's what we wanted to talk to you about." David eased into the chair across the table from her. "It is standard procedure in a murder investigation to keep track of expenditures on the victim's credit cards—"

"Did someone steal my Eugene's credit cards?" she blurted out. "Is that why he was killed?"

"No," David said. "It came to our attention that you booked a ten-day cruise to Hawaii on your husband's account this morning."

"It's a joint account," she said. "Was that wrong?" She looked at Bogie when she told him, "No one told me that I wasn't allowed to charge anything to our account. I paid a deposit for a lyre this morning too, to play for my Eugene's funeral."

"A leerer?" David shook his head in an effort to get everything to make sense. "You paid someone to leer—"

"Lyre," she said slowly. "It's a musical instrument, like a ukulele, only Nordic. Eugene wanted a Viking funeral. Did I do something wrong? Should I have waited to contract all that stuff now? Was I supposed to wait?" She waved her hands. "Oh, dear. I'm sorry. You have to forgive me." Sobbing into her hands, she stood up. "I'm such a newbie. I never had a husband murdered before…"

"That's okay, Marilyn." Bogie eased her down into her seat. "You didn't know any better." He shot a glare at David for upsetting her. "We have been through this before. We completely understand." Once she was seated, Bogie shot another chastising glare in David's direction.

The police chief responded with an expression that asked, "What-was-I-supposed to-do?"

"Well, I certainly hope I never have to go through this again. But if it does, at least I'll know better what to do and what not to do." Patting her chest with her slender hand, she sighed. "I mean, how many husbands can a woman have killed off before the police start getting suspicious?" She stopped and looked across the table at David, who squinted back at her. "That didn't come out right, did it?"

"Mrs. Newton, you have to understand how all this looks to us," David said by way of explanation to both her and Bogie.

"Eugene said he wanted a lyre and there is only one musician who plays the lyre in the whole state," she said. "I had to put down a deposit to book him. Do you know how many men want Viking funerals? I never would have thought—"

"Forget the Vikings and the lyre," David said.

"I can't," she said. "Eugene was very specific. He wrote it all down in his death book."

Bogie sat up straight in his chair. "Death book?"

"It's a book or file where you keep all necessary information for after your death," David explained. "Military people put one together before going overseas. It has all of your account information, will, or what you want for your funeral."

"My Eugene had everything written down in his book, plus he told me." With a gasp, she covered her mouth. "I also bought a truckload of firewood, twenty gallons of gasoline … and a pig this morning."

David shook his head. "A pig?"

"For the bonfire," she said. "I figured since we were having a giant fire that we'd roast a pig, too." Tears in her eyes, she smiled. "Eugene always said he wanted to go out like a Viking."

"Why a Viking?" Bogie asked.

"He saw it in a movie once," Marilyn said. "I don't remember the name. … It was a simple name and it had this big Viking funeral at the end."

"Was it *The Viking*?" David asked while rubbing his forehead.

"That's it." She snapped her fingers. "Am I right in assuming you wouldn't let me put his body in a boat, sail it out into the middle of the lake, and then have everyone shoot flaming arrows at it to set it on fire and sink it?"

Bogie covered his mouth with his hand to contain his laughter.

After recouping from his stunned silence, David said, "Your assumption is correct, Mrs. Newton."

"I thought so. That's why I'm having Eugene cremated."

"I hope you got a fire permit for the bonfire," Bogie said with a straight face. "With twenty gallons of gasoline, I recommend you have the fire company standing by."

She covered her mouth with her hand. "I didn't think about that. How many firefighters are there in the company? I wonder if I should buy a second pig. As long as they're standing by, it would be rude of me not to feed them."

"Don't you fret, Marilyn," Bogie said. "Doc and I will help you get everything you need to give Eugene a very fine Viking funeral. Have you thought of fireworks?"

"Can we get back to Eugene's murder?" David asked.

"Please do," she replied before answering Bogie. "Be sure to get back to me on the fireworks."

With a wink, Bogie acknowledged her request.

"Yesterday, your husband of—" David asked her, "How many years were you two married?"

"Twenty-five," Marilyn said.

"Your husband of twenty-five years was brutally murdered yesterday," David said, "and today you booked a ten-day cruise to Hawaii—a suite for two. Did you and your husband have any children?"

"No, we couldn't have children," she said. "Eugene shot blanks. But that was okay. We have dogs, which in many ways are better than real children. We didn't have to worry about saving for college, though we did have to put in a pretty pricey invisible fence because this twerp who moved in across the road was scared of Po Bear. Once he got out— Po Bear, not the neighbor—and he got in his yard and you should have heard him. He screamed like a little girl—the neighbor, not Po Bear." She added in a mockingly deep voice. "Po Bear has a real deep masculine bark. It's very impressive." She giggled at her impression. "But, because this twerp threw such a hissy fit, we had to have an invisible fence put in. But that wasn't enough for the twerp—"

"Mrs. Newton," David interjected. "Who's going on this cruise with you?"

"I don't know," she replied. "Why? Do you want to go? You look like you could use a good long vacation, Chief O'Callaghan."

Bogie replied, "The chief does work very hard."

"Mrs. Newton," David said, "you have to understand how it looks to us. Someone murdered your husband and, then, as soon as he's dead, you're booking an expensive trip to Hawaii and asking men to go with you."

Her mouth dropped open. "Chief O'Callaghan!" she gasped. "What kind of woman do you think I am? I'm in *mourning!* The only reason I'm not wearing black is because I don't have any black summer dresses. If I knew my husband was going to be murdered in the summer I would have been more prepared."

Rubbing his fingers against one of his temples, David asked. "Why did you book that trip? Why today—"

"Because it was a great deal," Marilyn said. "The travel agency was having a special. It includes one free shore excursion."

"But why did you suddenly go booking a trip as soon as Eugene was dead?" Bogie asked.

"Because my Eugene told me to," Marilyn said.

"Did he tell you this before or after he told you he wanted a Viking funeral?" David asked. "Don't tell me. He put it in his death book. Throw me a Viking funeral and then go on a cruise."

"No, it is not in his death book," she replied. "He told me to go on the cruise before he told me about the Vikings. ... I think." Her eyes narrowed in deep thought. "Actually, it could have been ... Was it after? We saw that Viking movie several years ago."

Cocking his head, David squinted at her. "Are you sure?"

"No, I'm not sure," she replied. "I've been talking about a cruise since we got married, so we could have talked about that before the Vikings. Is which came first important?"

"No," David replied.

"Good, because I can't remember."

"What were you doing between eleven o'clock and one o'clock yesterday, Mrs. Newton," David asked her.

"Oh, now that's an easy question." Pointing at him with a long index finger tipped in blue, sparkly polish, she flashed him a broad grin. "I had my yoga class from ten-thirty to eleven-thirty. Then, at noon I went to get my nails done."

"If you got a manicure only yesterday, why were you doing them just now?" David fought the chuckle working its way to his lips with how swiftly he caught his suspect in a lie.

"I didn't like the top coat she used," Marilyn replied. "It isn't shiny. Plus she didn't leave them under the dryer long enough and I got a smudge on my ring finger. I figured as long as you had me waiting, I'd go ahead and fix them." She laid both hand down on the table top and spread out her fingers. "How do they look now?" She bent over to closely examine the fingertips. "This is the first time I got blue sparkles. I know. It's too much. If I knew I was going to be in mourning I would have gotten something more demure. Do you think people will understand that I didn't know?"

"Maybe your manicurist will give you a redo," Bogie said.

"You're right," Marilyn said. "I mean, seeing how people can jump to the wrong conclusions—like your chief assuming I'm taking some young lover on a cruise and all …" She held out her long slender left hand for David to inspect. "Chief, O'Callaghan, do you think that's too much? Take a look at my ring finger. You would never know that I smudged it yesterday."

David touched the blue tipped fingernails. Instead of observing the hue of her nails, he took note of the diamond in her engagement ring, and the diamond encrusted wedding band attached. Together, the two rings took up the whole bottom of her ring finger, up to the first knuckle. She had to be wearing a total of four carats on that one finger.

I heard plumbers made a lot of money, but this guy must have used gold piping to bring in enough bucks for a ring like that … or dipping into the offering plate to keep his lady in diamonds.

"Be honest, Chief," Marilyn said to draw him from his thoughts. "Too much? Should I ask them for a redo?"

He didn't know if Marilyn Newton was a dumb blonde or a very cunning black widow. He turned his gaze from her glittery fingers to her lovely face. Marilyn Newton was a stunning woman. "I would."

Her eyes met his. She smiled. "You have such beautiful blue eyes, Chief O'Callaghan."

There it was. The charming black widow has revealed herself. Aware that he was at least fifteen years younger than she, David adjusted his assessment. *Maybe even a cross between a black widow and a cougar on the prowl.*

Before his suspicion could take root, her eyes filled with tears that spilled over the rims. "Not as beautiful as my Eugene's. He had such handsome green eyes. They were so soft and sweet and …" she choked. "… sexy."

As if her touch was electrified, David dropped her hand.

Bogie slid a box of tissue across the table to her and yanked out sheets to hold out to her. Taking the tissues, she asked the deputy chief, "Weren't they, Bogie? Didn't my Eugene have sexy green eyes?"

"I-I—to tell you the truth," Bogie stuttered, "I never noticed how sexy Eugene's eyes were."

She sobbed, "Now I'll never be able to look into them again."

While Bogie patted her arm, she blew her nose into the tissues before taking another tissue to wipe her face. "My Eugene had the sexiest butt you've ever seen, too."

Clearing his throat, David cast a glance at Bogie out of the corner of his eye. *I know the point of an interrogation is to gather information, but this woman is giving us too much.*

"He didn't like it when I bragged to my friends about how sexy he was," Marilyn continued while dabbing the tears from her eyes. "He was furious when I told my women's Bible study group about his butt." She offered them a smiled. "My Eugene was such a humble man."

"Marilyn," Bogie said, "I think if you had a lawyer present right now, he'd advise you to only answer our questions." He added in a whisper, "It would not be in *your* best interest to tell us—" He gestured to David and himself "—about how sexy Eugene's butt was."

"Can we get back to Eugene Newton's murder?" David asked in a firm tone.

"You do need a vacation," Marilyn said. "Can I suggest a cruise? Have you ever been on one, Chief O'Callaghan?"

David braced for an emotional response to a question that he was required to ask the spouse of every murder victim. "How was your marriage, Mrs. Newton?"

She uttered a low growl. "I'll bet you've been talking to Helga Thorpe."

The corner of David's mouth curled. "Why do you say that?"

"Because she's been spreading nasty rumors about my Eugene," Marilyn said. "One was about embezzlement. She claimed he was embezzling money from the church. Only Eugene insists on an audit every year. The auditors proved that was a lie. Then, this past year, rumors started about him and Edna."

"The office manager?" Bogie asked with a gasp. "No."

Marilyn nodded her head. "Of course, I heard them."

"Did you ask Eugene about those rumors?" David asked her.

147

"I didn't have to," Marilyn said. "Yes, Eugene and Edna worked closely together. He also worked with Pastor Deborah, and Edna and Deborah work together. They were all very good friends, but that's it. Edna is my best friend. She came to work at the church after her skunk of a husband ran off on her for a younger woman with size D cups." She hissed, "They weren't real."

She sat back in her seat. "Church folks are just like everyone else in that when you get a group of people together, there's always one or two troublemakers looking to drive a wedge between friends just for the sake of seeing drama."

She wagged a finger at Bogie and David. "I tracked down that rumor and it started with Helga Thorpe. Of course, if there was a scandal because the married chief trustee was having an affair with the divorced office manager, then he would be forced to resign—"

"Which would open the door for her to apply for the job," Bogie finished.

David was doubtful. "Is that what Eugene and Edna told you?"

"It's what I know," Marilyn said. "I know you have to investigate that rumor to make sure it wasn't true and that I didn't have a motive for killing my Eugene."

"I'm sorry to say you did have motive, Mrs. Newton," David said with a sigh. "You're booking cruises while his body is still warm."

"You have to understand my Eugene, Chief O'Callaghan," Marilyn said with a sigh. "Going on a cruise to Hawaii was at the top of my bucket list—"

Bogie nodded his head. "It's on your list of things to do before you die."

"No," Marilyn said. "Well, yes." With a sigh, she regarded her long fingernails. "I have two bucket lists. On one, I have a list of things I want to do before I die. But I also have a second one."

"What bucket list is that?" David asked.

"Things to do *after* my Eugene died," she said. "Going on a cruise was number one on the list." Seeing David and Bogie exchanging startled and suspicious glances, she laid her hands on her bosom. "I loved my Eugene with all my heart! He was the most compassionate, handsome, organized, practical, and sexiest man alive. He was honorable and faithful. But he was also something else."

"What?" Bogie asked.

"My Eugene was a stick in the mud." She gestured at Bogie. "You met him. My Eugene was so tight that he squeaked when he walked. He did the grocery shopping. Do you know why?"

"Because he was so cheap?" Bogie replied.

"Oh, we had awful fights," Marilyn said. "He would not believe me about how expensive groceries were. He swore that we spent so much on groceries because I didn't know how to shop. So he took over the grocery shopping a little over ten years ago. Suddenly," she smiled, "we stopped fighting over how much I spent on groceries because he was doing it. He was happy because he had control over the grocery budget. For years, he waited for me to get mad about it." She giggled. "Never happened. I hated grocery shopping and dreaded those fights when I'd get home." Her eyes teared up. "Now I have no one to go grocery shopping for me." Breaking down into heavy sobs, she collapsed onto the table top.

Bogie whipped a tissue out of the box and handed it to her. "It's okay, Marilyn. I am so sorry that you have to go through this. Eugene was a good, good man."

Sniffing, she dabbed her eyes. "Yes, he was. Eugene was a very good man. Even if he was a stick in the mud, I still loved him more than anything."

"It must have been very hard being married to such a frugal man," David said. "Didn't the thought ever occur to you that you might die first and not get to do those things on your bucket list?"

She laughed loudly. David and Bogie exchanged puzzled glances.

"What?" David asked over her laughter.

"Everyone knew Eugene was going to die first," she said with a wave of her hand. She sucked in her laughter. "Not that we *wanted* him to die first, but—it just went without saying." A weak smile came to her lips. "I always said that when he died, I'd find out I was an heiress."

"Were you?" David asked before correcting himself. "*Are* you an heiress?"

"Yes, my Eugene said he'd make sure I was very well taken care of and he did."

David and Bogie exchanged glances filled with suspicion.

Seeing this, Marilyn shook her head. "Don't you see? If my Eugene wasn't so tight, then I wouldn't be sitting pretty right now. I owe everything to him, and God for bringing him into my life. God knew I needed a stick in the mud like Eugene, and Eugene needed me to bring fun into his life. So God brought the two of us together."

"Really?" David cocked his head at her. "Most women like you would get impatient waiting for their husband to die to let them take advantage of their fortune."

"Maybe twenty years ago, before I grew up and came to appreciate all that Eugene did for me." Marilyn waved her hands with her long fingernails to gesture at her flowing blonde hair. "Look at me. I drive a red convertible. Eugene drove a green sedan. I was flash and excitement. Eugene was

150

a balanced budget and practicality. Eugene was news and in bed at nine o'clock every night. I was sexy romance books and sleeping in in the morning." She grinned. "But think about it. If I didn't have Eugene to keep me on the straight and narrow, I would have been out of control and dead before I was forty. And if Eugene didn't have me, then he'd have no fun or friends." Tears came to her eyes.

"Why wouldn't he have any friends?" David asked.

"Because he was a bad man."

"You just said he was a good man," David countered with a grin at catching her contradiction.

"He was." Seeing the spark in his eyes, she rushed on to add, "But his job was to be a bad man and Eugene was very good at it. He was the guy who had to make the hard decisions, both at home and in the church. You have to understand. You're probably the bad man here, Chief. There's always someone who has to make the unpopular decisions for the greater good. That was always Eugene. He would always get chosen to break the bad news and enforce the hard rules, which would get people mad at him."

"Like no to bake sales," David said while thinking of Chip Van Dorn.

"Oh, man," Marilyn said. "Talk about shooting the messenger there. We all called Eugene 'the bad man.'"

"What other kind of unpopular things would Eugene have to do?" David asked her.

"Tell me no," she replied. "No, we can't buy a Mercedes convertible. No, we can't get a fourth dog. No, *we can't go on a cruise.*" In a whisper, she added, "Actually, we could afford a cruise. He just didn't want to go on one."

"Who else did Eugene have to say no to?" David asked. "Who else was he unpopular with?"

Marilyn said, "Some of our church members are difficult to get along with. Like Helga Thorpe, for example. She always has an opinion about everything and sometimes she'll corner Pastor Deborah. Well, Deborah and Eugene have this thing—"

"What kind of thing?" Bogie asked.

"On Sundays, if she got cornered by someone, Pastor Deborah would shoot a look at Eugene and he would go over and make an excuse to take Deborah away. He did the same for Edna. Some of the church members, especially the lonely, older men, have become kind of dependent on her for company—you know, on account that she's so pretty and nice. So, if one of those poor old souls started monopolizing Edna's time to the point of being a pest so that she couldn't get her work done, my Eugene would move in to save her with an excuse about needing her for this or that."

"Did anybody object to Eugene doing that?" David asked.

Marilyn cast him a blank expression. "Not really. Like I said, Eugene was a bad man. It was what he did."

"What other unpopular decisions did Eugene make?" David leaned forward in his seat. "If he made a career out of being the bad man, he had to have had enemies. Did anyone give him any trouble—threaten him because of one of his hard decisions?"

Her beautiful blue eyes went blank. "No," she said in a very low tone. Realization seeped in. "But …"

"Who?" David asked.

Bogie was at the edge of his seat. "What are you thinking about Marilyn?"

"But he would have never gone through with it."

"Let us be the judge of that," David said. "Did someone threaten Eugene?"

"Bill Clark," she whispered.

"Bill Clark, as in chairman-of-the-town-council Bill Clark?" David felt the blood drain from his face.

"Twerpie." Marilyn Newton nodded her head. "That's what I call him."

"Twerpie," Bogie chuckled.

"Because he's a twerp," she replied. "He's the idiot across the road who Po Bear made scream like a little girl."

"Clark doesn't go to our church." Bogie asked, "Why did he threaten Eugene?"

"Because Eugene revealed him for the dirty snake in the grass that he is," Marilyn said. "Eugene made a fool out of him and cost him a whole lot of money to boot."

"How?" Bogie asked.

"Bill Clark wanted the church shut down," Marilyn said, "on account that our property is prime real estate, being right on the lake shore and all. Well, the Spencer family gave the property to the church over a hundred years ago."

Bogie was nodding his head. "Spencer history. Everyone knows that."

"Did you know that a real estate developer bought the property across the road from the church to put in condos? Of course, he could sell them for a higher price if he had a club-house and docks right on the lake. The only problem was the church was on that land." Marilyn shrugged. "No problem. The town council decided to petition to change the zoning for the church property to residential, claiming that we were violating the zoning, even though we've been there for a hundred years. Well, that failed miserably. Then, Bill Clark had his lawyer use all kinds of legal loopholes and challenged our non-profit tax status to have us shut down. No one expected Ed Willingham to represent us."

"Why did Bill Clark go to so much trouble to have you shut down?" David found his voice to ask.

"I thought it was vengeance against us because of Po Bear," Marilyn said. "But Eugene smelled something fishy and swore there had to be more to it than that. So he went digging. Sure enough, Eugene found out that Bill Clark was a silent partner of this development company. That was why he wanted us shut down. If we lost our tax-exempt status, we'd have no choice but to sell the property to pay our taxes. Then the development company could buy it cheap and convert the building into a clubhouse for the condos, which were residential, and put in docks."

"Snake," Bogie said.

"Eugene collected all of the evidence to prove it and Willingham gave it to the judge." She laughed. "In the end, Ed Willingham got Clark to pay the church's legal fees, too." She added in a low whisper, "I think Eugene and Willingham uncovered something else that Clark did that was dirty. I heard the whole thing cost him two-hundred and fifty thousand dollars in the end."

"Did Clark know Eugene was the one who uncovered everything?" David asked.

"Oh, yes," Marilyn said. "I heard him tell Eugene, right in the elevator after he got reamed by the judge for trying to shut down a church. Twerpie poked Eugene in the chest with his finger and said that he was going to make Eugene pay—one way or another—he was going to teach him a lesson for getting in his way." She gasped. "Could that be it? Do you think Bill Clark made my Eugene pay by killing him? Would he do something that evil?"

"The Bill Clark I know would," Bogie said.

CHAPTER TWELVE

"You knew nothing about Bill Clark's vendetta against the church?" Mac asked Bogie and David upon meeting with them in the police chief's upper floor, corner office after Marilyn Newton had left.

Marilyn was on her way to meet with Eugene's lawyer to set up some tax shelters for the bundle her cheap husband had left her; after which, she was going to the manicurist for a re-do. Tonya had suggested white tips, also known as a French manicure.

"It all happened before I started going there," Bogie explained, "and David was in Afghanistan. It was in the state court system and dealt with tax issues."

David lifted his head from where he was holding it in his hands. "So our department was completely out of the loop."

"Because of what Eugene uncovered," Bogie resumed, "the whole case was thrown out and according to the judge's ruling, it was never to be brought up again."

"And Bill Clark ended up exposed for the snake he is," Ed Willingham announced when he made his entrance into David's office. "I see you found out about your town council-man's motive for wanting to get rid of Eugene Newton."

Ed held the door open for Chelsea and her service dog to come in. Ben Fleming, the county prosecutor, was directly behind his assistant.

Upon seeing Molly, Gnarly leapt down from where he was getting a belly rub from Archie on the chief's sofa to gallop across the room to greet the white German shepherd. Their tails wagging, they danced around each other before settling down in a ray of sunshine beaming in through the window.

"While flying out here, I remembered Bill Clark's shenanigans." The high-priced attorney jerked a thumb in the prosecutor's direction. "Ben here and I talked about it on the way in from the airport."

Behind his desk, David laid his head back and massaged his temples with his fingertips until Chelsea went behind his chair to take over. "But that was all years ago."

Ben Fleming said, "You know as well as anyone in this room, David, that Bill Clark is an arrogant, vindictive—vindictive being the operative term here—SOB."

"Twerp," Bogie quoted Marilyn Newton.

Ben agreed. "Twerp."

"Did Clark know that Newton dug up the information that got his case against the church thrown out of court?" Mac asked.

"Yes," Willingham said, "but that wasn't half as painful as the other information that Newton uncovered." He chuckled. "Eugene Newton was almost as good as Archie."

"Almost, but not quite," she replied.

"What else did he find out?" Bogie asked.

"Bill Clark had not one," Willingham held up a finger, "but two," he held up a second finger, "overseas accounts in which he had a couple of million dollars hidden."

"From the IRS?" Chelsea asked.

"Almost as bad," Willingham said.

"His wife," Mac guessed.

Willingham nodded his head. "You see, back then Clark was in the process of a divorce. He had this money socked away and Eugene found it. He knew exactly what Clark was doing and that was when Clark threatened Eugene in the elevator."

"If word got to the right people about the millions he had hidden away, it would have cost him a whole lot of money," Mac said. "Did Eugene keep his mouth shut?"

Willingham shot Mac a coy grin. "Yes, *Eugene* didn't say a word."

"How about *you*?" Mac asked.

Willingham clasped his chest in a melodramatic manner. "Mac, I'm shocked that you would suggest such a thing. *I* am a lawyer. There are *laws* against divulging information—"

"Bill Clark was never your client," Archie interjected.

"He was trying to shut down a hundred-year-old church for his own financial gain." Willingham took in a deep breath before he said with a drawl, "I *may* have slipped a few account numbers to the mother of one of my daughter's little friends while waiting for the girls to finish their ballet lesson; and *maybe* that mother *happened* to be a divorce lawyer who *happened* to be representing Bill Clark's soon to be ex-wife, and it *may* have cost him a million or so dollars."

"Maybe." Mac grinned.

"Just maybe."

Mac turned to Bogie. "How long ago was all this?"

"Five years at least," Willingham answered. "It was long before you came to Deep Creek Lake, Mac. Your mother was still alive. She was the one who hired me to represent the church after Reverend Hess called her in tears about what was happening. That was when I met those folks at Spencer Church."

"They're all good people," Ben said in a somber tone.

"They certainly are," Willingham agreed.

David sat up in his seat. "Why would Clark have motive to kill Eugene *now?*"

"Revenge is best served cold," Archie replied.

"Clark never learned his lesson," Ben Fleming said. "About two weeks ago, wife number two walked in on Clark trying out an applicant for role of his latest mistress. The wife walked out, went straight to a divorce lawyer, and filed for a legal separation."

"Would Eugene Newton even care?" Bogie asked. "They don't hang out with the same crowd. They live across the street from each other—"

"The only reason Eugene uncovered Clark's dirty business before was because he came after Eugene's church," Willingham said. "That whole condo thing went up in smoke after the bottom dropped out of the real estate market."

"Then, as far as we know, Clark has no motive for killing Eugene now," David said with a sigh of relief. "Helga Thorpe has a stronger motive. Plus, she has access to a forty-five caliber semi-automatic—which happens to be missing, along with her."

"Then focus on Helga Thorpe," Ben Fleming said. "But I think it would be prudent to check out Bill Clark as well. He's not the type to let someone get away with upsetting his apple cart."

Bogie nodded his head to indicate that he understood. "I'll go digging around Clark's records to see if there's any recent activity that may warrant us questioning him."

Bogie and Mac noted an uncomfortable expression that filled David's face. Questioning the town councilman was the last thing the police chief wanted to do. It would serve to add yet another reason for the spiteful politician to want David O'Callaghan fired.

It was only due to the support of the other members of the town council who deeply respected David's military record and paternity that he had been hired for the position in the first place. Ironically, it was because of David's military record that Clark wanted to ruin the police chief he blamed for his sister's death.

Mac glanced up from David's face, which was pale, to see that Bogie was equally concerned about the prospect of questioning Bill Clark. He wondered if David had confided in the deputy chief about the reason behind Bill Clark's grudge against him.

With the rest of the staff out on patrol or keeping Ruth Buchanan under surveillance at the church, Tonya was alone at the front desk when the door flew open. The abrupt nature of the entrance made her reach for the weapon she wore on her hip.

Seeing an older couple walk in, she relaxed until she saw the hard expression on the man's face.

A head shorter than her companion, the female half of the couple was reed thin. Her frame appeared even thinner in her oversized dress that sported long sleeves. Clinging to her purse with both hands, she worked her bony fingers into the leather bag.

The sight of the uniformed female officer filled the male visitor with disdain. His dark eyes bore into her. He squared his broad shoulders and sucked in his bulging stomach to expand his barrel chest before demanding, "I want to talk to your police chief."

"I'm sorry, sir, he's in a meeting," Tonya replied. "Do you have an appointment?"

"No, but this is extremely important," he answered. "He's got a murderer right here in his town and I want to know what he's doing about it."

"It's never been proven that—" his companion interjected.

"Shut up!" He whirled around to backhand her across the face. "I've had enough of you yapping about innocent until proven guilty. That's a bunch of crap."

Tonya's jaw dropped. For a full moment, she didn't move. *Seriously? Did this guy just walk into a police station and slap someone right in front of me—a uniformed officer?*

Her nose bleeding, the woman dropped back against the wall.

"You're under arrest, sir!" Tonya jumped up from her seat and grabbed her handcuffs from the case on her utility belt. "Put your hands on top of your head."

"Go to hell!" He whirled around with a laugh. "Get me your boss!"

"You're under arrest for assault, sir! Lay down spread eagle on the floor and put your hands on top of your head."

Holding her bleeding nose, the woman stared wide eyed at Tonya.

"No!" He shoved the middle-aged female officer back with both hands. "You have no idea who you're dealing with, bitch!"

"That's where you're wrong, bucko!" Tonya whipped her baton out of her belt. "I know exactly what I'm dealing with." She rammed the end of the baton directly into his diaphragm. The air knocked out of him, he doubled over. With a twirl of the baton, Tonya wacked him across the base of the neck to send him down flat on the floor.

Refusing to be shown up by a woman, he grabbed Tonya's ankle and yanked her foot out from under her. But before he could gain an advantage, Tonya rolled over, dropped down on top of him, and wailed away at him with the baton to strike him on the head and shoulders.

"Hit him again!" Shocked by her outburst, the woman clapped both hands over her mouth.

Completely overtaken by fury over his arrogance, Tonya pinned one of her opponent's arms behind his back with his wrist wrapped around the baton. "Not so tough now!" she gasped out at him.

"Wait until your boss finds out what you did, bitch!" he grunted out. "You're going to pay!"

"No," Tonya said, "you are. I'll teach you to hit women."

With a hand on both ends of the baton, she twisted until she heard the snap of his arm out of his shoulder socket. His gut wrenching scream of pain sounded like music to her ears. When Tonya looked up at his companion, she saw a wide smile filling her bloody face.

"What's going on here?"

Tonya realized that they were no longer alone. The fight had drawn David, Bogie, and everyone out of his office on the second floor. She was still sprawled out on top of the man, pinning him to the floor, when she noticed her audience. "I'm arresting this man for assault, Chief."

"This bitch attacked me," the man yelled. "She broke my arm. I'm suing the whole lot of you."

David regarded the woman with the bloody nose. "Did this man strike you, ma'am?"

Seeing the blood, Chelsea had rushed to the water cooler to wet a paper towel to clean her up.

The woman looked around the reception area at the two uniformed officers, the two men in suits, and the two women. Plus, there were two German shepherds. The white one was licking her bloody hand.

"Tell us what happened, ma'am," Bogie urged her. "You're safe here. If he hurt you, we'll make sure it doesn't happen again."

Tonya was cuffing her prisoner. "Go ahead, ma'am. Tell him." She told David and Bogie, "I saw the whole thing. He backhanded her right in front of me. I couldn't believe it. Like he didn't see my badge and thought I wouldn't arrest him?"

"They're lying," the man objected. "You know how these bitches are. They stick together. The idiot walked into the wall!"

"No, I didn't!" the woman blurted out. "He slapped me." She pointed to the man on the floor. "And then when your officer told him that she was arresting him, he shoved her. That was when she took him down." She grinned. "Most beautiful thing I ever saw."

David squatted down to peer at the man struggling against the handcuffs. "You touched one of my police officers? In my station? How stupid are you?"

The cuffed man's face contorted in pain from the dislocated shoulder. "Just you wait. I'm Reese Fairbanks, the father of the man Scarlett Fairbanks shot in cold blood. Once my lawyer has a word with your prosecutor about how your officer treated the father of a murder victim, you'll be changing your tune."

"I don't think so," Ben Fleming said. "I am the county prosecutor and we don't take too kindly to men beating up women or shoving police officers in these parts. You're going to be spending some time in our jail. If you're smart, you'll learn some manners while you're there."

"Never!" he alternated between cursing and screaming out in pain when Bogie lifted him to his feet. While doing so, Bogie made no attempt to be careful of his dislocated shoulder.

"Let's make arrangements to transport him to the hospital to have his shoulder checked out." David patted Tonya on the back. "Good job, Tonya. I hope you taught this man a lesson."

"He'd have to have brains to learn anything," Tonya replied quickly before hurrying to where Chelsea and Archie were comforting the woman.

Kneeling in front of her, Ben Fleming was holding the victim's hand. "I give you my promise, Mrs. Fairbanks, no man lays a hand on his wife in my jurisdiction and gets away with it. I don't care how much money he has."

"You don't know how powerful Reese is," she said.

"Your husband can't touch anyone here," Mac said. "No one he can bribe, no one whose mortgage he can buy."

She gazed up at where Mac stood behind Ben with his arms folded across his chest. "You've been talking to Scarlett," she said in a hushed voice.

"Yes."

"How is she?" Her eyes filled with tears. "Holly?"

"She's fine," Mac said. "They're both fine."

"She's got a whole slew of friends who love and have been taking very good care of them," Archie said. "And she's got the best lawyer in the country to defend her."

"I'd like to think I'm the best in the world." Ed Willingham stepped forward.

"They say Scarlett killed my son," she said, "but no one understands what he had put her through. If they knew the truth about what he did to her and Holly then … If there's anything I can do to help in her defense …"

"We'll be glad to accept your offer of help," Ed said.

"In the meantime, Mrs. Fairbanks …" David said.

"Call me Jenny," she interjected. "Frankly, I've come to hate my husband's name."

"Jenny," David flashed her his most charming smile. "I'd like for you to go to the hospital so that they can check you out."

"My nose has stopped bleeding," she said.

David shook his head. "We're going to press charges against your husband and we're going to make sure we do everything by the book. Tonya will drive you."

"I'll come, too." Archie patted her hand.

"I'll send an officer to the hospital to take your statement and we'll make sure you have a safe place to stay," David said.

While the women gathered together to go to the hospital, Mac exchanged glances with David, Ben Fleming, and not the least, Ed Willingham. By the time they had left, taking Gnarly and Molly with them, the defense attorney was openly grinning.

"I guess things are really shaping up for Ruth Buchanan, or Scarlett Fairbanks, whatever you want to call her," Ed said. "The mother of the victim has volunteered to help in her defense. Once a jury hears that, they'll refuse to convict."

"If the case gets to a jury," Mac said.

"You don't think…" Ben asked.

"I don't think she did it," Mac said. "Ruth Buchanan says she shot her husband twice. Shoulder and leg. He was shot three times. Plus, he had a blood soaked towel in his lap where it looks like he was tending to one of the shots. That indicates time between the first two shots and the kill shot to the head."

"Why didn't Ruth say she was innocent from the beginning?" the prosecutor asked.

"I don't think she knew," Mac said. "Archie only found out about the third shot in the police reports."

David said, "Most likely, the investigators kept the number of shots from the media."

"All these years, Ruth thought she killed her husband and the father of her child," Mac said. "In reality, someone came in to finish the job and let her take the blame."

"Any idea who that someone is?" Ed Willingham asked. "The best case for her defense is that she didn't do it. If we can finger someone else—"

"Jason Fairbanks liked to beat up women," Mac said. "I'd like to start with his mistress. Who else would he call after his wife shot him?"

"I can tell you right now that if you set foot in that town to defend the accused killer of Jason Fairbanks, you're going to have trouble," Ed Willingham said. "According to my background check on the Fairbanks, Reese Fairbanks rules that town—literally. He owns the bank and mortgages. I suspect he has the county prosecutor in his pocket, as well as the sheriff. That's why Jenny was so hesitant to admit that he slapped her. It took her a while to realize that we were out of her husband's reach."

"Then I guess when Archie and I go up there," Mac said, "we're going to have to go in through the back door."

"And while you're up there going through the back door," David said, "Ben and I will keep Reese Fairbanks locked up down here."

Rubbing his hands together, the county prosecutor uttered an evil chuckle. "I love this part of the job."

CHAPTER THIRTEEN

"Where's Brewster and Fletcher?" David asked Chelsea as if she would know the answer when he pulled his SUV into the church parking lot to find their cruisers empty. It was difficult locating the cruisers in the lot filled with cars, SUVs, and trucks. It looked like every light in the church was on. Christian rock music wafted from inside.

"They must be having some sort of event," Chelsea told him when he opened the door to help her out.

"On Wednesday night?" David opened the rear door. Molly jumped out and took her place at Chelsea's side.

"Some churches have services in the middle of the week."

David draped his arm across her shoulders. "Well, I just want to check on Fletcher and Brewster, and then we'll go out to dinner."

"Good, I'm starved." Wrapping her arms around his waist, she gazed up at him.

The naughty arch of her eyebrow, framing her light blue eyes, excited him. He pulled her in closer to press her body against his. "Well, we're going to have to do something about that," he breathed before covering her mouth with his to give her a long kiss.

When they finally parted, she sighed. "Dessert at my place?"

But David wasn't paying attention. Behind her, he recognized Bogie's cruiser parked next to Mac's red Dodge Viper. "What's going on here?" He pushed her away when he spotted Ben Fleming's black Ferrari.

"Oh, Chief O'Callaghan," Edna greeted him when he flew through the doors, "just in time." Carrying a plate filled with food, she was heading toward her office. "Carmine brought out a fresh lasagna. It's got Italian sausage in it." She pointed her fork across the foyer to the fellowship hall. "You better hurry. Your men finished off the last platter in twelve minutes flat." She patted Molly on the head. "Carmine also baked a batch of dog biscuits this afternoon. You'll find Gnarly in the children's chapel doing tricks for cookies."

David stepped into the fellowship hall to find it filled with tables and people eating, talking, and laughing. Board games were set up on some tables. People overflowed into the sanctuary where some young people were playing Twister. "Is this a party?" He turned to Edna. "Where are my officers? They're supposed to be keeping an eye on Ruth Buchanan."

"They are." Edna stepped into the hall and pointed toward the fireplace. "They couldn't keep any closer of an eye on her if they were sitting in her lap."

David followed the tip of her fork to a table where Officer Fletcher was standing up to tell a story while gesturing wildly with his arms. The table was filled with uniformed officers—some of whom had not been assigned to watch Ruth Buchanan, but appeared to have stopped in for their dinner break. The next table over contained Brewster, Bogie, Mac, Ben Fleming and his wife Catherine, Ed Willingham, Reverend Deborah, and Ruth Buchanan. Plates of food, in various stages of consumption, filled the table.

Edna was right. They couldn't keep a closer eye on Ruth Buchanan.

"Chief O'Callahgan!" Carmine grabbed David into a tight bear hug. It wasn't until he let David up for air that the police chief saw that Carmine was wearing a white apron and chef's hat. "Eat! Eat! And you need to hurry. This group doesn't let any food sit for long. Lucky for you, I have been cooking all afternoon. Good thing I got a delivery from the wholesaler today."

He led David by the elbow to the steamer tables filled with hot food. Three more tables were filled with covered dishes, including huge desserts. "Make room for the Big Cheese!" Carmine called out while plowing through the mob that had surrounded the buffet tables. "The Big Cheese gets to go through first."

Abruptly, Carmine stopped, let go of David's arm, and turned around. "Where are my manners? Ladies first." He reached out to take Chelsea's hand to guide her to the buffet table and, with a deep bow, handed her a plate. "Make room for the Big Cheese's lovely lady, and then the Big Cheese!" He threw out his arms. "Enjoy!" It sounded like an order.

In spite of the humongous array of food, all within inches of her snout, Molly remained next to her master's side, showing little reaction to the dozens of hands that petted her while they made their way along the table. Giving suggestions for dishes to try, Carmine ushered them along. Refusal was not an option. If they showed any hesitation, Carmine would grab the serving spoon and heap some onto their plate regardless.

After their plates were filled to overflowing, Carmine gave them one final order. "Don't forget to leave room for dessert." With a gravy ladle, the chef pointed over to two tables filled with cakes, cookies, and what David recognized as a dessert made up of brownies and whipped cream called Death by Chocolate.

Chelsea was already weaving through the tables to the center attraction in front of the fireplace. Brewster jumped up out of his seat and held out his chair for her. Next to Ruth, Bogie was doing the same for David.

"What's the occasion?" David asked Reverend Deborah who was eating an array of desserts resting before her.

"I guess if you want to name it, it's a vigil of justice," the pastor said. "Ruth can't leave the building without being taken into custody. So she's trapped here. Everyone came out to show her that she's not alone. Then, Carmine brought his catering truck filled with food. We decided to play some music. Our youth group broke out the games." She gestured to the crowd that had gathered. "It just sort of happened."

"Best surveillance I've ever been on," Fletcher said over his saucer of Death by Chocolate while standing behind the police chief. If he dropped his dessert, it would have landed on David's head. "They should all be like this."

Edna returned from her office to whisper into Deborah's ear.

Sadness crossed Deborah's face. "Being among all of our friends, I forgot all about Eugene … and Marilyn." She choked.

"I think that maybe you should talk to her," Edna said with a sob in her voice. "I told her where to go, but I think she needs a little bit more than that."

"I'll talk to her," Deborah replied while wiping her mouth. "I'll go over there, too. She really shouldn't be alone tonight." She told those around the table. "It's Marilyn."

"She's lost," Edna explained.

"Lost?" Catherine Fleming asked.

"In the grocery store," Edna said. "She couldn't find where they hid the maple syrup, and then it seemed to hit her that Eugene will never be bringing home the maple syrup ever again and she broke down—right there in the middle of the tissue aisle. The store manager took her to her office and she called us."

"Well, I guess if you're going to break down, the tissue aisle is as good of a place as any," Fletcher muttered behind David's back.

Edna paused to swallow. "It's those little things that bring it all home."

After Deborah left the table, Brewster held out her chair in an offer to Edna. "Would you like some dessert, Miss Edna? If you wait too long, Fletcher will polish it off before you get any."

The raven-haired assistant hesitated while regarding the muscular officer with dark curly hair. His mustache stretched across his face when he grinned at her. An expression of uncertainty crossed her face. "Well, I'd hate to hurt Carmine's feelings by leaving some of his Death by Chocolate behind." She slipped into the offered chair and Officer Brewster hurried off to get her dessert.

"I hope you're not mad, Chief," Fletcher said. "More and more people were coming in. We heard the music. And then Pastor Deborah came out and told us that we could keep a closer eye on Ruth inside and there was no reason why we should go hungry." He shrugged. "She had a point."

"I was the one who suggested they contact the rest of your officers to come get some dinner," Edna confessed. "I mean, why should they miss out on such a fun stakeout? Right?"

"True. Why should they?" David agreed while looking at his forkful of lasagna. "Thank you for inviting them. That's very nice of you considering that they're waiting to arrest Ruth."

Behind David's back, Fletcher shot a thumbs up to his partner when he returned with a plate of the chocolate dessert. The officers around the table smiled at each other. They weren't in trouble after all.

Uncomfortably, David became aware of Chelsea bowing her head to murmur a prayer. *I guess I should say grace?* He noticed Bogie peering at him from under his bushy eyebrows. The deputy chief cocked his head.

David dropped his head to look at his hands. *Oh, Lord, thank you for this food and get me through this case without getting my head slapped by a church lady.*

"Where's Archie?" Chelsea asked Mac.

"She's flying up to New York to prep things for our investigation," Mac said.

"I can't believe all these years I've been carrying around this guilt for killing Jason when I hadn't," Ruth said. "It makes sense now. I couldn't understand how he had died from a shot to his leg. My first shot hit his shoulder, not his chest."

"Have you given any more thought as to who Madame X could have been?" Mac asked her. "Or would Jason have called his mistress after you left to come help him?"

"Obviously, Jason had enemies," Willingham said. "The copy of the autopsy report shows that he had been shot with a stun gun."

"That sounds like maybe his mistress," Ruth said. "They had to have had a fight. I think that was why Jason came home early. He accused me of talking to her. He must have gone to see her and she wouldn't see him."

"Worse, if he had electrical burns from a stun gun," Willingham said.

"Did she have enough money to give you fifty thousand dollars to start over?" Mac asked her.

"She did seem to have a lot of money," Ruth said.

"But would she be willing to part with that much cash to frame you for killing Jason?" Mac asked. "That seems like going overboard for revenge on a man for beating her?"

"If a woman is abused long and hard enough, they are capable of anything," Chelsea said. "They can become so desperate for relief, and yes, revenge, that they stop thinking straight."

"Like maybe she had an abusive lover before," Mac mused, "and when Jason hit her, it was the last straw?"

"Maybe," Chelsea said.

"We'll take a closer look into her background," Willingham said.

"What about Eugene's murder?" Edna reminded them of the tragedy that had brought Ruth's past to light.

"We do have a couple of suspects," David said.

"Are you sure it wasn't Chip?" Edna asked.

"Positive," David said. "His gun was the wrong caliber and he was already dead at the time of Eugene's murder."

"How bizarre," she said with a shake of her head. "So much tragedy on the same day."

"Studies have shown that violent crimes increase during a full moon," Chelsea said. "Like the rising and lowering of the tide, they will happen in waves."

"They also say things happen in threes," Edna said, "but I don't believe that."

"I don't either," Chelsea said, "but the whole full moon theory has been researched and it has been determined that some people do have a chemical imbalance when the moon is full as opposed to other phases of the moon."

"I can attest to that," Bogie said. "All my years on the force, I can tell you, when the moon is full, that is when people go nuts. Crime rate will shoot up and the cases will get crazier."

"As unreasonable as Helga is, I just find it so hard to believe she would actually shoot Eugene because she believed she stood a chance of becoming chief trustee with him gone," Edna said. "That's crazy." She shrugged. "But then, she always did strike me as a little delusional about her importance. But I never thought she was capable of killing anyone." She took a bite of the dessert and smiled. "Thank you, Officer Brewster."

"Anytime, ma'am." He grinned back at her.

"I just can't believe a member of our church would do such a thing." Edna glanced around the table. "Everyone loved Eugene—especially Marilyn."

"Who has already booked a cruise to Hawaii," David said.

"I know," Edna said. "She invited me to go with her. I'd go but I don't know what I'd do with my daughters."

"Daughters?" Brewster's face fell.

"Two," Edna said. "Nine and a seven year old."

"Edna is divorced," Bogie said in Brewster's direction.

The smile returned to the officer's face.

Seemingly oblivious to the point of Bogie's communication, Edna continued eating while saying, "You have to understand about Marilyn and Eugene, Chief O'Callaghan."

"I know," David said, "a cruise was on her bucket list of what to do after Eugene kicked the bucket."

"She's got an air-tight alibi," Bogie said. "Plus, Marilyn hasn't skipped town. It looks like Helga Thorpe has."

"That explains why Sirrus looked so happy when he came in this afternoon," Edna said.

"Sirrus Thorpe was here?" Mac asked. "Why'd he come in?"

"Oh, he comes in practically every day," Edna said. "He's relatively new to the church. Helga has been coming for several years." Pausing in her eating, she stared at her half-eaten dessert before resuming. "Thirteen years. I've been here five years. I moved here from Pennsylvania after my husband walked out on us. It wasn't until the last year and a half that Sirrus started coming."

"And he comes in every day?" Mac asked.

"He's got a very successful business to run—" David said.

"From what he tells me, Helga is the one running the business," Edna said.

"What does he do while he's here?" Mac asked.

"Fix-it up type stuff," Edna said. "Very often new Christians will dive in. It's like they want to make up for a lifetime of sin and they want to absorb everything connected to the church. So they'll contribute in every way possible to the church—their time, their money, their talents. Not a day goes by that Sirrus doesn't come in to fix something. As old as this building is, and as short as we are on funds, there's always something that needs fixed. Today, he came in to fix the leaky toilet in the lady's room."

"Was he one of the members that we fingerprinted?" David asked Bogie.

The deputy chief shook his head.

"Oh, you'll find his fingerprints all over the building," Edna laughed. "But he doesn't have a key, so he couldn't have let himself in—unless he used Helga's. All of the trustees have keys to the building."

"When he came in today," David said, "did he mention that we had officers at his house searching for his gun?"

"Never mentioned it," Edna said. "He did say how devastating it was about Eugene getting shot. He kept asking if there was anything he could do for me or the church." She squinted. "Now that you mention it—" She turned to Bogie. "Do you think Helga skipped town for good?"

"That's what it looks like."

"Well, Sirrus was in a *really* good mood when he came in." She moved the last bite of her dessert on her plate. "He actually had a little nip to his step. He once told me that the very sound of Helga's voice made the hair on the back of his neck stand on end." She giggled. "He said that after telling me what a nice, sultry voice I've got."

174

"Sultry is a good word for it." Brewster's gaze never left her face.

"Down, boy," Bogie said under his breath.

"How about Bill Clark?" Mac asked Edna.

"We haven't seen him in years," Edna said. "And we'd like for it to stay that way."

David pushed his plate, with all the food eaten, away. "As much fun as this might be for now, Ruth can't stay here in this church indefinitely."

"Who says she can't?" Edna asked.

"The guys from New York will not sit idly by," David said, "even if Carmine's lasagna is to die for."

"You haven't tried the Death by Chocolate yet," Fleming said.

"Give me twenty-four hours," Mac said.

"Twenty-four hours to do what?" David asked.

"To go to New York and rattle a few chains," Mac said.

Mac gave the signal to David to walk out to his car with him when Carmine started lining the guests up to do the bunny hop. While everyone was hopping into the sanctuary, Mac and David scurried out to the parking lot.

Once they were able to hear each other speak over the music, Mac asked, "If the police were searching your house for a murder weapon, would you leave them behind to go to the church to fix a toilet?"

"That struck you as strange, too," David replied.

"His wife is a murder suspect," Mac said. "She's in the wind and he doesn't care?"

"All he's worried about is that she'll come back," David said. "I really don't think this guy is into his wife or anything she does. You heard Edna. He has left the business for Helga to run and the very sound of her voice makes the hair on the back of his toupee stand on end ..."

Slowly, Mac shook his head while opening his car door. "In theory, that makes sense. But I was a homicide detective for twenty years. Never do I remember someone taking off, except to run, while their house was being searched for a murder weapon."

"Sirrus isn't the suspect," David said. "His wife is."

"Have you found any real evidence against her yet?" Mac asked.

"As in the gun? No," David said. "Forensics didn't find anything against her on the laptop that we can use. She took off before we could get her fingerprints and they aren't in the system. They did find a lot of information that the IRS can use against her and Sirrus. She was fast and loose with the company funds. She put down her masseuse as a company expense." He added, "But we do have a strong circumstantial case. There were a ton of emails that she sent out regularly stoking the fire for Eugene and Edna having a love affair. But it looked like only a few church hens put any stock in it."

Mac's response was silence. With his arms folded across his chest, he stared beyond David into the night. "Wouldn't Sirrus still stick around during the search, even if only out of curiosity?"

"Unless he honestly didn't care," David said. "I interviewed this man, Mac. He's extremely strange. Strange people react ... strangely."

Resigned, Mac shrugged. "You're right ... I guess. I mean, Sirrus may have a motive for killing his wife, but why Eugene Newton?" He slipped into the driver's seat of his sports car.

"Exactly." David held the car door open when Mac reached out to close it. "Can I ask your opinion on something?"

"Since when have you had to ask for my opinion?"

"Our victim ... Eugene Newton ..."

"Yes?" Squinting up at him, Mac waited.

"He was the chief trustee of this church," David said. "This church that, according to the pastor, doesn't even have enough money to replace the plumbing, and has enough fix-it jobs to keep Sirrus Thorpe occupied practically daily. And yet, Newton's death made his widow an heiress."

"I see what you're saying," Mac said. "You're thinking that our victim was in a prime position to help himself to church money."

David nodded his head. "Won't be the first time that a trusted member of a church embezzled all of their money. And if one of his fellow trustees or Reverend Deborah found out, they could have gotten pretty mad at him. All of them had keys to the building. They could have come in to catch him with his hand in the cookie jar, things escalated, and Eugene got killed."

"Didn't Deborah say there were regular audits?" Mac asked.

"If he was smart, he could have found a way to get past the audits."

Mac grinned at him. "Sounds like you already have it figured out."

"I'm checking into Eugene's personal finances to find out exactly where all this money that made his wife an heiress came from."

"I'll be interested in what you find out," Mac said.

Grinning at Mac's approval, David released the car door for him to close. "Don't take any unnecessary chances in New York."

"Hey, Chief," Brewster hurried up to them, "do you mind if I ask you and Mac a question?"

"I thought Bogie already answered your question," Mac said through the open window. "She's not married. She's divorced with two little girls."

"I was that obvious?" Brewster asked.

David held up his finger and thumb to indicate a small amount. "Only a little."

"You didn't offer to bring me dessert." Mac pretended to be offended.

"You don't have bedroom eyes," Officer Brewster said.

"Yes, I do," Mac said. "Archie told me just last night."

"My question is," Brewster said, "is Edna a suspect? I mean, would I get into trouble if I were to ask her out to lunch or? Nothing fancy. Or do I need to wait until you make an arrest?"

Mac and David exchanged questioning glances.

"Bogie checked her alibi," David said. "She was with her mother, sister, and two daughters at the time of the murder." He asked Mac, "Can you see any issue with Brewster taking Miss Bedroom Eyes out?"

"Asking her," Brewster corrected him. "She may say no and break my heart. Or even worse, say yes and we can end up getting married and then she'll rip out my heart and put it in a blender."

David smiled. "Brewster, she works for a church. I don't think that while you're on the graveyard shift, she's going to be cruising the bars looking for quickies in the men's room like your ex-wife."

"You better hurry," Mac said in a low voice. "There's Miss Bedroom Eyes now. She's leaving."

Brewster glanced over his shoulder. Seeing Edna loading two little girls in the back seat of her red sedan, he ducked back behind David.

"I thought you wanted to ask her out on a date," David said.

"What if she says no?" Brewster asked.

"What if she said yes?" David replied.

"Forget it."

Mac leaned out the car window to say in a low voice, "Brewster, ask her to dinner at the Spencer Inn. Your dinner will be on the house and she'll be impressed."

"But I'd still have to ask her out," Brewster said.

"Be a man, Brewster," David said. "That's an order."

"She's leaving," Mac hissed when they saw her climb into the driver's seat of her car. "I'll give you a hundred dollars if you go over now and ask her. When she leaves, my offer is off the table."

When Brewster hesitated, David stepped around and shoved him in the direction of the car.

Seeing him stumble toward her car, Edna rolled down her car window. "Officer Brewster, is everything okay?"

"Yes." Brewster cleared his throat. "I was just getting some last minute instructions from the chief." He bent over to peer at the girls in the back seat. "Are these your daughters?"

The two dark haired little girls smiled and waved at him while their mother introduced them. "That's Allison," Edna said. "She's seven years old. And the big sister is Kiersten. She's nine."

Brewster was uncomfortably aware of Mac and David watching him from across the parking lot. *It's do or die.* "Edna ..."

"Yes, Officer Brewster?"

He stared into her face. Her voice sounded as sultry as her dark eyes framed in thick black lashes that matched her lush hair.

"Officer Brewster ..."

Aware of her hand on his arm, he realized that he had been staring at her.

"Did you want to ask me something about Eugene's murder?" she was asking.

"No."

"Then what is it, Officer Brewster?" Her dark eyes were filled with concern.

"Uh, would you be willing to have dinner with me this Friday night ..." Fearful of a possible rejection, he rushed to add, "At the Spencer Inn."

"Are you asking my mommy out on a date?" Allison, the younger of the two girls, squealed from the back seat. "Ee-ewww!"

"Quiet, dummy!" Kiersten grabbed the back of the seat in front of her. "Say yes, Mom! He's dreamy!"

"Is that a real gun?" the younger girl called out. "Have you ever killed anyone?"

"Will you two be quiet?" Edna yelled to be heard over their argument. "Gee-whiz!" When she turned back to Officer Brewster her cheeks were bright pink. "Do you want to reconsider your invitation?"

He laughed. "No. Friday night okay?"

"Friday night," she replied.

"All right, Mom!" Kiersten yelled. "Way to go!"

"Don't worry, Officer Brewster," Edna said, "I'll get a babysitter. I promise."

"Call me Nate," the officer said. "Friday night then. I'll pick you up at seven-thirty?"

"Do you know where I live?"

"I'm sure the chief got that when he ran a background check on you," Officer Brewster said with a smile. "I'll get directions from him."

"I don't know if that's a good thing or bad."

Once she was out of sight, Mac held his hand out the window of his red sports car as he drove past Officer Brewster. With a grin, Officer Brewster snatched the hundred dollar bill from his hand.

CHAPTER FOURTEEN

New York—Next Morning

Mac woke up with a blazing headache. Pushing through the pain, he remembered where he was when he had drifted off to sleep. The sound of someone throwing up in the next cell brought it all back with a jolt.

The draft through the cell accentuated the cold of the cement floor and steel bars in his tiny room. Hugging himself, he shivered to fight off the chill. The shiver stung when it traveled across two raw spots in his back.

Oh, yeah, now I remember. He clutched his neck where the sheriff's deputy had grabbed him from behind before shooting him in the back with the stun gun. When Mac came to, he was handcuffed and being tossed into the back of the police car.

How long have I been asleep? He looked around the holding cell area in search of a clock. There was none. *Twenty-four hours isn't much time. David's right. Ruth can't stay in the church forever. Eventually, she'll have to turn herself in and when she does, she'll end up here, unless we can expose the truth.*

181

He was on the verge of drifting back to sleep when the clang of a baton on the cell bars yanked him back to consciousness.

"On your feet, Forsythe! There are some people who want to talk to you!" the guard continued to bang on the bars with his baton while Mac slowly climbed out of the cot, stood up, and then stretched his arms up over his head.

While the guard eyed him with disdain, Mac picked up his sports coat, casually slipped it on, and then sauntered over to the door. "I'll take my coffee black and tell the chef that I like my eggs medium, over easy."

The guard took in a deep breath. His lips curled up into a sneer that Mac recalled feeling on his own lips when he'd gone up against men who had complete faith that their fat wallets contained a license that allowed them to operate above the law.

"You're no different than the rest of them." His beady eyes looked even smaller due to his extremely wide jaw, which resembled that of a robot Mac recalled on a children's cartoon from his childhood.

Mac swallowed down the churn he felt in his stomach. He was making himself sick. "You have until the count of ten to open this door or next week you're going to be working the school crossing."

"Next time you lay a hand on your wife in this town will be your last," the guard hissed.

"Is that a threat?" Mac asked in a low voice.

"It's a promise." The guard yanked open the door.

Keeping distance between himself and the guard, who was begging to be given an excuse to "defend himself," Mac side-stepped out of the cell and went down the short hallway to the door leading into the check-in area for the holding cells.

On the other side of the door was a small receiving area, beyond which was another door leading to the stairwell that went up to the sheriff's department. The guard poked Mac in the back with his baton to send him stumbling into the door. "They're waiting for you upstairs, big man."

Turning to him, Mac held up his hands. "Don't touch me again."

The guard stepped in close to him. Mac could feel his hot, foul breath on his face.

"What are you going to do about it, big man? Whack me around like you did your wife?"

Without saying a word, Mac glared at him. For just an instant, he dropped his eyes to check the name on his nametag pinned to his breast.

Stacey. Sheriff's Deputy Stacey.

The deputy uttered a laugh. "Yeah, that's what I figured. Not man enough to fight a real man. For them, you let your lawyers and your money do your fighting. When you need to feel like a real man, then you slap around your woman."

"What I do with my wife is none of your business," Mac said in a low threatening voice.

With a final glare, Mac went up the stairs and waited while the guard unlocked the door to lead him down a corridor to the door at the end. Throwing open the door, Deputy Stacey stepped aside and jerked his head to indicate that he was to enter.

Mac stepped inside to see two men. The barrel-chested one with a gray military buzz cut was clad in a uniform and wearing a gold police shield of sheriff. His companion was short and scrawny with dark hair that was silver at the temples. The smaller of the two men was dressed in a tailored suit.

Crooked lawyer.

The sheriff gestured at the empty chair facing the two-way mirror that filled one wall in the room. "Sit down, Mr. Forsythe."

With as arrogant an air as he could muster, Mac strolled to the chair, dropped down into it, crossed one leg over the other, and folded his arms. Attached to one corner of the ceiling, he saw the green light on the surveillance camera indicating that the interview was being recorded.

Winking at the lawyer, he said, "I guess now is where you tell me what a naughty boy I've been."

"Mickey Forsythe," the man in the suit said with an air of formality, "I'm Winston Hawkins, the county prosecutor, and this is Sheriff Quinton Nichols. He's investigating your case and it is my job to decide how we are going to proceed with the evidence that he has uncovered."

"County prosecutor, huh?" Mac looked from one of them to the other. "Brought out the big guns already? I'm impressed. They don't usually break out the lawyers until I bring in mine."

Sitting across from Mac, Hawkins thumbed a folder under his hand. "You've been through this before, huh, Mr. Forsythe?"

"Once or twice," Mac said with smirk. "I assume you ran a background check on me." With a laugh, he turned to the sheriff. "They all do."

Sheriff Nichols leaned over the table. "Rape and murder are not a laughing matter, Mr. Forsythe."

"I didn't rape anyone," Mac said.

"That's not what your victim says," the lawyer said.

"That *victim* is my *wife.*" Unfolding his arms, Mac sat up in his seat. "For the record, she says a lot of things." Chuckling, he brought in his chair. "When we met, she said she was a virgin. Now how a whore can be a virgin, you tell me."

"We have witness statements to back up her statement that you forced her," Sheriff Nichols said.

"Who else was in our suite?" Mac asked. "So she got loud. She's always loud. And as for the bruises on her arms? She likes to be held down." He shrugged. "It's our thing."

"Is her running down to the hotel lobby in hysterics claiming that you killed her lover also your thing?" Prosecutor Hawkins asked.

"Did she see me kill him?" Mac asked. "We had a fight a couple of days ago. Kendra got mad and decided to make me jealous, so she picked up some guy and came here—after stealing a hundred thousand bucks of my money. I followed them here and had a word with this other man. Once I told him the score, he decided it was in his best interest to leave. So my driver took him to the airport and dropped him off." He shrugged both of his shoulders with an exaggerated look of puzzlement. "I don't know where he went from there. Did you ask Brutus?"

"His story is the same as yours," Sheriff Nichols said.

"Then it must be true," Mac said. "After Brutus took this guy for a drive, Kendra and I fought it out—we're quite a passionate couple—then we had makeup sex, which is very physical. That was where she got the bruises."

"Then why did she go running down to the hotel lobby afterwards?" Sheriff Nichols asked.

"Because she's nuts." Mac waved a finger across the table at the prosecutor. "If you're looking to charge someone with something, then charge Kendra for stealing a hundred thousand dollars of my money. She took it out of my account—without authorization. Check with the state police in Maryland. I did press charges against her." Folding his arms across his chest, he sat back in his seat. "As for your case against me … it's her word against mine on the rape and you have no body or evidence for the murder."

185

Sheriff Nichols and Quinton Hawkins regarded each other in silence before looking back at Mac. Hawkins narrowed his eyes in question at the sheriff who offered a slight nod in response to the prosecutor. The county prosecutor then turned his full body back to Mac while the sheriff crossed the room to the panel of light switches on the wall. He flipped one to turn it off.

Mac saw the green light turn off on the surveillance camera.

They were now off the record.

Quinton Hawkins opened the folder that had been resting on the table. "You have quite an impressive portfolio, Mr. Forsythe. According to my check into your background, you're worth half a billion dollars."

"I have a knack for making wise investments," Mac said.

"We see that," Hawkins said. "You seem to have your fingers in everything. Computers, banking, aeronautics … politics."

"I've hired a few politicians for consulting on occasion," Mac said with a wicked grin.

Sheriff Nichols and the prosecutor exchanged smiles.

Mac smiled back at them.

"How much do you pay your political consultants?" Quinton Hawkins asked him.

"Depends on how good they are. …" Mac replied. "How many of my problems they're able to fix."

"Let's just say," Quinton Hawkins said with a drawl, "we could help you. Suppose we could make this matter go away? You're right. We have no body to back up your wife's claim that you had your driver take her lover out and kill him. We found no evidence in your limo to support that. The rape kit shows that you did have sexual intercourse with your wife, but nothing to indicate that it was forced."

"But if we chose to press forward with the investigation," the sheriff said, "what if we decided to go out looking for that dead body?"

"What if we decided to put your tearful wife on the stand to tell her story and let the jury decide?" the prosecutor asked. "What if we put our deputy on the stand to tell about how you threw a punch at him when he went up to your suite to question you? They'll see a rich bully and a brow-beaten wife."

"But—under the right circumstances—we could make this whole matter go away," the sheriff said. "Maybe if you hired a couple of consultants …"

Mac asked, "How much would these consultants cost?"

"Two million," Quinton Hawkins replied. "One million to hire Sheriff Nichols' services and one million for my legal services."

"And if I'm not looking to contract for any consulting?" Mac replied.

"Then you're going to have some serious issues," the prosecutor replied. "Sure, your big lawyers may prevail, but you'll be having to come back to our lovely area time and again for court hearings and the media is going to paint you to be a wife-beating monster."

"Even if that is what you are," the sheriff said, "do you really want everyone to know?"

"Two million dollars? I spent more than that playing poker one night in Monte Carlo." Mac flashed them a grin. "Give me my phone."

"We have it right here." The prosecutor slipped Mac's cell phone from under a sheet of paper in the folder and slid it across the table. He then took the sheet of paper that had been covering it and laid that down next to the phone. "The account numbers where you are to make the two deposits are

187

right here. Once the money is transferred, then you'll be free to go."

Mac was bringing up the banking account holding the money. "And what about my wife?"

"She's your problem," Sheriff Nichols said.

Mac raised his eyes from the cell phone to ask in a low voice, "Are your people going to be sticking their noses into our business when I get back to the hotel to discuss this matter and how much it is costing me with her? I want to make sure she doesn't do this again."

"I suggest you be quiet about it or leave town before you discuss it," the prosecutor replied.

The sheriff and prosecutor were practically dancing in their seats while they watched Mac working his cell phone. After the pressing of a few buttons, he turned the phone around for them to see the green line indicating the moving of the money and the words, "Transfer Completed" flash on the screen.

"Are we done?" Mac asked.

The prosecutor and sheriff rose from their seats and offered Mac their hands. "It's a pleasure doing business with you, Mr. Forsythe."

"I'm glad we were able to sort things out, gentlemen." Mac shook their hands in turn. "Can I go now?"

Sheriff Nichols hurried over to the door. "I'll even have one of my deputies drive you back to your hotel." He yanked open the door to find a group of men in suits and wearing badges indicating their status as federal agents standing on the other side.

The sheriff sputtered, "What the—"

"Oh, these men are with me." Mac dug his finger into his ear to remove the ear bud that had recorded their entire conversation. "Let me introduce you to Special Agent Sid

Delaney with the FBI. They have something they need to tell you two. It starts with, 'You're under arrest for soliciting a bribe ...' and ends with 'anything you say can be held against you.'"

CHAPTER FIFTEEN

David dreaded Chelsea's silence. Unlike Archie Monday, who waited patiently and with understanding for Mac to come around to making the big commitment, Chelsea Adams yearned for more stability in her life.

Why wouldn't she? David understood. Her brother disappeared shortly after high school, to turn up after several years living as a recluse in an abandoned castle on top of the mountain. Chelsea's mother died shortly after his disappearance.

To add to the family upheaval, her first love had broken her heart. The fact that *he* was the first love who had broken her heart compounded his guilt. *Who would have thought that fifteen years later we would reconcile?*

David welcomed Mac and Archie's engagement with mixed emotions. He was happy for them, but anxious about what it would mean for him and Chelsea. *Is she going to start chomping at the bit for us to walk down the aisle, too? I love her, but am I ready for that?*

With anxiety, David would take note every time his lovely lady with platinum blonde waves would cast her pale blue eyes at him while she thought he was sleeping.

The morning after Mac had left for New York, David found her sitting at the picnic table on the back deck of her two-story condo staring out at the tranquil lake, which was still in the early hours of the day.

Deep Creek Lake was in the height of the summer season. At eight o'clock, the vacationers and summer residents were still getting ready to enjoy the sunny day. There was only one fishing boat on the water when David carried his hot steaming coffee out onto the deck. In a nearby tree, a bird was chirping excitedly. David wondered if the tabby cat that belonged to one of Chelsea's neighbors was on the receiving end of the bird's apparent tantrum.

Oblivious to the bird's chatter, Molly was dozing in the middle of a sunbeam. Gnarly, who had spent the night while his owners were in New York, was stretched out with his head resting across her neck. When David emerged through the French doors to join them, the German shepherd eyed him without lifting his head, as if he didn't want to wake his female companion from her nap.

Molly's master was dressed for work in a pale blue business suit with a matching blouse and pumps. The hue of her suit seemed to be tailor made to match her pale eye color.

David laid his hand on her shoulder. His touch startled her out of her stare across the water. Feeling her jump, he paused in bending over to kiss her on the lips. "Sorry, I didn't mean to scare you."

"I was thinking," she stammered before reaching up to pull him back down to kiss her. "Good morning." She brushed her hand down the front of his white shirt and across the badge pinned to his chest. "If you're going to keep spending the night here, you need to bring more shirts to keep in my closet."

"Maybe." Sipping his coffee, David sat down in the seat next to her. "What were you thinking so hard about?"

"Last night," she said. "Those were all such nice people ... and how they all came out to support Ruth and ... fun. I always thought church people were stuffy and no fun but—" She giggled. "I've never done the bunny hop before."

"Neither have I."

"Do you believe in God, David?"

"Of course, I do." Avoiding her gaze, he took a long sip of his coffee.

"Why don't we go to church then?"

"Because we're living in sin," David replied in a mocking tone.

"But aren't we all sinners?" she shot back. "You and I are having premarital sex. There's a killer out there who murdered their trustee. Gnarly stole a sausage off my neighbor's grill last week. You and I run into people who lie, cheat, and steal every day. Some of us are bigger sinners than others, but isn't that why God sent Jesus? To pay for our sins so that we can be saved?"

David lifted his eyes to look at her. "I wondered what you were in such a deep conversation about with Reverend Deborah last night."

"Where do you stand, David?"

He looked out at the still water on the lake. He was aware of her eyes searching his face. After a long silence, he swallowed. "God and I aren't exactly on good terms right now."

"Why's that?"

"You weren't here when Dad was dying," David said. "He was in excruciating pain and he died slowly over a very long time. You remember him. He was the backbone of this lake. He did so much to help so many people ... he devoted himself to helping others ... he made so many sacrifices, including giving up the love of his—" Feeling his fury rising, he stopped and took a sip his coffee. "And God let him suffer like that."

She hung her head in silence.

"Then there's the evil I saw overseas—horrible things done to good people," David said. "What kind of God lets things like that happen?"

"God doesn't do those things," Chelsea said. "People do those things. A person killed Eugene Newton. Evil people organized, trained, and planned for those planes to fly into the World Trade Center buildings and the Pentagon. *Not God.*"

"*He* could have stopped it." David drank down the rest of his coffee. "Are you ready to go?" He stood up and went back inside.

"Yes." She stood up.

Molly was instantly awake. Gnarly jumped back to allow her to climb to her feet to rush to her mistress.

Carrying Chelsea's laptop case and purse, David came back to the door.

"I'm going to start going to church, David," Chelsea announced.

David groaned. "And you expect me to drive you?"

"No," she said. "Bogie volunteered to take me. He and Doc go to Spencer Church. Molly and I will ride with them, so you don't have to go."

"Good."

She laid her hand on his chest. "I'd like for you to come with me, though." She smiled coyly.

David's phone buzzed on his hip. Perfect timing. Without answering her, he brought his phone to his ear. "O'Callaghan here." The news from the other end of the line brought a smile to his face.

"Have Bogie meet me at the station in fifteen minutes." He disconnected the call.

"Good news from Mac in New York?" Chelsea asked about his grin.

"No," David said, "but it is good news. We got a hit on one of Helga Thorpe's credit cards. She used it this morning to check into a motel in Breezewood, Pennsylvania."

"That's a major stop on the Pennsylvania turnpike," Chelsea said.

"Exactly." David handed her the laptop case. "She must have been laying low—waiting for things to cool off." He ushered her and the dogs to the door. "I hope you don't mind if I leave you at the station and ask Fletcher to take you on to work. Bogie and I need to go meet the Pennsylvanian State Troopers in Breezewood before she moves on. They've got a unit staking out the room until we get there to pick her up."

"Don't say a word," Quinton Hawkins warned Sheriff Nichols before hissing in Mac's direction. "You set us up." He shot a sneer at FBI Special Agent Sid Delaney. "This case will never see the inside of a court room."

"I wouldn't be so sure of that," the federal agent said. "We recorded the *whole* conversation. You made the offer to Mr. Faraday. *You* solicited a bribe."

"Forsythe isn't even your real name?" Sheriff Nichols asked.

Mac slowly shook his head. "Mickey Forsythe is a fictional character in a series of books written by Robin Spencer. We set up a phony identity using his name. A very rich man who thinks he's above the law, beating up his wife in your jurisdiction—sort of like Reese and Jason Fairbanks. That's how they got away with beating up their wives all those years without anyone doing anything to put a stop to it."

"Entrapment." The county prosecutor's tone betrayed his impatience with them inconveniencing him.

"I don't care," Mac said. "Everyone is going to know what type of men you really are--very willing to forget your sworn duties and look the other way while a woman was being abused—just like you did for years with Scarlett Fairbanks."

"Scarlett Fairbanks killed her husband," the sheriff said. "Everyone knows that."

"No, she didn't," Mac said. "And if she had, then you put her in the position where she was forced to defend herself because you refused to protect her from that animal."

"You have no proof of that," Prosecutor Hawkins said.

Special Agent Delaney said, "I'm sure a jury is going to see the connection between Reese Fairbanks' generous financial support for both of your election campaigns and the lack of action on your part to ever charge his son even though Mrs. Weber, the Fairbanks' neighbor, called the police a dozen times over the years to report the domestic disputes. Jason Fairbanks broke his daughter's arm and the doctor reported it. He was going to testify against him."

"And he recanted," Hawkins said with a laugh while crossing his arms. "Not my problem."

"He recanted thanks to Reese Fairbanks intimidating him," Mac said.

"Now that was Fairbanks' doing." Sweat was rolling down the sheriff's flabby cheeks.

"Shut up, Nichols," the prosecutor ordered before telling Mac. "Legally, Reese Fairbanks did nothing illegal. He never laid a hand on that doctor and he never threatened him."

"He threatened to foreclose his parent's mortgage on their home and throw them out on the street if he testified," the special agent said. "We have statements from both of them and their son."

"Meanwhile, you strong armed Scarlett Fairbanks and threatened her with jail time if she didn't drop the divorce," Mac said.

"She skipped town and took Fairbanks' daughter with her," the prosecutor said, "which is against the law."

"So is beating someone to a pulp!" Mac shot back.

"What do you want?" With a handkerchief, the sheriff mopped the sweat from his forehead, cheeks, jaws, and down under his chin.

"I told you to shut up, Nichols," the prosecutor said. "Don't say another word."

"You shut up, Hawkins," Sheriff Nichols said. "It's over. From here on out, it's every man for himself."

The prosecutor scoffed at the sheriff before directing his laughter at Mac. "And we'll just see who is left standing."

"Get him out of here," Special Agent Delaney ordered his partner to remove the prosecutor. "Put him in a holding cell with a violent criminal and turn your back for an hour or so," he said for the lawyer's benefit. "Let's see how he likes it."

While they escorted the cuffed prosecutor out of the interview room, Mac glared down at the sheriff from where he stood on the other side of the table.

Even while Sheriff Nichols hung his head in shame, the former homicide detective was sickened by images of abused women and children—a few who had been killed—who he had encountered during his career. Here sat a man who had taken an oath to protect them, who could have helped Scarlett, Holly, and Reese's wife Jenny, and he didn't—for money.

"I want a deal," the sheriff broke the silence to say.

"I'm not in a position to offer any deals." Mac turned the chair around and straddled the back to sit across from him. "But I can put in a good word for you. I want to know about Jason Fairbanks' murder."

"There's nothing to it," Sheriff Nichols replied. "His wife shot him and ran off. He had hunted her down and dragged her back before. She figured if he was dead, that he couldn't hunt her down again."

"Someone threw water on him and shot him with a stun gun." Reminded of the shot he had received from the arresting officer the night before, Mac involuntarily rubbed the welts the stun gun had left on his back. He imagined the pain of the extra jolt from being wet when the electric current was shot through him. *Not that Fairbanks didn't deserve it.* "I want to know who did it."

Sheriff Nichols slumped. Slowly, he shook his head. "I don't know that for certain. Fairbanks ordered us to focus on Scarlett and getting Holly back right away."

"So you didn't really look anywhere else," Mac said. "Weren't you even curious about why Fairbanks clothes were damp? Didn't you read the autopsy report where it said he had welts in the groin area consistent with being shot repeatedly with a stun gun? Don't tell me you thought Scarlett had done it."

"We knew Scarlett would never have gotten close enough to Jason to have done that," the sheriff said.

"Then who?" Mac asked. "Who could have gotten that close?"

"No woman alone," the sheriff said. "Not without help."

"This injury seems to be very personal," Mac said, "like the type of injury a woman would wish on a man for hurting her."

The sheriff shifted uncomfortably in his seat. "I never got evidence to confirm anything concrete."

"But you did hear something." Mac leaned across to him. "You want a recommendation from me, you better give me something."

"Portia Hagar." The sheriff's jaw worked as he clinched his teeth. "Jason Fairbanks made the mistake of slapping around the wrong woman. She worked for the Fairbanks and had an affair with him. Then she made the bigger mistake of trying

197

to leave him. He didn't like that and slapped her around. She called the police—"

"Who did nothing," Mac said.

"She did succeed in getting a restraining order."

"But that does no good when the monster you are restraining owns the police," Mac said.

"No one owns me," the sheriff objected.

"What do you call it when you refuse to uphold the law on the say so of a man who is giving you money?" Mac's lips curled into a snarl. "How is it that Scarlett's lawyer didn't know anything about this restraining order keeping her husband away from his mistress when she was trying to divorce him?"

When Sheriff Nichol's hung his head, Mac knew the answer. "Really? Fairbanks had Scarlett's divorce lawyer under his thumb, too?"

Sheriff Nichols grumbled.

With a sigh of disgust, Mac asked him, "What happened with Portia after she got the restraining order against Jason Fairbanks?"

"She got her butt fired from Fairbanks' bank," the sheriff said. "Fairbanks then got her blackballed all over town. I heard that she was planning to move out of the area. One night, Jason got drunk and went to her place. She says he raped her."

"Did you believe her?"

"She had bruises all over her," the sheriff said. "He claimed she liked it rough." He wiped his sweaty forehead. "I thought for sure Hawkins would have to indict Jason. He went too far that time, but Hawkins didn't do a thing. Less than a week after Hawkins had made that decision, Jason Fairbanks was dead."

Mac studied the man across the table. His face was drenched in sweat. He refused to meet Mac's gaze. "What are you not telling me?"

"Let's just say that through the years, the morale in my department has been less than high."

"Your deputies know what's been going on," Mac said with a nod of his head. "How could they not?"

"If they didn't know," the sheriff said, "they certainly suspected."

"Could some of them have decided to teach Fairbanks a lesson?" Recalling the anger he saw in the deputy's eyes, the same one who had shot him, Mac once again fingered the welts on his ribs.

"None of my people had anything to do with Jason Fairbanks' murder," the sheriff insisted.

"What about Fairbanks' mistress?"

Sheriff Nichols raised his eyes to Mac's. "She had an alibi for the time of the murder. She was at a job interview an hour away."

"She could have arranged for someone to kill Jason Fairbanks for her," he said.

"No money trail to indicate that," the sheriff countered.

"Maybe whoever killed Fairbanks for her was looking for a different sort of revenue," Mac said. "Where is Portia Hagar now?"

"A big bank in Albany," Sheriff Nichols said. "I heard she got married."

Mac referred to his notes on the case. "Did you even bother questioning the Fairbanks' neighbor to see if she saw someone go in to finish off Fairbanks after his wife had left?"

Sheriff Nichols nodded his head. "Tuyon Weber."

"Did she see anything on the day of the murder?"

Nichols was already shaking his head. "She saw nothing. She spoke with a thick Vietnamese accent, but there was no mistaking her in that she heard no shots at any time that afternoon. Nor did she see anything." He added, "I wouldn't have been surprised if she was lying though."

"Why?"

"Because she was the neighbor who kept calling the police every time Fairbanks beat on Scarlett or his daughter," Sheriff Nichols explained. "More than once she chewed out the officers responding to the call for not doing anything." He chuckled. "Even with her thick accent, there was no mistaking what she was saying to them. She could very well have seen the whole thing go down and claim not to know anything in order to protect Scarlett Fairbanks."

"Does she still live at the same address?"

"She's dead." Sheriff Nichols went on in response to Mac's fallen expression. "She was an old woman. She died a couple of years ago of a heart attack. Her niece lives in that house now."

Located at the midway point on the Pennsylvania turnpike, Breezewood was an immensely popular stop for truck drivers and other travelers. By mid-morning, most of the weary trekkers passing through the town were finishing their breakfasts, gassing up their vehicles, and gearing to continue their travels.

At the largest of the many roadside motels, the staff was busily cleaning the now empty rooms in preparation for the next influx of guests. Upon the arrival of the Pennsylvania State Troopers and Spencer, Maryland, police chief and deputy chief, two older looking cleaning women pushed their carts around the corner of the building and ducked for safety.

After leading the police to the room on the ground floor, the motel desk clerk gestured to indicate that this was the one. After easing him out of the way with his arm across the older man's chest, David stood to the side of the doorway and pounded on the door with his fist. "Helga Thorpe! This is Police Chief David O'Callaghan! We have a warrant to take you in for questioning. Open the door!"

"Police?" A woman's high-pitched shriek came from inside the room.

A crash that resembled the sound of furniture overturning came from inside the room.

"What the—" A young man's voice followed the crash. "You have the wrong room! There's no one here by that name!"

"That doesn't sound like Helga," Bogie whispered from where he was perched with his gun drawn on the other side of the doorway.

David looked questioningly at the desk clerk who checked the clipboard under his arm. "It was our night clerk who checked her in." He ran his finger across a line on the roster. "This is the room assigned to that credit card."

"This is the police!" David called out. "Open the door and come out with your hands up!"

"I can't go to jail!" the woman screamed.

"Shush! Be quiet and they'll go away!"

"Where's my bra?" she yelled. "I need my bra, damn it!"

"Here!"

"That's a shirt, you idiot! Don't you even know what a bra looks like?"

The curtain covering the window rustled.

"We're going in!" David gestured at the desk clerk. "Open the door."

The clerk rushed forward, unlocked the door, and dropped back with his hands over his head. Guns drawn, David, Bogie, and four troopers from Pennsylvania's state police rushed inside to find a young woman standing in the middle of the room wearing only a pair of black lace panties. Her long dark hair fell down into her face and over one shoulder.

Upon the all-male police entrance, she clapped her hands, in which she clutched a black lace bra, over her naked breasts. Her eyes were wide and her mouth hung open. "Don't shoot! I didn't do anything!"

After tossing her head to get her hair out of her eyes, she glared at the young man sitting on the edge of the bed. He was dressed in nothing but a pair of red silk boxer shorts. In their hurry to get dressed, the blankets had fallen off the bed to land in a heap.

"I mean," she said, "I did nothing illegal. He did it all."

"Did what?" David asked.

"Whatever you're here to arrest him for."

"First of all," David said, "who are you?" He held out a shirt that he had picked up off the floor to the woman still covering her bare breasts with only an unhooked lace bra.

"Candace Stengel," the girl said. "And this is Kendell Richards—"

In spite of his effort to shush her, she rattled on with pride. "He's a famous male model. He's replacing Michael Jordan in the Hanes underwear commercial. Next week, they're going to put his picture up in Times Square wearing nothing but his briefs. We met and fell in love last night in the motel lounge. He's traveling through from New York to visit his mother in Ohio and I'm on my way to New York to break into theater."

Lurking in the doorway, the desk clerk laughed. "Male model? New York?" He gestured at the man cowering in the bed. "You're good, Kenny."

"Do you know this man?" David asked the clerk.

"He's a bus boy in the hotel diner," the clerk said. "His good for nothing older brother is the night clerk who checked in the guest with that credit card you had flagged."

"You lied to me!" Candace dropped her bra to the floor and lunged for Kenny. "Have you even been out of this burg? You probably don't even have an agent. You took those pictures of me for yourself."

While the troopers stood in stunned shock at the suddenly topless woman, Bogie threw both arms around her waist and lifted her from the floor to cut off her attack. "Come on, sweetheart, let's get you dressed and calm you down." Whirling her around, he carried her kicking and cursing from the room. One of the troopers followed with a blanket to cover her up outside.

Still laughing, the motel clerk sauntered out of the room and back to his office.

David turned to the man on the bed covering himself up with the sheets. He had long blond hair and a goatee. "Get dressed, Romeo. You have a lot of questions to answer." The police chief picked up a pair of blue jeans from the floor. They still had the factory creases and stiff texture of new pants. He tossed them at him. "Where did you get Helga Thorpes' credit card, Kenny?"

"I *am* going to be a model ... someday." Kenny turned his back to the police officers to put on his pants.

"I'm not here about your dreams and aspirations." David set his foot on a chair next to the bed. "I want to know where you got that credit card that you used to book this room."

"I found it." Kenny turned around and zipped up his pants. "I found a purse in a booth in the diner yesterday when I went on duty. It was still there when I finished my shift. No one called or came back for it. So I opened it up and there was a wallet with cash and credit cards and—"

"Cash? How much?"

Kenny hesitated before answering. "Five-hundred and fifty-four dollars."

"Where's the cash?" David asked even though he knew the answer.

"I didn't steal it." Kenny gently fingered a tribal tattoo that covered his entire shoulder and traveled the length of his arm down to his wrist. Depicted an assortment of brightly colored bird feathers, the tattoo showed signs of being freshly re-touched.

The police chief cocked his head to take note of an oily lotion that had been applied to the fresh artwork. "You spent it."

"Hey, I would have given the purse back if someone had come in asking for it," Kenny said. "I waited all day, and when no one did …" With a shrug of his shoulders, he admired his new tattoo. "Besides, finders keepers."

"And in this case the finder is also going to be a weeper." David stepped up to him so that his face was inches from Kenny's. "I want to see exactly where you found this purse."

Kenny swallowed. Beads of sweat formed around the mustache of his freshly trimmed goatee. "Am I in trouble?"

A wide grin crossed the police chief's face. "Kenny, don't be silly." In response to Kenny's sigh of relief, he added, "Of course, you're in trouble."

CHAPTER SIXTEEN

"Do you think Kenny is guilty of anything beyond credit card fraud?" Mac asked David on his cell phone while keeping an eye on their rental car's GPS.

Mac kept the other eye on the road weaving through an upper scale subdivision littered with small mansions on landscaped lots. Archie, who was driving, was notorious for getting so involved in hands-free phone conversations that she would ignore the GPS instructions.

"Turn right up here, Arch," Mac directed.

"I've got it." She turned on the right turn signal. "If someone stole Helga's purse, then why did they leave over five-hundred dollars and her credit cards?"

"I doubt if it was stolen," Mac said. "More likely she dumped it."

"That makes more sense to me," David said. "Kenny found the purse in a booth in the busiest restaurant at the biggest truck stop in Breezewood, a major stop on the Pennsylvania turnpike with people going in all different directions. If Helga had been lucky, a dishonest traveler would have found the purse and used up the cash on his travels before resorting to the credit card, hundreds of miles in the opposite direction from where she was heading."

"Which would have sent you on a wild goose chase," Mac said. "But as luck would have it, a less-than-swift busboy found it and used it up right there in town."

"He spent over three hundred of the cash on a tattoo," David said.

"Over three hundred dollars?" Mac replied. "For a stupid tattoo that's going to sag into an ink blotch when he gets old and wrinkled?"

Seeing by the GPS that they were approaching their destination, he tapped Archie's arm and pointed. "We're here." Enthralled in the phone conversation, Archie hit the brake pedal so hard that they jerked to a stop. Mac's cell phone clattered to the floor. "Easy!"

"I am taking it easy," she yelled. "Geez! Next time you're driving." Grumbling about backseat drivers, she eased the car over to the curb.

Mac picked up the cell phone from the floor to discover that his call to David had been disconnected. He cursed. "I didn't get a chance to tell him about the feds arresting Hawkins and Nichols and our lead on Portia."

"Portia Hagar had an alibi." Archie parked in front of what had once been Jason and Scarlett Fairbanks' home.

The sprawling French country home rested at the end of a paved circular driveway in the middle of which rested a rhododendron bush. A four-foot brick wall marked the boundary between the home and the property next door that sported an elaborately landscaped garden, which included a goldfish pond and footbridge.

"Jason Fairbanks allegedly raped Portia Hagar." Mac followed Archie when she strolled over to the edge of the driveway to the house next door. "He got away with it because his father owned the law in this county. She was fired and her career over. Don't you think it's possible that she got mad enough to take matters into her own hands to get the justice she deserved?"

"And frame an innocent woman in doing so?" Archie dared to step up the driveway.

"Maybe that wasn't her intention," Mac said. "How was she to know that Scarlett—"

"Ruth," she corrected him from over her shoulder before stepping over to the flowers surrounding the fish pond.

"Ruth—was leaving on that day at that time—unless she was Madame X. Maybe she intended to frame Ruth all along."

Archie bent over to peer more closely at the red flowers.

"Smells like a set up," Mac said. "What are you doing? Nichols said Mrs. Weber passed away."

She smelled one of the flowers. "Are these bloodflowers?"

Mac was about to respond with "Who cares?" when a feminine voice replied in broken English from the home tucked behind the exotic garden, "Yes. You have good eye." A young Asian woman with black hair that hung down to the middle of her back stepped from among a bed of rose bushes. Her gardening gloves and worn clothes coated in potting soil and other planting substances revealed that they had interrupted her yard work. "You admire garden? Yes?" Her voice was laden with an oriental accent that revealed her foreign upbringing.

"Very much so," Archie said. "These gardens are lovely. You must have a green thumb."

"Yes, I do," she replied, "but I can't take all credit. Most of garden was planted by my aunt many year ago. She pass away. Now I care for it."

"I'm sorry to hear that," Archie said.

"Was your aunt Tuyon Weber?" Mac asked her.

Instead of answering, she cocked her head and looked him up and down with suspicion in her eyes.

"I'm Mac Faraday." He offered her his hand, which she ignored. "This is Archie Monday. We're investigating Jason Fairbanks' murder for the lawyer representing his widow, Scarlett."

"Everyone call me Lee." Relaxing, she took off her gardening gloves to shake his hand. "I remember Scarlett. Yes. Nice lady. Pretty daughter named Holly."

"Then you lived here," Mac replied.

"I was at university when Mr. Fairbanks die," she said. "I was raised in Vietnam. Aunt Tu come to United States with American soldier. She had promised to send for all of us after she become citizen but, when that happened, they did not have money. After uncle die, Aunt Tu send for me." She frowned. "My mother too sick to come. She pass soon after I come." A smile came to her lips. "But Aunt Tu take good care of me. She send me to school so I run her business."

"What business is that?" Archie asked.

"Nursery." Lee waved her arm around to indicate the elaborate gardens. "Aunt Tu start plant nursery after uncle die. Biggest in whole area. Right off interstate. Everyone go there."

"Did your aunt ever talk about Fairbanks' murder?" Mac steered her back to the reason for their visit.

"He wasn't nice man," Lee said. "No one sad when he die. Very mean. He hit Scarlett and Holly. Aunt Tu call police and they do nothing. She said it shameful thing for man when his death set living free."

"How profound," Archie said.

Gauging the distance between the two homes, Mac narrowed his eyes. "Was your aunt here at the time of the murder? Was she working in her garden—"

"Aunt Tu always gardening," Lee said. "But she say she see and hear nothing."

During their conversation, Archie was squatting next to the bloodflowers to admire the red blooms. "What kind of mulch do you use?" She brought a handful up to her nose to sniff.

"It is a special mixture that I make myself," Lee said with a grin full of pride. "Aunt Tu created it. Spend many years mixing and experimenting."

"What's in it?"

"Many things. Make flowers big and bright."

"Do you sell it at your nursery?" Archie asked.

"Yes," she said. "Stop by and tell them I send you. They give discount."

While Archie gushed at the offer of a discount, Mac once again eased them back to the reason for their visit. "We were hoping that the current owners of the Fairbanks' home would let us in to take a look at where the murder happened."

"I'm sure they would, if home," Lee said. "They on vacation. Disney World with two children. So sorry."

Mac was ushering Archie back to the car when he said, "I guess now we have to stop by the plant nursery."

"We probably should." She brought her hand up to his nose for him to sniff. Smelling the sour scent, he rubbed his hand over his nose to wipe out the odor. "What is that?"

"Many things." Archie wiped her hands together. "I'm willing to bet one of them is chicken feces—which means our killer walked through Aunt Tu's garden on his way into the Fairbanks home to kill Jason."

Mac noticed the brick fence separating the two properties. "That wall is the perfect place to hide behind while waiting for the ideal opportunity to slip inside once Jason was alone to take him out."

"And frame Scarlett in the process."

"Ruth," Mac corrected her with a smile.

"Ruth." Playfully, she shoved the rental car's keys into his chest. "You're driving."

From the driver's seat of his cruiser, Bogie glanced over at David when he heard him curse upon reading the text that came in on his cell phone. They were less than ten minutes from Spencer police station. "Bad news?"

"Is there any other kind?" David shoved the phone back into its case on his utility belt. "We have visitors. Two detectives from New York and Bill Clark, who is raising Cain because I'm not there to kiss his butt."

"I'll kiss him if you want me to." Bogie shook his fist in the air to signify the type of kiss he would lay on the arrogant town councilman.

The corners of David's mouth tugged up at the thought of the muscle-bound deputy chief taking on Bill Clark, who was built like a rail.

It was clear to everyone by how the councilman avoided Bogie that he was afraid of him. Desk Sergeant Tonya had noticed that over the years, Bill Clark would never stop in when Bogie, the deputy chief, was there but David was not. If he called in for David, he would refuse to speak to Bogie, whose job was to cover when the chief was unavailable.

At first, everyone assumed that the councilman avoided Bogie because he considered dealing with the second in command beneath him. Then, Mac suggested an experiment. When David was ordered to make an appearance at a town council meeting to answer questions about various minor issues, Bogie appeared in his stead with the excuse that David was ill. Bill Clark tried to excuse Bogie, only to have the rest of the council, familiar with the law officer's long association with the police department, argue for the deputy chief to stay.

Like Gnarly sniffing out a bad guy, Bogie sensed Clark's fear of the deputy chief who could physically snap the twerp in two like a toothpick. The councilman refused to make eye contact with him. During the meeting, when Bogie moved in his direction, beads of sweat formed on Clark's shiny forehead while he backed away.

Not unlike Gnarly, Bogie fed on Clark's fear.

No one knows what Bogie said, or did, to the chairman of the town council in the men's room at the Spencer Inn after the breakfast meeting. When asked, he said simply, "We discussed the high cost of medical care nowadays." He also expressed that he had a very enjoyable breakfast to boot.

Whatever was discussed, after that breakfast, Bill Clark made fewer appearances at the police station, and never when he saw Bogie's cruiser in his reserved parking space.

"Everyone knows why Bill Clark has it out for you," Bogie told David.

David felt a lump form in his throat. Images of the gentle face, and the touch of the soft flesh of a woman from long ago came to his mind. The memory of her whispered words of love to him were drowned out by her terror-filled scream as it blasted through his earbud and filled his head when the undercover operation went south.

Lisa Clark.

Because I got his little sister killed—that's why. David swallowed. "Wh-why is that?"

"Because he knows no matter how much money he throws around in this town, he'll never leave the type of legacy that your daddy left behind … or that you're going to leave," Bogie said. "All the bucks he's got, and all the fancy friends he's paid for, can't make up for the big thing he ain't got. You know what that is?"

"What?" David asked with a sigh.

"Character. Clark's got no character and that's not something that you can buy with any amount of money." Bogie swung the steering wheel to turn into the Spencer police department parking lot. "He knows it deep down and he's jealous—that's what."

"Maybe." David took in a deep, cleansing breath while dreading the next few minutes.

"Does he ever blink?" The larger of the two detectives, both dressed in dark suits and ties, eyed Gnarly occupying the couch.

Poised to pounce, the hundred-pound German shepherd directed his unblinking eyes at the visitors—as if to dare any of them to try to take a seat on *his* sofa.

Meanwhile, the two detectives and Town Councilman Bill Clark were sitting in the three straight back chairs left in the reception area.

"Depends," Tonya replied from her desk.

When she didn't elaborate, the smaller of the Mutt and Jeff pair of detectives asked, "On what?"

"On who he's staring at."

"This is ridiculous." Bill Clark bit off each word. "He's a dog, damn it. This is a police station, not a kennel. That sofa is for visitors, which is what we are."

"Then tell him to move." Anticipating a bit of entertainment, Tonya sat back in her chair and twirled the pen she had been using to write.

The three men eyed each other. Two of the three were armed, but that didn't seem to matter. In silence, they looked from one to the other.

"You know him," the smaller law officer who had introduced himself as Detective Fred Oliver told Bill Clark. "You order him off the sofa."

His partner, Detective Morris Probst, agreed. "And while you're at it, tell him to share those cookies he's been hoarding, too."

The councilman's beady eyes grew wide. Sitting up straight he turned toward Gnarly. The German shepherd was staring right at him. His ears stood tall. Even in his lying position, he was poised to take any action at a split second's notice.

Bill Clark sat back in his seat. "That sofa's probably covered with dog hair anyway and my suit needs to be dry cleaned."

Making a sound from deep in his throat that could have been a laugh, Gnarly laid his head down to rest on the arm of the sofa. The fresh batch of dog biscuits, delivered by Carmine that morning, rested only inches from his snout.

Detective Oliver chuckled. "That's what I thought."

"But I want to try one of those chocolate cookies," Detective Probst said with a whine in his voice.

"If you want a cookie, go get it," his partner said.

Detective Probst stood up and took a step toward the box on the end table.

His eyes narrowing and his ears falling back to lay flat on top of his head, Gnarly uttered a low growl.

"On second thought, my wife has been telling me to lose weight." The detective retook his seat.

Giggling openly, Tonya returned to her work.

When David came through the door, Bill Clark was the first on his feet. "O'Callaghan, where have you been?"

"I was out following up a lead on a murder investigation," David replied.

"Meanwhile, these two detectives who have come all the way from New York to pick up an escaped killer have been made to wait." Clark gestured at the two men standing behind him. "A murder suspect who you were notified about more than twenty-four hours ago. Yet, you didn't hesitate to lock up the grieving father of her victim."

"No, I didn't hesitate to arrest that man," David said, "because he was stupid enough to assault a woman right here in this police station in front of one of my officers and then was such an idiot that he assaulted a uniformed officer when she tried to arrest him. If stupidity was against the law, we'd be arresting him for that as well."

"But you haven't arraigned him yet," Clark said. "What's the hold up?"

"Me," Ben Fleming announced before closing the door behind him. "If you have any issues with how Reese Fairbanks' case is being handled, Clark, talk to me."

"You can start talking by telling me why you're so quick to lock up the family of a murder victim but slow to arrest that victim's killer."

"I take it Fairbanks is a friend of yours," Bogie said. "Figures."

"As a matter of fact we're fraternity brothers," Clark said, "but that makes no difference in the fact that a man came all the way here from several states away to see that justice was done in his son's murder and he ends up behind bars while the woman who killed his only child is running around scott free."

"You haven't picked up Scarlett Fairbanks yet?" Detective Probst asked. "You got a copy of the arrest warrant."

"Her church is giving her safe haven," David said. "We can't take custody of her as long as she's on their property."

"Bull!" Clark said. "Go in, cuff her, and drag her out."

The prosecutor stepped up to look down in the councilman's face. "Unlike how they do things where your friend comes from, we don't take orders from small men with big wallets."

"What's that supposed to mean?"

"Fairbanks' empire has crumbled," Prosecutor Ben Fleming announced. "His wife is pressing charges against him for assault, which he was stupid enough to have committed in front of a Spencer police officer. In addition to that, I'm pressing charges against him for assaulting a police officer and resisting arrest. The prosecutor and sheriff in New York have been arrested for soliciting a bribe, and they're singing like pop stars about Reese Fairbanks' dirty dealings throughout the years." He cocked an eyebrow. "Fact is, Clark, your friend's ship is sinking. Do you really want to stay on it? I recommend you jump this ship with the rest of the rats."

Bill Clark backed up from Ben Fleming. He jerked his chin up and eyed each of them while considering how best to save face.

Even Gnarly rose up to await his reaction.

Deciding to reinforce his position of power, he told David, "I want to be kept informed about how this case progresses."

"Oh, you will be, sir," David replied.

When Bill Clark turned to hurry for the door, he found Bogie blocking his path.

"In a couple of minutes, I will be questioning another suspect in Eugene Newton's murder," David said.

With a sweep of his arm, Bogie gestured down the hallway to the interrogation room.

"Come, step into our chamber, councilman," Bogie said.

"I've never—" Clark said.

"That's not what I hear," Ben replied. "By the way, I'm going to be sitting in on this interrogation, so be careful about what lies you tell."

When Bogie clasped his arm, Clark shook it off. "You'll be hearing from my lawyer." With that threat, the councilman stomped down the hallway.

"Our sheriff is now in jail?" Detective Oliver asked. "Is it true that the FBI is investigating Fairbanks for bribing him and Hawkins? Then what are we supposed to do about Scarlett Fairbanks?"

"Smoke them if you got 'em, gentlemen," Ben said. "I've been negotiating with Scarlett Fairbanks' lawyer and the New York attorney general's office about how they want to proceed. New evidence in the Jason Fairbanks murder is coming out. As for you two, I took the liberty of reserving a penthouse for you at the Spencer Inn."

"Penthouse?" Detective Oliver's eyebrows rose up on his skinny face.

"Sweet," Tonya said.

"Well, you did come all this way," Ben said. "I talked to the Inn's manager, Jeff Ingles. Go up to the Spencer Inn and make yourselves comfortable. Have some lunch, and then check in with your office to see what they want to do. Maybe we'll have some developments by close of business."

"How is the food at this Spencer Inn place?" Detective Probst asked.

"The best," Bogie said.

"It's a five star restaurant," Tonya told them. "You have to save room for their chocolate lava cake dessert."

Puffing out their chests and smiling ear to ear about snagging such a luxurious assignment, the two detectives bumped fists. "Take your time, my friends," Detective Probst said.

Once they were out the door, Ben Fleming allowed a sly grin to come to his lips. He turned to David, who peered at him with an arched eyebrow.

"Penthouse suite at the Spencer Inn?" David asked. "Looks like you bought Ruth Buchanan some time and at a pretty high price. Don't even think of charging that to the police department."

"Don't worry," the prosecutor said. "Mac's covering it. It was his idea to buy more time. Let's pray he starts making headway in New York on finding Fairbanks' killer."

CHAPTER SEVENTEEN

The last place Mac and Archie expected to meet a rich man's mistress was at a Chuck E. Cheese, but that was where Portia Anderson, formerly Hagar, agreed to meet the two of them during a birthday party for one of her young son's friends.

Since her torrid relationship with Jason Fairbanks, Portia, like Ruth, had put her past behind her. She moved two hours north from Newcomb to a small seashore town, where she met and married the town pharmacist. Even after having two children, she held a slight touch of the sensual beauty that had attracted Jason Fairbanks. Her shapely curves were still visible under her old jeans, button down top, and comfortable shoes. She wore her long dark hair twisted and pinned to the top of her head and lightly touched her face with a hint of make-up. Other than that, she looked like all the other mothers fighting to keep track of their children racing around the children's restaurant.

Mac and Archie leaned across the table to hear Portia's story over the roar of children of every age and size and the musical entertainment by animal characters. Portia divided her attention between them, a baby in a car seat, and

217

her young son who was crawling at top speed through the tubes that snaked through the pizza and amusement place.

"Jason Fairbanks got exactly what he deserved." In contrast to her message, she smiled and cooed at the giggling baby girl. "Didn't he?" she asked the baby in a sing-song voice. "Bad things happen to bad people."

"Are you talking about him getting killed or before he was murdered?" Mac asked in a serious tone.

Portia hesitated before replying, "I'm not sure what you mean."

Mac told her, "A couple of hours before he was murdered, someone shot Jason Fairbanks with a stun gun—several times."

"It wasn't me," she said. "I would have liked to. That animal raped me, just' to show me that he owned the town, the law, the courts, and me. That's why I moved away."

"And I'm sure the thought of revenge never crossed your mind when he got away with raping you," Mac asked.

"How could it?" Portia asked. "His father owned the county prosecutor. Reese Fairbanks fired me and had me blackballed from every reputable business in town."

"That must have made you very angry," Archie said. "It would have made me mad."

Portia glared at both of them. "Didn't you talk to the police? They did question me already. I had a solid alibi. I was at a job interview."

"We did and they did." With a sigh, Mac leaned across the table to catch her eye. "How about if we start over? ... I know you didn't kill Fairbanks."

Suspicion filled her face while she held his gaze. "Then why are you here?"

"I want to know who tortured him for you," Mac said. "Maybe whoever it was decided to take matters into his own hands and ensure Fairbanks would never hurt another woman again."

"No," Portia said.

"No to what?" Mac asked. "No you won't tell us, or no he didn't kill Fairbanks."

She glared at them. After a long silence, she said, "I don't have to talk to you." She gathered her baby bag.

Mac reached across the table to grab her arm. "I'm not looking to get you or your friend into trouble. I'm simply trying to get the facts to help Scarlett Fairbanks clear her name."

"No one blamed her for killing her husband," she said. "As a matter of fact, I would be glad to testify in her defense about the monster she lived with."

"If you really want to help her, tell us what happened the day he was murdered," Archie said.

"Let *me* tell *you* what happened," Mac said. "Fairbanks raped you but the prosecutor refused to press charges. Someone came to you—someone who was equally disgusted by seeing all that Jason Fairbanks got away with—and offered to teach him a lesson, on your behalf. You called Fairbanks and offered an apology and to make it up to him with an afternoon of fun and games at your place. Then, you went to your job interview, which gave you a solid alibi. When Fairbanks arrived at your apartment—vengeance was waiting for him." He narrowed his eyes at her. "How did I do?"

Archie looked from him to Portia and back again.

Portia was gazing silently at Mac. Finally, she said, "He assured me Jason was alive—madder than hell, but alive, when he left my place."

"Can you give me a name?" Mac asked.

"No," she replied.

"You can't—"

"I *won't*," she said. "Arrest me, sue me, whatever. He was the only one who stood up for me and got me some justice for what Jason had done to me. He went to bat for me when no one else would. No way will you make me sell him out."

The chair of Spencer's town council, Bill Clark could not resist scoffing when Police Chief David O'Callaghan entered the interrogation room, even if the county prosecutor was directly behind him.

"You do realize, O'Callaghan, that I will remember this day when it comes time to renew your contract as police chief."

"Try it, Clark," Ben Fleming said, "and the local media will get the low-down about the town councilman who tried to close down a church, and your soon-to-be ex-wife's divorce lawyer will find out about all of the skeletons in your closet. So, I suggest you adjust your attitude … unless it's twisted beyond adjusting."

Silently, Bill Clark eyed David O'Callaghan who was sitting directly across from him at the table.

The police chief's eyes met his. "I'm only doing the job I was hired to do. That's all I ever try to do."

"No matter what the collateral damage is," Clark said.

"There are some things that are beyond my control," David said.

Clark's eyes narrowed to dark beady slits.

"We have witnesses who heard you threaten Eugene Newton," Ben Fleming said. "Now he's dead."

"Did you kill him?" David asked.

"I despised the cretin," Bill Clark said. "He could not understand that my trying to get his church closed down was not personal. It was business. They've been sitting on that prime property doing their pagan worship to some supreme mythological being since Spencer was founded. Do you know how valuable that property is—right on the lake with a building that could easily be converted into a club house? But those people are too pathetic to make good use of it. What use does Spencer have with a church anyway? But Newton took it all personal and decided to get even by digging into my business—"

"Which ended up costing you an arm and a leg in your last divorce," David noted.

"That was when it got really personal," Clark said in a cold tone.

"And now that you are in the process of a second divorce Eugene Newton is dead," Ben said.

"Are you waiting for me to express remorse?" Clark asked with a smug grin on his face.

"I don't think that's possible for you," Ben said. "Makes me wonder if maybe Newton's death was to prevent history from repeating itself."

"Just ask your police chief," Clark replied.

Confused by the comment, Ben glanced over at David, who was gazing past the councilman to the wall behind him. Before Ben could inquire, David raised his voice to ask, "Where were you Tuesday between noon and one o'clock?"

Clark whipped out his cell phone and checked his calendar. "I was home alone. Since my wife walked out on me and my mistress realized she wasn't going to be wife number three, I spend a lot of time alone." He chuckled. "I'm sure that's only a temporary situation, though."

"Too bad," David said. "It's hard to alibi yourself when you're alone."

"Unless your soon-to-be-ex-wife is a blood-sucker," Clark replied. "I'm sure her private investigator can verify where I was and what I was doing, complete with time-stamped pictures." He paused to enjoy the disappointed expressions on the police chief's and prosecutor's faces. He especially enjoyed it on David's face.

"Well, if you have no other questions …" Clark rose to his feet and, without waiting for a dismissal, he threw open the door and left.

Ben Fleming shot David a look that demanded an explanation for the cryptic exchange between him and the councilman before shoving back his seat and going after their suspect. In the hallway, Fleming turned around so fast that he bumped into David. "If there's something going on between you and Clark, then you better fill me in."

"Nothing more than a personal dislike for each other," David said.

"Never lie to a politician, O'Callaghan," Fleming said. "The first lesson in political science is lying, so I can spot one from a mile away … in the dark."

Before David could think of a response, a high pitched scream, partnered with laughter, came from the reception area.

"That sounds like Clark," Fleming said.

Pushing past the county prosecutor, David rushed down the hallway and into the reception area where Bill Clark was pushed down onto the sofa with what appeared to be a small black bear on top of him—licking his face.

"You're right, Marilyn. He does scream like a little girl." Bogie had his arms folded across his chest.

"Po Bear isn't picky," Marilyn Newton said with a wicked grin. "He loves garbage. Doesn't he, Twerpie?" She was digging through her purse at the reception desk.

"Get him … off … me. Now!" Bill Clark begged between licks that included tongue action from the huge dog covered with thick black fur.

Po Bear was approximately seventy pounds bigger than Gnarly, who watched the attack from under Tonya's desk. With wide eyes, he appeared to be thinking, *That's one big dog*.

Displeased with Bogie's lack of action in saving the councilman, David grasped Po Bear's collar and pulled him off.

Once he was freed, Bill Clark's arrogance returned. While wiping the dog drool from his shirt, he sputtered out his threat to Marilyn. "I was attacked! You all saw!" He pointed at each one of them. "This woman has no right owning a dog of that size! It's clear to everyone that she can't control him. He attacked me, knocked me down, and tried to eat my face."

"Here it is!" Marilyn sang out while pulling a brilliantly colored brochure from her purse. "Here you go, Bogie! Now, I have already booked the suite for double occupancy. I have the dates circled on this brochure." She thrust the brochure into Bogie's hand. "Tell Doc to call me. We'll have a blast."

"To tell you the truth, I think if Doc was to go on a cruise, I'd want to go with her," Bogie said.

"No men allowed," Marilyn said. "I'm in mourning. It just wouldn't be right for me to go on a cruise with a man."

"I was thinking her and me," Bogie said, "on our own cruise."

"Then who's going to go with *me*?" With her bottom lip sticking out in a pout, she stomped one of her feet.

"I have legal recourse!" Bill Clark yelled louder as if to get through to Marilyn.

"I'm sure you do," she replied. "You also have illegal recourse, which I'm well aware of." She turned to David. "Have you asked Twerpie for his whereabouts at the time of my Eugene's murder?"

"He claims he has an alibi," Ben said, "which his soon-to-be-ex-wife's PI can confirm."

"Oh, do you mean Brenda?" Marilyn asked. "I just saw her at zumba."

"Zumba?" David asked.

"It's an exercise class," Tonya said.

"I thought you took yoga," David said to Marilyn.

223

"That's on Tuesdays." One corner of Marilyn's lips curled upward. "Ivana is in my yoga class."

Bill Clark's eyebrows rose.

The other corner of Marilyn's mouth kicked up. "Ivana is Twerpie's first wife."

Bill Clark's eyebrows met in the center between his eyes.

"After zumba today, we all went to the power café at the club—all four of us. What was the fourth lady's name?" Marilyn pointed a French manicured fingernail at the town councilman. "Francine!"

Bill Clark's jaw dropped open.

"Who's Francine?" David whispered to Ben Fleming.

"Clark's latest mistress," Ben said, "and the manager for his last campaign."

"They all felt really bad about Eugene dying and wanted to know what I was going to do now," Marilyn said. "I told them I really didn't know. So Ivana suggested that maybe I would like to get into politics. She said that she knows for a fact that any idiot can run for office and be on the town council. All you have to do is have the support of the right people. Well, you would not guess who came in after her Pilates class."

"Who?" Tonya asked.

"Catherine Fleming!"

"My wife." Ben held back a chuckle as he imagined what happened when his wife, a United States senator, walked in on Marilyn's power luncheon.

"She said that she would give me her full support!" Marilyn threw up her arms like a cheerleader concluding her grandest performance.

"Senator Catherine Fleming is supporting you!" Bill Clark gasped.

"Yep, Twerpie!" Marilyn sang out. "I'm throwing my top into the political ring and running against you!"

It took a full moment for Ben Fleming to realize. "It's *hat*, Marilyn. You throw your *hat* into an election."

"But I look terrible in hats," Marilyn said. "So I guess I'll have to throw in my top." She looked down at her abundant bosom. "I hope I don't forget to wear my Victoria's Secret when I do that for my campaign kick-off party."

She winked at Bill Clark, who looked gray. "See you on the campaign trail, Twerpie!"

Marilyn Newton spun around on her high heels and waved a slender hand. "Come along, Po Bear. Our work here is done." The humongous dog fell in next to Marilyn and the two of them sashayed out the door.

Bill Clark collapsed onto the sofa.

"This is one election for town council that Spencer will never forget," Ben Fleming murmured.

Chapter Eighteen

"Well, that was a wasted trip," Archie said upon their return to the police station in New York. Glancing across to Mac in the driver's seat of their rented sedan, she noticed him staring through the windshield at the sheriff's deputies coming out of the station. "Did you hear me?"

Blinking, a slow grin crossed his face. "Yeah."

"Portia told us nothing."

"That's right," Mac said. "She told us *nothing*. But she *didn't* tell us a lot." He unbuckled his seat belt, threw open the door, and hurried toward the entrance of the police station.

"*What* didn't she tell us?" Archie rushed to climb out of the car and keep up with him.

"Where to start looking for the person who avenged her." Grasping her hand, Mac practically dragged her up the steps and into the police station. "We need to take a look at the police report for when Jason attacked her."

226

David O'Callaghan couldn't get Marilyn Newton's diamonds out of his mind. *How does a retired plumber acquire so much wealth that his death makes his widow an heiress?*

The logical answer was embezzlement.

If David's suspicion was correct, then that could prove to be a motive for one of Eugene Newton's church-going friends killing him. He could understand how angry Eugene's fellow trustees could become if they realized he was stealing from the church, threatening its closure, in order to keep his lovely wife in diamonds and glittery fingernails.

The best place to start asking questions about the church's finance was their accountant, Thomas Letterman.

Since retiring as an executive from the IRS, the widower spent most afternoons at the Spencer Inn golf course. A jovial, gray-haired man with a thick mustache and glasses, Thomas was delighted to answer any questions the police chief had about Eugene's murder as long as David could keep up with him on the golf course in the hot summer sun.

The accountant may have been an elderly man, but he didn't let that stop him from carrying his golf bag across the course. "Golf carts are for wimps," he told David before slinging his filled golf bag across his back and marching off to the fourth hole.

With watery eyes, he said with a choked voice, "Eugene was a good man. There was nothing he wouldn't do for anyone. Even if it seemed impossible, Eugene believed that if we had the will, we would find a way. And if the church couldn't do it … more than once, he would pay out of his own pocket to help a fellow church member out."

As if to take his mind off the tragedy, Thomas proceeded to try to line up his shot to tee off at the fourth hole. Blinking the tears out of his eyes, he sniffed and wiped his nose on a handkerchief.

227

"I guess," David said as casually as possible, "that was one of the questions that I have to ask about Eugene Newton."

"What?" Thomas asked with his head down while lining up the shot.

"He was a retired plumber."

"Yep," Thomas said, "sold his plumbing business and retired ten years ago."

"I know plumbers make a lot of money," David said, "but according to Marilyn, he left her an heiress—extremely well off."

"That's what I heard, too," Thomas said.

"Yet, the church is flat broke."

"*Was* flat broke," Thomas said.

"Was?"

"Yep." Thomas nodded his head before calling out, "Fore!" He swung the club to send the ball flying over the green course. It bounced onto the green. With a pleased grin, he shoved the club into his bag, slung it across his shoulders, and proceeded toward his ball.

David jogged to catch up. When Thomas failed to offer further explanation, he asked, "'Was' as in past tense. Are you telling me that the church is not broke anymore?"

"That's right," Thomas said. "Eugene left his whole estate to the church's operating fund. Estimated at two-point-three million dollars. Deborah told the trustees this morning."

David felt his mouth hanging open. He was forced to swallow before finding his voice again. "Are you sure?"

With raised eyebrows, Thomas nodded his head. "It was in his will. The house belonged to Marilyn, as well as the lakeshore property. But Eugene's liquid assets go to the church."

"How does Marilyn feel about that? Did she know?"

"Of course she knew." Stopping, Thomas placed a golf gloved hand on his hip. "Why would Eugene not tell her?"

"Well, considering that she expected to be an heiress …"

"Expected?" Thomas uttered a hearty laugh. "Marilyn *is* an heiress. She told me this morning that she's worth about eighty million dollars … thanks to Eugene."

David shook his head in order to clear up the confusion in his head. Maybe he could shake everything into place. "How—"

"Ten years ago, Marilyn's folks passed," Thomas said in a somber tone. "They had been married for over fifty years and passed within two weeks of each other. Her mother had a stroke and, two weeks later, her father died of congestive heart failure. Guess you could say he died of a broken heart." He leaned on his golf bag. "Well, Marilyn's father was almost as tight as Eugene when it came to money. She inherited eight million dollars. Of course, Marilyn wanted to go wild—"

"Like go on a cruise?"

Laughing, Thomas shook his head. "You couldn't pay Eugene to get on a cruise ship. The guy was not a party animal in any sense of the word." His smile dropped. "But he and Marilyn were a good couple. They understood, appreciated, and respected each other's differences. You don't see that very much in couples nowadays. That's why there's so many divorces. People don't respect their spouses' differences."

"No, they don't."

Thomas said, "Eugene did agree to selling their little house out in the country and moving into a big, fancy place here on the lake. They'd go out more and Marilyn got a snazzy sports car, but that was it. Eugene sold his plumbing business, and they lived on his money, while he invested Marilyn's inheritance." He chuckled. "I guess he did pretty good because she found out from her lawyer that he had multiplied her inheritance ten times."

"While the church was failing," David noted.

With narrowed eyes, Thomas cocked his eyes at the police chief. "What are you implying?"

"Eugene controlled all of the church's finances," David said. "Has anyone noticed that his nest was getting bigger while the church had leaky toilets and—"

The police chief stopped when Thomas burst out into such hard laughter that he was forced to bend over at the waist. Glancing around, David was glad to see that no one could see the hysterics his question had prompted. "You have to admit it's suspicious."

Thomas grasped David by the shoulder. "Obviously, you never met Eugene. You have no idea what type of man he was."

"No, I didn't meet him."

"Eugene didn't *take* money from the church," Thomas said in a firm, serious tone, "he and Marilyn were the ones who kept it going—kept it opened. Over the last few years, Spencer Church lost some of our most generous donors. Some died. Some moved away. Others just plain got mad about something or other and left."

"Like Chip Van Dorn," David said.

"Perfect example. Look at how he ended up." Thomas leaned over to whisper to David, "Bill Clark and his friends had been spreading vicious rumors to people moving into the area that didn't help. Sour grapes about losing the case trying to close us down so that they could buy our property dirt cheap."

"I'm sure," David said by way of agreement.

"They figured that if they couldn't close us up in the courts, that they would run us out of business by making people quit. It almost worked. Last year, donations were so low that we couldn't pay our bills. The only way we could keep our doors open was to lay off our office manager, fire Ruth, and sell the guest cottage. The trustees left that meeting very upset."

Standing up tall, Thomas peered at David to hold his gaze. "Well, it was right after we had made this horribly painful decision that Eugene contacted the board to say that Marilyn insisted on paying Edna's and Ruth's salaries."

"Did he talk her into it?" David asked.

"*Now* what are you implying?"

"Could Eugene have been upset about Edna getting laid off due to personal reasons?"

Thomas placed both hands on his hips. "What personal reason?"

"Sources says Eugene Newton and Edna Parker were quite close."

"Yeah, they were," Thomas said in a matter-of-fact tone. "Eugene was also close to Reverend Deborah. They had to be in order to work together as well as they did. We wouldn't want a chief trustee who didn't work closely with the pastor and the head of member services. That's what we call Edna. Sort of an unofficial title. Eugene wouldn't have been a good chief trustee if he didn't give a darn about a couple of single mothers losing their jobs."

"I'm talking about rumors of Eugene having an extra-marital affair with Edna Parker."

Thomas' face went momentarily blank while he digested what David had said. Gradually, his cheeks turned red. His thick gray eyebrows looked like storm clouds over his piercing eyes. "How dare you even think that about Eugene?" He waved one of his golf clubs as if he considered using it on David. "Edna, Deborah, and Ruth were like sisters to him … and he loved Marilyn more than anything!"

Apologizing, David explained, "When it comes to a murder investigation, I have to investigate rumors, no matter how ludicrous friends and family of the victims may consider them. You'd be surprised how often they turn out to be true. I'm sure you've heard the line, 'Where there's smoke, there's fire.'"

"Well, I know where this smoke started," Thomas said. "Helga Thorpe. Which explains why you're implying that Eugene embezzled funds from the church. Helga started that rumor, too."

The accountant continued waving the golf club. "Well, I assure you, it was quite the opposite. Not only did Marilyn cover the church's bills when we were so far in the red that we couldn't pay our bills, and cover Ruth's and Edna's pay—without any sordid hanky-panky required—" he added with a growl, "but Marilyn paid their medical coverage, as well. They insisted that it was to be an anonymous donation. Edna and Ruth have no idea who is making those donations that kept them employed."

"But that was *his wife's* money, not Eugene's," David said. "It sounds like they kept their money separate."

"Eugene was very sensitive about being a plumber and marrying a rich woman," Thomas said. "He didn't want anyone, in any way, thinking he was a gigolo." He allowed a smile to cross his lips. "Not that he looked like one." He stood up tall. "But there's more."

"What is that?"

"Even with that, the church has not always been able to make its bills with donations from members alone," Thomas said. "Eugene insisted that when that happened, he increased his own donation above and beyond his regular tithe to make sure those bills were covered." He added, "Does that sound like the actions of an embezzler to you?"

"You have to admit its suspicious how he took eight million dollars and turned it into eighty million," David said.

Thomas laughed. "Completely straight up and above board." He went back to lining up his next shot. "According to what his lawyer told me, Eugene could teach Warren Buffett a thing or two."

With another boisterous laugh, he swung at the ball. "Eugene? Embezzler? I can hear him laughing up at the Pearly Gates now." Bending over, the elderly gentleman continued to laugh.

While the accountant was having his hearty laugh, David considered the church's standing. A year ago, they were on the verge of closing—until Eugene and Marilyn Newton had bailed them out. Now that Eugene was dead, the church was sitting pretty and able to pay all of its bills.

Sounds like a motive.

"Thomas," David said, "did any of the trustees know about Eugene making the church a beneficiary in his will before his death?"

"What do you mean?" Thomas said.

"Who will manage Eugene's money now that it's going to the church?"

"Eugene's lawyer is the executor," Thomas said. "I guess as far as managing the money and paying the bills now that Eugene is gone, the trustees have been talking about giving that job to Edna Parker. She had always been part time before because that was all we could pay her. Now that we have so much money, we're already talking about expanding the church's programs, which means we need a full-time administrator." He grinned. "We can now afford to give Edna Parker and Ruth Buchanan full benefits, too. Thanks to Eugene."

"Looks like Edna and Ruth really benefited from Eugene's murder," David said. "Did either of them know that Eugene had made the church his main beneficiary?"

Thomas shrugged. "I really don't know. They were all close. I guess it's possible. Marilyn knew. Maybe she mentioned it."

Sheriff's Deputy Guy Stacey looked like a beaten dog when he entered the interview room to find Mac Faraday sitting at the conference table with a case file resting in front of him.

Mac rose from his seat and invited the deputy who had shot him with a stun gun only the night before to sit across from him. "Thank you so much for coming in."

"My supervisor made it sound like I didn't have a choice," the deputy said while taking his seat. "Look, if this is about my shooting you last night …"

"No," Mac replied, "I completely understand. I've been on your side. Last night, I had to make it look good in order to uncover the truth about what's been happening here."

"It's all over about Hawkins and Nichols," Deputy Stacey said. "I'd suspected before, but had no definite proof. So if you asked me to come in for that, I wish I could help you, but I really don't know anything, except how certain people in this county have had a free pass as far as the law's been concerned."

"Actually, I want to talk to you about a different issue." Mac's eyes met those of the deputy's. "The murder of Jason Fairbanks."

Mac paused while the sheriff's deputy stared wordlessly across the table at him.

"Portia Hagar alleged that Jason Fairbanks raped her," Mac said. "According to the police records, you were the first officer on the scene when she called the police. When Hawkins refused to press charges against Fairbanks, you made numerous calls to the sheriff and even Hawkins' office about the lack of action."

When the deputy said nothing, Mac explained, "I've been there, Stacey. I've investigated cases and arrested violent suspects where I had everything I needed for the prosecutors to move forward but, because of some political maneuvering or deal making behind the scenes, nothing was done and the bad guy walked away."

Deputy Stacey asked, "What's this about?"

"I think when the system refused to stop Jason Fairbanks, you decided to do it yourself."

"I did not kill Fairbanks," the deputy said.

"I talked to Portia Hagar," Mac said.

His mouth drawn tight, Deputy Stacey gazed straight ahead.

Mac lowered his voice. "I'm not trying to get you into trouble. I simply want to know what happened."

"I want to talk to my union rep," Stacey said in a deadpan voice.

"Deputy, I assure you, this meeting is completely off the record," Mac said. "I don't think you killed Jason Fairbanks."

"I'm not a rookie, Faraday," the deputy said. "I know how to manipulate suspects. So don't you sit there—"

"You threatened me this morning," Mac reminded him. "You risked your career and criminal charges to avenge a rape victim when the system refused to give her justice. I don't think you would purposely frame an innocent woman for murder. And I suspect that if you killed Fairbanks and accidentally framed her, that you would have found some way of clearing her name—maybe even confess to the murder yourself?"

Deputy Stacey looked around to ensure that their conversation was not being recorded. "Let's say, I did ambush Fairbanks the afternoon he got killed …"

"Hypothetically?"

"Hypothetically," Deputy Stacey said.

"Hypothetically, if you were to lure him into an ambush," Mac said, "would you have done it alone?"

"I would have had to have had help," Deputy Stacey said. "But I would have no idea who."

"Of course not," Mac replied. "Would any of your accomplices, if you had any, have wanted to go further to put an end to Fairbanks' abuse?"

"No," Deputy Stacey said. "No one would have wanted to kill him. We didn't think an animal like that deserved to live, but all we would have wanted to do was send a message to him that while his father may have owned the law in this town, he didn't own every officer and we were going to take our vows to heart—we were going to protect every person in this town, even if we had to do it on our own—without the support of the sheriff and prosecutor."

Mac worded his question carefully. "If you and your fellow officers were to have done this, how would it have gone down?"

"I imagine," the deputy said, "Fairbanks would have had to have been lured to his mistress's apartment. He would have been told to let himself in with a key that would have been hidden under a mat and come inside and get comfortable in bed. The shower would have been running to give him the impression that she was there. He would have been so anxious to get to her that he would have stripped down and gone in. That would have been when he would discover that it was not her in the shower, but a group of cops not on his daddy's payroll."

"At which point he was drenched in water and shot repeatedly in the groin area with a stun gun," Mac said.

Careful to avoid a confession, the sheriff deputy said, "That would have been an effective payback for rape."

"What would have kept Fairbanks from identifying the vigilantes?"

"He would have been immediately blindfolded and his hands tied around his back. He would have been restrained until it was over."

In deep thought, Mac peered across the table at him. "Would all of you have left together?"

"Yes."

"And Fairbanks would have been alive."

"Madder than mad," the deputy said, "but he would have been alive."

"What would have kept him from taking out his anger on Portia Hager?" Mac asked.

"It would have been made very clear to him that if he ever contacted her or if so much as a hair on her head got a split end," the deputy said, "that we would be back and it would be worse than this time around."

"And then hours later, he ended up dead," Mac said. "When the call came in that Fairbanks had been shot, did—would, the thought have crossed your mind that one of your—"

Deputy Stacey was shaking his head. "Yes, the thought would have crossed my mind and—if I and my fellow officers were to have avenged Portia Hager's rape, then we would have gotten together and checked into it ourselves. I can assure you—no one on this police department killed Jason Fairbanks."

"You're positive about that?" Mac asked.

"Positive." The deputy shrugged. "You know, when the legal system breaks down—or like in our case, refuses to work at all—it can get very frustrating—"

"I know," Mac said.

"A person can only take so much before they decide to take the law into their own hands and do something about it. Ironic, ain't it, that so many people all on the same day decided to put an end to Jason Fairbanks."

CHAPTER NINETEEN

"How do I look?" Jenny Fairbanks asked while checking her reflection in the mirror of her compact.

"I'm sure Ruth and Natalie will think you look wonderful," Bogie turned around in the passenger seat of David's cruiser to tell the older woman who was sitting in the back seat.

"Even if I didn't, they wouldn't tell me." She put the compact away in her handbag. "How they must hate me for never having the nerve to stand up to Reese and Jason to protect them."

As if to comfort her, Gnarly whined and laid his head in her lap. She stroked the top of his head and ears.

Casting a suspicious glance in Bogie's direction, David said, "I'm sure they understand."

He noted that two empty Spencer police cruisers were in the church parking lot. With a grin, he assumed Fletcher was inside getting lunch made up from the food leftover from the night before, while Brewster was spending time with Edna, the church office manager with the "bedroom eyes." Ed Willingham's rented car was parked near the main entrance.

"Are we ready?" David asked their passenger in the rear seat.

Jenny sucked in a deep breath. "As ready as I ever will be."

Bogie slid from the passenger seat and opened the rear door. Unlike what he did for Mac, Gnarly was polite enough to wait for Jenny to climb out before jumping out of the cruiser and galloping up to the door.

Ruth and Natalie were waiting in the foyer for her. Upon seeing her grandmother, the teenaged girl burst into tears and ran into her arms. The first tear shed caused a waterfall of emotion that climaxed into a group hug.

Fearing the tears were contagious, which seemed to be evidenced by Edna and Deborah yanking tissues from a box to dab their eyes, David and Bogie moved to the other side of the fellowship hall where they spotted Ed Willingham eating a piece of chocolate cake.

"Any word from Mac?" David asked with a note of hope.

"As a matter of fact, he called a few minutes ago," Ed said between bites of the cake. "I told him I'd call back when you got here with Jason Fairbanks' mother. He had a few questions for her since she found the body."

"Hey, Chief," Fletcher called from the kitchen doorway. "You need to try some of this refrigerator salad."

"Later," David said.

"I just had the vegetable soup," Ed said. "It has squash in it. That, and the fresh loaf of Italian bread, make me want to convert. My parish doesn't feed its parishioners like this."

"Where does Mac's investigation stand now?" David asked. "Those cops from New York aren't going to wait around forever."

"As long as Mac is putting them up in his suite at the Spencer Inn, they'll wait," Ed said before taking the last bite of his cake.

"Even if they're willing to wait, Ruth can't live inside this church building indefinitely," Bogie pointed out.

"Then let's get this show on the road." Ed took his cell phone from his pocket. "Deborah said we can meet in her office."

The lawyer led David and Bogie across the fellowship hall, where they discovered that the church pastor had already ushered Ruth, Natalie, and Jenny into her office located at the end of the business wing.

As expected, through the glass door, they saw Officer Brewster leaning on the counter in front of Edna's desk while making chit chat.

Unable to resist, David threw open the door. "Everything okay, Brewster?"

The officer jumped to his feet. "Fine, sir!"

"You do know you were assigned to keep an eye on Ruth?" David fought to keep the stern tone in his voice.

Blushing, Edna said, "I'm sorry, Chief, I called him in to help me …" Standing up, she searched her office. "… to get a catalogue that fell behind this file cabinet. It's way back there and I can't reach it. I think someone is going to have to move the cabinet to get it and I really need that catalogue to order office supplies."

"And I was about to do it when you walked in, Chief." Brewster went over and grabbed the heavy file cabinet with both hands.

"Do you need help?" David asked.

"No," Brewster and Edna said in unison.

With a laugh, David turned around to collide into Sirrus Thorpe, who had come through the door at the same time that he was going out.

The old man's weathered face was screwed up. "What's going on here?" he demanded to know.

"I've just about got it," Edna called out from where she was kneeling to reach behind the cabinet. "Pull it out just a little bit more, Nate."

"You got it." Grunting, Officer Brewster tugged on the cabinet.

"Nate? Who's Nate?" Sirrus asked with a firm tone.

"Officer Brewster is helping Edna retrieve her office supply catalogue," David explained.

"Maybe that's why you haven't found Eugene's killer yet," Sirrus said. "You and your officers are too busy hanging around here eating our food and sniffing around the women. Do you have any idea how heartbroken every member of our church has been since Eugene got murdered? That man was the backbone of this church and someone walked in and blew him away. Where were your officers then, Chief? Sniffing around some woman somewhere or eating donuts someplace?"

Ignoring the insult, David asked, "Have you heard from your wife, Mr. Thorpe?"

"Nope. Doubt if I will." Sirrus jerked his head in Brewster's direction. "So why don't you take Nate here and go look for her?"

With a squeal of success, Edna stood up and waved the catalogue in the air. She and Officer Brewster bumped fists before clasping their hands together to thrust them into the air in a sign of victory.

"You would call me if you did?" David interrupted Sirrus' glare to ask.

"Why wouldn't I?" Sirrus asked. "I despised that woman. Only reason I married her was because she lied and told me that she was pregnant. ... I should have learned then to never believe a word that came out of her lying mouth." Grumbling, he turned around and went out the door.

"You coming, O'Callaghan?" Ed Willingham came down the hallway to fetch him.

"Sure, Ed."

When they passed the office where the chief trustee had been murdered, Ed asked over his shoulder about their progress on that case.

"We have a BOLO issued on a suspect," David said. "So far all that we've dug up is an idiot."

"At least you have a suspect," Ed said.

"Mac doesn't?" David asked.

"Nothing that's panned out." Ed paused at the office door. They could hear the women talking inside. "But they suspect the killer hid out in the neighbor's garden while waiting for Fairbanks to be left alone—after Ruth left—before making his move."

"Why does he think that?" Bogie asked from where he had folded his massive frame to sit in a comfy padded chair on the opposite side of the comfortable office decorated in soft lilac.

On the long sofa, Ruth and Natalie huddled on either side of Jenny, who continually dabbed at her eyes with a damp tissue while clinging to her granddaughter's hand. Ruth clutched the elderly woman's arm.

"Forensics had found traces of plant fertilizer at the murder scene." Willingham pressed the button on his cell phone to call Mac.

When Mac answered on the other end, the lawyer advised him that he was putting him on speaker phone. "Jennifer Fairbanks is here, Mac. She has agreed to answer any questions you have about her son's murder."

"Not that I know very much," Jenny said. "Reese and the police immediately focused on Ruth and refused to consider anyone else, even when I insisted that she would never kill Jason."

Mac's voice came from the speaker of Ed's cell phone. "But you found the body and called the police. You got there shortly after four o'clock. You called nine-one-one at four-oh-four."

"That was less than a half hour after we left," Natalie said.

"Did you see anyone leaving the house as you arrived?" Mac asked. "Maybe you saw someone heading over toward the neighbor's house, through her gardens."

Jenny was shaking her head when Ruth asked, "Do you mean Mrs. Weber?"

"Yes," Mac said. "There were traces of her special fertilizer found in footprints on the floor and on the gun."

"Well," Ruth said slowly, "if the killer was hiding in the garden, wouldn't Mrs. Weber have seen him or her?"

"She told the police that she didn't see or hear anything," Mac said. "I'm thinking that means she was inside the house at the time of the murder."

"That's not true," Natalie blurted out.

"Natalie …" Ruth warned.

"But, Mom, she heard the shots," her daughter argued. "Don't you remember? She came running up the driveway when you came running out of the house." She directed her voice in the direction of Ed's cell phone for Mac to hear. "She was not inside her house. She was outside gardening. She was wearing her gardening gloves. I saw her putting them back on when we were driving away."

"Gardening gloves?" Mac repeated. "Are you sure?"

Natalie nodded her head. "She asked if everything was all right and if we wanted her to call the police again. Mom said it was fine and not to call the police. She told you to go, Mom. Don't you remember? She came running up because she heard the shots. She had, too. I heard them."

"You heard the shots?" Ed asked. "How many shots did you hear?"

"Two," Natalie said firmly. "Not real close together like you hear in the movies. One. And then there was this awful silence and I was afraid Mom was dead. I didn't even know she had a gun. And then the second. Then Mom came running out. I was afraid Dad would be behind her."

"Let me get this straight," Mac said. "You, Natalie, heard two shots. The neighbor, Mrs. Weber, came running up the driveway and asked if she should call the police, which, according to the record, she had done many times before when Fairbanks would hit you or your mother. Ruth told her that everything was fine and that she had to go. Mrs. Weber then said for you to go … Yet, after the murder, she told the police that she saw and heard nothing."

"That's what it sounds like," Ed said.

"Why don't you talk to Mrs. Weber?" Ruth asked. "If the killer was hiding in her garden—"

"Unfortunately, Mrs. Weber is dead," Mac said.

"How awful." Ruth hung her head. "I know that if there was any way for her to help, she would have. She was a very kind lady. She knew everything that was happening. She offered more than once to testify for me in court to get Jason put away."

"Then why did she lie, Mom?" Natalie asked. "She told the police that she saw and heard nothing and that's a lie! Why did she lie?"

"Maybe Reese got to her," Jenny said. "I wouldn't be surprised."

"She must have lied to protect me," Ruth said. "She heard the shots. She must have assumed I killed Jason and said she knew nothing so that she couldn't be made to testify against me."

"Maybe," Mac said in a low voice.

"Can I ask a question?" David blurted out.

"If it will help to clear things up," Ed responded.

244

David crossed the office to stand over the three women huddled on the sofa. "Jenny, why did you go to see your son that afternoon?"

Jenny gazed up at the police chief. "I don't quite remember."

David folded his arms across his chest. "You don't remember? You found your only son dead. Yet, you have no memory of why you went over to see him?"

Ruth and Natalie turned to look at the older woman.

"Ruth," David asked, "did your mother-in-law have a tendency to stop in to visit very often?"

"Not really. She and Jason didn't have a good relationship." Ruth gazed over at Jenny. "Why did you come over? You called the police shortly after four? Jason usually worked until five o'clock. Why would you come to the house at four to see him?"

"Tell them, Jenny," David said. "You're safe here. Your husband is in jail and we're all here to protect you. Tell them."

"Tell us what?" Natalie asked.

Jenny hung her head while tears streamed down her face. Sensing the woman needed comforting, Gnarly climbed out from under the coffee table to place his head in Jenny's lap. She stroked the top of his head while he gazed up at her.

David told Ruth and Natalie, "She went to your house to do whatever she had to do to ensure that you two were able to get away. It was Jenny who arranged for the fake identification and gave you the money and set up this job to help you to escape from her son. She sent the gun to Ruth to protect herself against her own son."

In shock, Ruth and Natalie stared at the woman sitting between them.

"Is that true, Jenny?" Mac's voice came out of the phone.

"How did you figure that out, Chief?" Bogie asked.

"In the cruiser on the way over here," David said. "In New York, they were Scarlett and Holly. That was what Jenny knew them as. But on the way here, you called them Ruth and Natalie. A natural reaction would have been for Jenny to ask, 'Who's Ruth and Natalie?' But she didn't, because she knew their new names already. She arranged for their new identities."

"I had been saving money for years to run away," Jenny said. "I had it all socked away. Stealing a little here and a little there. I planned so carefully how I was going to do it, too. No way was anyone ever going to find me and I was going to start a whole new life. But then, when Jason broke Holly's arm—my only grandchild—and Reese helped him get away with it—then I knew I had to do something. The only thing I could do. But then, Scarlett ran away and took Holly with her."

Sighing, she patted Ruth's and Natalie's hands. "I prayed every day that we would never find you. But then, Reese's PI did and dragged you both back. After Jason raped his mistress and Reese helped him get away with that, too, things got worse. Jason became completely convinced that he was invincible. There was nothing that he couldn't get away with and Reese did everything to confirm it." She sniffed. "My son was gone—transformed into a monster. But I had a grand-daughter. She still stood a chance."

"It was you who saved us," Ruth said with tears in her eyes.

"Yes, it was me," Jenny said in a hushed tone. "Once I made my decision about what had to be done, I moved forward with my plan, only instead of me changing my identity and running away, it was my granddaughter and her mother. I remember I was so surprised with how easily it all came together. My church pastor arranged for the job here. He was the only one I trusted to know what I was planning to do.

He had seen an advertisement in a church paper and believed that it was the answer to our prayers."

"It was," Ruth said. "Natalie and I have been so happy here." She kissed her on the cheek. "Thank you, Jenny."

"Don't thank me," Jenny said. "The gun was mine. I had gotten it years ago to protect myself from Reese—but I never had the nerve to use it." She sobbed. "I never expected Scarlett to use it. I thought that Jason would back down once he saw it. How I wish I had never sent it to you."

"I didn't kill him, Jenny," Ruth insisted.

"I know." Jenny took her hand. "You didn't kill him. Reese did, by raising him to be a monster, just like him. He put that bullet between our son's eyes the minute he taught him that women were put on earth to be abused."

The three of them collapsed into a sobbing mob.

Taking the cell phone with him, Ed gestured for David and Bogie to meet him outside to leave the women alone. In the hallway, Ed asked Mac, "Did you get all that? Still think that it's possible that Madame X set Ruth up?"

There was a long silence on the other end of the line. "What do you think, David? You're there. What did Jenny look like to you?"

"She's genuinely remorseful for her son's death and the way he had turned out," David said. "She's passionate about saving her granddaughter and Ruth."

"I believe she's carrying a heavy burden for not stopping her husband from turning him into the monster that he grew up to be," Bogie said.

"Do you think she killed her son to save her granddaughter?" Ed asked.

"I think she would have confessed to that a long time ago if she did," David said. "She feels responsible enough as it is for supplying them with the murder weapon."

LAUREN CARR

"Maybe she didn't confess because she was afraid of what her husband would have done to her," Ed said.

"Jenny didn't do it," Mac's voice shot from the cell phone. "She didn't kill her son."

They could hear in the tone of his voice that realization had struck him.

"I know who did it," Mac said. "I know who killed Jason Fairbanks. I just need Archie to dig up some information to prove motive."

248

CHAPTER TWENTY

The lawyers from the New York Attorney General's office and New York State Police were still arm wrestling to determine who was in charge when Mac and Archie, equipped with reports and case files, barged in to speak to whoever it was that had the power to void the arrest warrant for Scarlett Fairbanks, aka Ruth Buchanan.

In the hallway leading to what had once been the county prosecutor's office, FBI Special Agent Sid Delaney pointed them in the direction of Howard Stafford, who was standing behind the prosecutor's desk in his spacious corner office like a conqueror staking his claim.

Mac was not happy to see that he looked to be about twelve years old. But he had to deal with him. With Archie directly behind him, Mac rushed in, "Mr. Stafford ..." He offered him his hand. "Mac Faraday."

Ignoring his hand, the young man with the baby face announced, "So you're the one who started all this."

"Kind of." Offering a sheepish grin, Mac thumbed the two case files he hugged to his chest. "It had to be done. With all the years that Reese Fairbanks was running this county, there's no telling how many people fell victim to the lack of justice here. I'm willing to bet Scarlett Fairbanks is just the tip of the iceberg. You have a lot of work to do."

"That's what I'm afraid of," Stafford said. "Every conviction that Hawkins won can now be overturned, which means the state will need to retry them—if we have the manpower and time to do it."

"Well, I think I have an easy one for you … if you'll take the time to look at it with me." Mac opened one of the case files and laid it down on his desk. "Scarlett Fairbanks. Hawkins issued an arrest warrant for the murder of her husband, Jason Fairbanks."

"Reese Fairbanks' son." Stafford sat down behind the desk and turned the folder around to study the report.

"Right now, there are two detectives from here in Maryland waiting to take her into custody," Mac said. "But I think once you see what I've uncovered, you'll realize that she didn't kill her husband. Someone else did and you can save your people a lot of time and money if you will file a motion to drop the charges and let those detectives come back to New York without her. And they can save you a lot more money by bringing back Reese Fairbanks, who the Spencer police are currently holding in their jail."

"You'll need to have some pretty convincing evidence to prove she didn't do it, Faraday."

"Scarlett Fairbanks took her daughter and left on the day of the murder," Mac said. "She admits she shot her husband twice." He held up two fingers. "Once in the shoulder and the second time in the leg. The autopsy report states that he would have survived those two shots. As a matter of fact, they were minor enough for him to get a dishtowel and apply pressure to his leg wound."

Archie yanked a picture of the crime scene from her folder and handed it to the prosecutor. "The bloody dishtowel is right there, which proves that time passed between those two shots and the fatal one to the head."

"So the killer is the one who fired the third shot," Mac said.

"Do you know who that person is?" Stafford asked. "And do you have any proof that they did it?"

"Yes."

"Who and what proof do you have?"

"Tuyon Weber," Mac said, "the Fairbanks' next door neighbor."

"The neighbor? Why? Were they having some sort of—" Stafford looked up at Archie. "Do you have any proof that this Tu-guy did it?"

"Tuyon," Mac said. "She was an elderly woman, a Vietnamese war bride, who came over to the United States in the seventies with her American husband."

"According to the Fairbanks file," Archie said, "she called the police dozens of times to report Jason Fairbanks for assaulting his wife and daughter. She argued with the police for not doing anything to stop it."

"What made it especially frustrating for her was that she herself had been an abused wife, so she knew intimately what Scarlett was going through." Mac opened up the second folder for Stafford to read.

Stafford pulled the file over to scan the information.

"These are hospital reports for Tuyon Weber," Mac said. "She had been in and out of the hospital for broken bones for several years from the time she came to the states until her husband died after a long illness."

"Her husband's illness was never diagnosed," Archie said, "but the symptoms are consistent with arsenic poisoning."

"You may or may not want to exhume his body for an autopsy," Mac said.

Stafford sat back in his seat. "So you're thinking—"

"Tuyon Weber was working in the garden when she heard the shots," Mac said. "She came running into the driveway to make sure Scarlett and her daughter were fine. They left. Then, determined to end their suffering, the same type of suffering that she had to endure for years, she went into the Fairbanks home where she found Jason tending to his gunshot wounds. Being the type of man he was, he probably said something abusive to set her off. Whatever happened, she knew that if he lived Scarlett and Holly would never truly be free."

"Her niece told us that Tuyon had said that it was a tragedy that Jason Fairbanks had to die in order to set Scarlett and Holly free," Archie said.

"So," Mac said, "after Scarlett and Holly ran away, Tuyon Weber set them free by picking up the gun and killing Jason Fairbanks."

"An argument could be made that she killed him to save them," Archie said.

"Proof of any of this?" Stafford asked.

"The killer could not have been hiding in the garden like we first thought," Mac said, "because both Scarlett and her daughter stated that Tuyon Weber came running up the driveway when she heard the shots."

"Yet, she told the police she saw and heard nothing," Archie pointed out.

"She lied to protect Fairbanks' wife," Stafford said.

"The killer couldn't have been hiding in or come from the garden without Mrs. Weber seeing him because she was gardening," Mac repeated. "However, physical evidence proves that the killer had been in the garden." He flipped a page in the Fairbanks case file. "The proof is in the chicken poop."

"Chicken poop?" Stafford almost brought the page up to his nose to read it.

"Tuyon Weber made her own custom plant fertilizer," Mac said. "One of the ingredients is chicken poop. Forensics found traces of it in footprints found at the scene. They also found traces of it in dirt left on the grip of the gun. Holly Fairbanks remembers seeing Tuyon Weber putting on her gardening gloves when they were leaving. She wore them when she pulled the trigger."

"And the chicken poop proves this?"

"If the killer had simply walked through her garden or hidden there, then the chicken poop would have ended up on his shoes to leave footprints." Mac pointed at the forensics report in the case file. "But, it wasn't found only on the floor. It was also on the grip of the gun, which proves the killer handled the fertilizer, as well—which is what Mrs. Weber was doing at the time she heard the gun shots."

Stafford closed the two folders. "I guess we need to issue a warrant to bring this Weber woman in for questioning."

"Won't do you any good," Mac said. "She's already dead."

Stafford looked from Mac to Archie and then back again.

"Stafford, the attorney general is on the phone for you," a young woman called to him from the doorway. "Defense attorneys are flooding the circuit court with appeals."

Seeing beads of sweat on Stafford's forehead, Mac pressed. "If I were you, I'd drop the charges against Scarlett Fairbanks, file the Fairbanks murder under suspect dead and unavailable for prosecution, and throw the book at Reese Fairbanks for causing this mess in the first place."

"Sounds good to me." Stafford slapped the case file closed. "We'll have an arrest warrant first thing in the morning. Tell those detectives to not leave Spencer without Fairbanks in custody."

Within an hour, Spencer Church erupted with a joyous cheer that could be heard out on the lake. Natalie hugged her grandmother while Ruth hugged Carmine.

Everyone was so busy hugging and crying tears of joy that no one noticed when Gnarly jumped up onto the buffet table to steal a chicken breast and escape to the children's chapel with it.

In her office, when she heard the news, Edna threw her arms around Officer Nathan Brewster to kiss him on the lips. Realizing the unexpected display of affection, she just as quickly pulled away. "I didn't mean to do that." Flustered, she explained, "I'm just so thankful to you and everyone for being so patient and not pushing …"

"No problem, ma'am."

"Edna," she corrected him.

"Truthfully, I'm kind of sorry that this assignment has ended," Brewster explained. "The view here is really pretty, and I kind of liked it."

"Even pulling out my file cabinet?"

"Hey, if you ever need anything pulled out, day or night," Brewster jerked his thumb toward his chest, "I'm your man."

"I wouldn't promise things like that, if I were you." Blushing, Edna looked down at her feet. "Need I remind you that I'm a single mom with two little girls? My honey-do list is quite extensive."

Brewster grinned back at her. "I'll be glad to look at your list anytime. I'm off work tomorrow."

"So am I," she said. "I have Fridays and Saturdays off since I work on Sundays."

"How about if I come over to your place and take a look at your honey-do list?"

Expectantly, Sirrus Thorpe rushed into the office with a plate filled with chicken and potato salad and beans. "I saw that you hadn't gotten any dinner yet, Miss Edna, so I took the liberty of fixing a plate for you. If you waited any longer, then you were going to miss out on my potato salad."

Edna's cheeks turned pink. "Thank you, Sirrus, but I already ate."

Sirrus' face fell when he saw the dirty plate already resting in the center of Edna's desk. He looked up at Officer Brewster.

"I'm sorry, Sirrus," Edna said.

With a wide grin on her face, Deborah came into the office. "Oh, great, Sirrus, I see you made a plate for me. I was so busy talking to everyone that I didn't get a chance to get any. Is this your potato salad? I was afraid I was going to miss out." Taking the plate in one hand, and Sirrus by the arm with the other, Deborah turned him around and they headed out the door. As they turned the corner to go into the fellowship hall, the pastor winked at them.

"I like Pastor Deborah," Brewster said.

"So do I."

Leaning against her desk, he asked, "Now, where were we?"

"My honey-do list."

"Am I being too forward by offering?" Brewster asked.

"No," she replied. "There's a ton of small things that need fixed. Starting with a hole in our privacy fence so that Rack, Shack, and Benny can play outside."

"Rack, Shack—"

"And Benny," Edna said. "Our dogs. They're Chihuahuas. Two sisters and a brother. My daughters named them after characters in a Veggie Tales movie. Benny dug a hole under the fence and as soon as he gets out, he takes off. Plus, the railing is loose on our deck and I worry that the girls are going to fall—" Stopping, she shook her head. "Oh, I'm terrible. You must think that I'm taking terrible advantage of you."

"Hey, I'm begging you to take advantage of me." He stuck out his chest. "I'll bring my tool chest and we'll get Benny penned in tight before you can say 'Gringo.'"

"And I'll make you lunch," she said.

"Don't make it a big one," Brewster said. "We have reservations for the Spencer Inn at eight o'clock."

She kissed him again. "I can't wait, Nate."

He kissed her back. "Neither can I."

"Hey, Brewster!" Bogie slammed his palm against the wall when he came in, causing both Brewster and Edna to jump at the abrupt noise.

Even Gnarly, sitting at Bogie's side, was cocking his head at the two of them with a suspicious glint in his brown eyes that made them feel guilty enough to back up a full step from each other.

"I know you're going to be sorry to hear this, but the state prosecutor in New York has dropped the charges against Ruth. That means you and Fletcher can go back to the station and check in with Tonya before signing out. Have a great weekend and see you when you're back on duty Monday morning." He winked at the office manager. "You, too, Edna."

"Thank you, Bogie," she replied, "for everything." She gazed up at Brewster. "You guys are the best."

Brewster's face felt warm. To hide his blush, he turned his attention to Bogie. "What about the detectives from New York who came down to pick up Ruth? How are they taking the news about going back to New York empty handed?"

"That's right," Edna said. "I forgot all about them. Aren't they going to be angry that they came all the way down here for nothing?"

"They're not going back empty handed," Bogie said with a laugh. "The FBI and New York Attorney General both want Reese Fairbanks. David called the detectives. They both have appointments with the masseuse at the Inn's spa for tomorrow morning and asked that everyone take their time."

CHAPTER TWENTY-ONE

"What's wrong with this case?" David asked Gnarly, who was riding in the front passenger seat of his cruiser.

As if he expected to hear the dog answer, David glanced over at where Gnarly was staring straight ahead through the windshield. He seemed to be scanning the dark road ahead of them in search of his home, Spencer Manor.

David O'Callaghan lived in the same guest cottage at Spencer Manor that Archie Monday had lived in for years. Robin Spencer had stipulated in her will that Archie was permitted to live in the guest cottage for as long as she wanted, even though Mac Faraday inherited the estate. As their relationship grew, Archie had no desire to leave and Mac didn't want her to move anywhere—except into the main house.

The timing worked out well. At the same time that Archie moved into Spencer Manor, David O'Callaghan's mother was committed to a nursing home. Unable to live any longer in his run-down childhood home, he accepted Mac's invitation to move into the stone cottage.

Lately though, he had been spending most of his nights at Chelsea's lakeside condo.

The news of the charges against Ruth being dropped should have been reason for a night of celebration with Chelsea.

Yet, David's mind was elsewhere.

The pressure was on. Mac Faraday had solved the murder of Jason Fairbanks. Ruth Buchanan was in the clear. Now the police chief was determined to solve his case sooner rather than later.

Part of the stress was due to a touch of sibling rivalry. He and Mac Faraday may not have grown up together, but there was a familial connection that clicked the instant they met that day when Mac had driven his new, red sports car up to Spencer Manor.

David O'Callaghan didn't expect to have the instinct and expertise that Mac had developed over twenty years of working as a homicide detective in Washington, D.C. *Man, Mac was working murder cases before I had even learned to drive.*

This sudden realization did little to ease David's resolve to solve Eugene's murder on his own. *This is my case and I want to solve it—without my big brother's help.* Sarcastically, he thought, *How mature is that?*

After a celebratory dinner with Chelsea, David begged off with the excuse that he was tired, which he was. Dragging Gnarly away from his "date" with Molly, David climbed into his cruiser to head back to Spencer Manor.

"I know what's wrong," David answered. "Helga Thorpe is not that bright. She's not smart enough to give us the slip the way she has. Nothing's on her laptop to indicate that she was planning to do this. Zero activity on her bank accounts and cell phone since she left Wednesday morning. Leaving her purse in Breezewood with all that cash and credit cards? That contradicts her motive." He shook his finger in Gnarly's direction. "If Helga's motive was to take over as chief of the trustees, then why run off?"

David slammed the brake pedal to bring his cruiser to a screeching halt. Gnarly was propelled to the floor. Casting a dark glare at the driver, the dog climbed back up into his seat.

"That's it! It makes no sense! Either she killed Eugene for another reason or she didn't do it! I need to take another look at Eugene Newton's murder."

David put the cruiser into reverse and backed up into a driveway along the lake shore road to head back to Spencer Church.

Using the key that Reverend Deborah Hess had given him, David let himself in the front door of the darkened church. After switching on the lights, he made his way past Edna's office and down the business wing.

Gnarly led the way.

"Someone could have killed Eugene so that the church could inherit his fortune," David murmured while making his way to the business office. "But then, where was Helga during the time of the murder? Maybe she did kill him, planning to frame Chip Van Dorn, who had threatened him, then, after the murder-suicide, realized that we would be looking at her again." He stopped outside the office.

Gnarly sat down in front of the locked door with the yellow crime scene tape stretched across it.

Using his key, David unlocked the door and swung it open. He turned on the lights and peered inside. Ducking under the tape, he stepped into the office and went over to the desk. Mentally, he re-enacted what had to have been Eugene Newton's final hour.

"It can't be that complicated," David heard a voice come to him from the end of the hallway.

Grabbing his weapon in his holster, David whirled around to find Mac's silhouette standing in the doorway.

"I thought you weren't coming back until morning," David said.

"I chartered a jet to bring me into McHenry. Archie isn't happy that I dropped her off at the manor and came straight here." Mac ducked under the tape to enter the office and went behind the desk, being careful to step over the taped outline and blood stains behind the desk.

Sitting at attention, Gnarly sat in the hallway like a guard on duty.

"Where did you park?" David asked.

"Over on the other side of the parking lot." Mac indicated with a jerk of his thumb. "I beat you here by only a couple of minutes. You came in while I was turning the corner of the building."

David said, "This building is big enough and has so many rooms and dark corners that someone could have slipped in the back door without Ruth seeing him, sneaked up here to shoot Eugene, and then left without anyone knowing."

"She swears she didn't hear the shots."

David was shaking his head. "Possible if the office door was shut and she was vacuuming on the other end of the building."

"She didn't see Eugene's car until she came to this wing after hearing Gnarly barking when she turned off the vacuum." Chuckling, Mac folded his arms across his chest. "You aren't buying that Helga Thorpe killed Eugene Newton."

David countered. "Why aren't you buying it?"

"Because her taking off doesn't fit with her motive for killing him."

"Eugene left everything to the church," David said. "Before his murder, they were existing on borrowed time. Now, since his death, all of their money problems are taken care of. Edna Parker is on her way to being a full time church administrator of a million-dollar church."

"You mean the church lady with the bedroom eyes that Brewster is chasing after?" Mac asked.

"Exactly."

"But she has an alibi," Mac argued.

"She has a key to the building," David said. "She knew Eugene was going to be here alone counting on Tuesday morning. A looker like that, she could have given a gullible man a key to come in to kill Eugene while she established an alibi with her mother and sister."

"A femme fatale masquerading as a church lady," Mac said with a grin.

"Edna Parker isn't certain that she wants the job of full time church administrator," Reverend Deborah's voice came out of the darkened corridor. She stepped into the doorway. "I saw the lights on and decided to investigate."

"Why would she refuse?" David asked. "She's a single mother with two kids."

"And her dead-beat husband is years behind in child support," Deborah said. "But when the board offered her the job, she said she had to think about it. Edna puts her girls first. She likes the flexible hours and being able to come and go as they need her. She's afraid that she'll lose that flexibility if she accepts a full time position with so much responsibility. So, as for that being a motive for her killing Eugene—you're completely off the mark."

David and Mac exchanged glances before the police chief asked, "How about you, Reverend? Did you know that Eugene was leaving millions of dollars to the church?"

"Yes," she said, "and I guess I have no alibi since I was just coming in from running at the time he was killed."

"How did things change for you since Eugene's murder?" Mac asked.

"Overall, not good," Deborah said. "Yes, the money takes away the stress of worrying from one month to the next about if we are going to be forced to close, but if I wanted a life free of financial stress I would have become a mathematician like my father wanted and I would have married the lawyer my mother tried to fix me up with. Then I wouldn't have been widowed to raise a child alone before I was thirty because my husband felt called to go build a church in the jungles of South America where he got tortured and executed by guerillas."

She shrugged her shoulders. "To answer your question, financially, God has always blessed me with all I need." Her eyes teared up. "I needed Eugene's friendship and emotional support more than I needed his money."

Feeling like a jerk, David hung his head.

Gnarly licked the pastor's hand. She knelt down to pet the German shepherd who licked her face. "I thought you had decided on Helga Thorpe as a prime suspect."

"We're trying to piece everything together," Mac said.

Feeling his phone vibrate on his hip, David ducked under the crime scene tape to slip out into the hallway and down the hall to take the call.

"I'm sorry I didn't finish marrying you and Archie the other day," she said while stroking Gnarly. "I completely forgot about that until this evening when Carmine and Ruth announced that they were getting married."

"Are they?" Mac smiled. "That's good news."

"God does have a way of turning things around," Deborah said. "Ruth could never accept his proposal before because she was afraid that applying for the marriage license would flag her in some way that the police would find her. But now that you've cleared her name—none of that would have happened if Eugene hadn't been murdered."

David hurried back into the doorway. "They found Helga."

"Now maybe we'll get some answers," Mac said.

"Actually, I think we're going to get more questions before we get more answers," David said.

Police Chief David O'Callaghan was heading back to Pennsylvania. This time, Mac was riding in the passenger seat while Gnarly rode in the back. Bogie tagged along in his cruiser behind them.

The stark night of the Pennsylvania forest was illuminated by the lamps set up by the emergency vehicles surrounding the tan four-door sedan parked in the turn-off of what appeared to be a long-forgotten boat launch of a tiny lake. The sounds of heavy traffic and the semi-truck horn blasts from the turnpike road less than a mile away pierced the wilderness.

"She's at the end of the road," a Pennsylvania state trooper directed David when he climbed out of his cruiser after parking it off the dirt road in hip high brush. "The sergeant will fill you in. He's up there with the crime scene folks."

Leaving a window down for Gnarly, Mac, David, and Bogie made their way along the road overgrown with brush and untrimmed branches from trees that threatened to overtake the road completely.

Using his flashlight to lead the way along the path, David warned Mac, who was behind him. "Watch out for snakes."

"Snakes?" Mac halted.

Bogie bumped into him from behind. "Woods like these are filled with them." He gently pushed Mac to go ahead. "If one bites you, be sure to not to let him get away. We'll need to take him to the ER with you so they'll know what antivenom to give you."

"Do I look stupid to you?" Mac asked Bogie.

"Only when you're trying to train Gnarly."

Up ahead, David laughed. "Come on, you two. We have a murder to solve."

The dirt-covered, tan sedan came into view where it rested in the spotlights set up by Pennsylvania's crime scene investigators.

The fate of Helga Thorpe seemed to cry out to them when they spied a thick hose taped to the rear tailpipe of the car with the other end threaded through the front driver's side window where it was held in place with duct tape. The window had been rolled up as far as the hose permitted.

"One of our people found her when he pulled off the main road to take a leak," the sergeant came around the car to explain to them when he noticed David's and Bogie's uniforms. "Of course, she was parked way down here off the road, but his cruiser's headlights caught off her rearview mirror. He decided to drive up to investigate. The ignition is on. She had to have been dead long before her car ran out of gas."

Using his flashlight, Mac peered in through the windows at the woman slumped over in the driver's seat of the car. "I don't see a suicide note, but I do see her cell phone in the center console. She may have left a note there … if she killed herself."

"I'll ask our forensics people if it's okay to open up the car yet," the sergeant said.

"Bogie," David asked, "did you check out Helga's calendar on her laptop?"

"She had nothing on it," Bogie said. "Looked to me like she didn't use it."

"Chelsea uses the calendar on her cell phone," David said, "because she has that with her all the time. She isn't as attached to her laptop as Archie."

"Why do you want to see her calendar?" Bogie asked.

"Because Helga disappeared before we had a chance to ask her about an alibi for the time of Eugene's murder," David said. "Her assistant said she came back from lunch that day flustered—"

"Which a person would be if they had just committed murder," Mac said. "But there could be other reasons for her being flustered besides murder. She had an argument with a friend, she got a speeding ticket on the way back to the office, she was using her lunch hour to have a rousing roll in the hay with her lover only to have the hundred -pound dog break down the door and jump on the bed in the middle of it—"

"Yeah," Bogie said, "that happens to me all the time. Have you ever thought of putting a lock on your bedroom door?"

The sergeant called to them from the other side of the car. "We're opening it up now."

"Helga wouldn't have committed suicide," Bogie whispered to David and Mac as they made their way around to where the troopers were prying open the passenger side door while being careful to not disturb any evidence. "She was too arrogant. She would have been confident that she could have beaten any murder wrap."

"If she was going to kill herself, why plant her purse in Breezewood to lead the police away?" Mac asked.

"You're both right." David slipped on a pair of evidence gloves. "She was murdered. But who did it?" With a nod of gratitude, he took the cell phone from the trooper who had reached inside to retrieve it. He pressed the button to turn it on.

"We've had no credit card or cell phone activity for the last two and a half days?" David glanced over at Bogie while waiting for the phone to turn on.

The deputy chief answered with a nod of his head. "We've been watching. Nothing."

Mac peered into the darkness surrounding them. "This place is really out of the way." He pointed to the small lake where the car was parked. "What lake is that?" he asked the sergeant.

"It's called Miller's Pond. It used to be a pretty nice lake. My grandfather used to bring me fishing, but then it got all overgrown and mucky. Now, mostly kids come out here to smoke and drink and have sex in the back of cars. We're running them out of here all the time."

"It's up." David thumbed through the applications on the phone to take him to the calendar. "Yep, she uses this to keep her calendar." He thumbed through the pages to go back three days to the day of the murder. When he read the screen he let out a breath. "According to this, she had a twelve-thirty appointment with a doctor in Oakland on Tuesday."

"If she kept that appointment," Mac said, "then she would have an alibi, which means she would have had no reason to run off or commit suicide."

"But Eugene spoke to someone when he called her at the store right before he was killed," Bogie said. "He talked to someone for more than a minute and a half."

"Maybe he talked to her right before she left for the doctor's office," David said. "And that call has nothing to do with Eugene's murder. Fact is, she may have an alibi."

"Or maybe not," Bogie said. "Does she have the phone number for the doctor in that thing? I'll call their office first thing in the morning to confirm that she made it there."

"Did Eugene call her office number or her cell?" Mac asked.

"Her office number," Bogie said.

"And Helga's assistant was out to lunch," David said. "Eugene talked to someone and no one else knew he was at the church." He handed the cell phone to the forensics officer to be bagged while asking the officer searching the inside of the car. "Is there a gun in there?"

The officer reached under the seats. "I don't see any."

"Helga Thorpe was our last suspect," David said. "Every suspect we've had—the very few that we've had—have come up clean—from Chip Van Dorn to Marilyn to Ruth to Edna—"

"Edna!" Bogie let out a loud objection. "Edna would never—"

"I'm reaching, Bogie," David said. "I admit it, I'm reaching. I've never had a murder victim like this—the guy is completely clean and yet someone shot him three times for what looks like no good reason."

"Can I make a suggestion?" Mac asked.

"Please," David replied.

"I have gotten to points like this before on cases more times than I like to admit," Mac said. "When that happens, I go all the way back to the beginning and start all over." He turned on his heels and went back to the cruiser.

"Start all over," David repeated in a dejected tone.

As he disappeared into the darkness, Mac waved to David and Bogie to follow. "Back to the beginning, gentlemen."

CHAPTER TWENTY-TWO

"Murder." David slammed his cell phone down on the kitchen counter in Spencer Manor before picking up his coffee mug. "The ME in Pennsylvania has already determined by the blood tests on Helga Thorpe that she had enough sleeping pills in her that she was completely unconscious before the carbon monoxide killed her." He went to the coffee maker and filled his mug.

"Could she have taken them herself so that she'd be asleep when the carbon monoxide killed her?" Archie clutched her hot coffee mug in both hands.

"Wouldn't that be double dipping?" Mac replied. "If she intended to kill herself, why not just let the overdose of sleeping pills kill her. Stringing that hose from the exhaust pipe and through the window—that had to be a lot of work."

Thinking about her husband's obvious hatred toward her, David said, "It isn't like Sirrus was going to try to save her if she had simply taken a bottle of pills and laid down in bed."

Each of them donning bathrobes and slippers, they stared straight ahead in deep thought. After getting back to Spencer Manor in the middle of the night, David and Mac

269

had only slept a few hours before questions about Eugene Newton's murder woke them up.

The only sound in the kitchen was Gnarly gulping his breakfast.

"Who would want to kill Helga Thorpe?" Archie asked.

"A lot of people," David said. "Bogie found a ton of venomous emails on her laptop. How she ever found time to work for the sporting goods store, I don't know. It's like she managed the church's rumor mill. She antagonized the children's ministry director. She offended Carmine. She would send out and receive hundreds of emails a day—all griping and gossiping about the church and how it was run."

"That's what my mother hated about church," Archie said. "Every one we ever went to, there was always one flock of gossipy old hens—"

"Isn't that true of any place where you get a bunch of people together?" Mac took his and her mugs to the coffee maker for refills. "In the police department, there were some officers who were just as catty as a bunch of old church ladies. If you ask me, it's the human condition—not confined to churches."

"You're right there," she said.

Mac turned to David who was leaning against the kitchen counter. "What's the estimated time of death?"

"Sometime Wednesday morning."

Handing Archie her coffee mug, Mac slid into the chair next to her. "Okay, let's think about this."

"Sirrus claimed Helga had packed her bag and left early Wednesday morning when he was on his way out fishing," David said.

"Fishing?" Mac repeated.

"Sirrus is a die-hard fisherman," David said. "When I questioned him on Wednesday, he was very pleased because he had caught a twelve-pound largemouth bass that morning."

"Did you see this fish?" Mac asked.

"No, but I guess I will," David said. "He took it to the taxidermist. He wouldn't have told me that if there wasn't any. It'd be easy enough to check out."

"Why don't we call that taxidermist to see when Sirrus brought that fish in?" Mac asked.

"You always look to the spouse first," Archie joked.

"I do that for a reason."

"Sirrus has no motive to kill Eugene," David said. "They did find Helga's suitcase in the trunk of the car."

"Why pack your bag to kill yourself?" Archie asked.

"What did she pack?" Mac asked.

"Huh?" David replied.

"Did the police send you an inventory of what they found in her suitcase?" Mac asked him.

"I'm sure they will." Pondering Mac's questions, David took a sip of his coffee.

"There are certain things that people will never leave on a trip without," Mac said. "If we take a look at that list, we could determine if Helga had packed that suitcase or someone else—"

"Like her husband," Archie said.

"Sirrus has good reason to kill Helga," David said. "Just plain hatred. But he has no motive for killing Eugene Newton. As far as I can see, they had no connection. Sirrus does volunteer small jobs at the church, and seems to be very fond of the women there, but he doesn't benefit from Eugene Newton's death."

As a thought came to his mind, he stood up straight from where he had been leaning against the counter. "Unless maybe he killed Eugene to frame Helga, with the intention of killing her and making it look like a suicide because she didn't get away with Eugene's murder … but I don't think Sirrus is that diabolical."

"I'm thinking about where the police found Helga's car," Mac said.

"On a rural country road two miles from Breezewood," David said.

"An abandoned fishing pond," Mac said.

"How did I miss that?" David muttered.

Smiling into his coffee, Mac asked, "What did you say?"

"Nothing," David replied. "I grew up around here and I never knew about that pond."

"You're not a die-hard fisherman," Mac said.

"But then there's the logistics of getting back to Deep Creek Lake," David said. "Breezewood is almost two hours away. The killer—"

"Probably Sirrus," Archie said.

"—could have hitchhiked to Breezewood from the fishing pond, and then got a bus ticket to get back into our area."

"Which tells me that this murder took a lot of planning," Mac said. "More planning than Eugene's murder."

"Maybe Helga was the intended target all along," Archie said.

"Which points to Sirrus Thorpe," David said. "That man makes no secret about hating his wife." He muttered, "I'd hate to be in that marriage."

"But if Sirrus hated Helga enough to want her dead," Archie asked, "why kill Eugene Newton?"

Mac suggested, "Why don't we ask the reverend?"

Bogie met Mac, David, and Archie at Reverend Deborah Hess's house, in the pastoral residence next to the church building. Archie had to keep a tight hold on Gnarly's leash when he spotted a calico cat curled up on the bench on the rustic porch.

Completely uninterested in the dog, the cat remained curled up and ignored Gnarly, which perturbed him more than if the feline had hissed at him.

Clad in shorts and sandals, Deborah's son Chase invited them inside the comfortable log home. Sliding glass doors opened up to a deck, off which was a dock. A group of young people were enjoying the sunny, summer day on the lake. Clad in a one-piece swimsuit, Natalie was one of the young ladies.

"Mom's working on her sermon for Sunday." Padding through the great room to the dining area, Chase yelled up into the loft. "Mom, the police are here to see you." He turned back to them. "Do you know who killed Eugene yet?"

"That's what we wanted to talk to your mother about," David said.

"Man, the world sure has gone nuts," Chase said. "Who would do that? Who would kill a nice guy like Eugene?"

"We're trying to find that out," David said.

"I promised your mother that we would find out who did this," Bogie said, "and we intend to keep that promise."

"I know, Bogie," Chase said. "We're all worried about what people are going to think about our church—two of our trustees dead. Natalie's mom ended up being wanted for murder. Of course, people are going to find out about that."

"But her name is cleared now," Archie said.

"And now she's getting married." Natalie trotted in from outside. Her wide grin told everyone that she approved of her mother's new husband-to-be. "I'm getting a new daddy." Squealing when she said "daddy," she hugged Chase.

"Only now I can't just jog down the path to see Natalie," Chase said. "They're moving in with Carmine over in McHenry. I'm going to have to ride my bike all the way over to the other side of the lake."

"A lot of lives are changing," Deborah said as she came down the stairs from the loft. "It's good to see some blessings coming from this tragedy." The dark circles under her eyes betrayed the stress the murders had on the pastor.

After Chase and Natalie had gone outside to rejoin their friends, Deborah revealed that the phone had been ringing ever since the news hit about Helga Thorpe's body being found in Pennsylvania. "But they aren't saying if it was suicide or murder—only that her death is being investigated."

With a sigh of exhaustion, she invited her guests to sit down in the living room. She took a seat next to the stone fireplace.

"It was murder," David said. "Helga Thorpe had an alibi for the time of Eugene's murder."

"She was at a chiropractor's office in Oakland," Bogie said. "Her appointment was at twelve-thirty. No way she could have killed Eugene here and made it there in time for her appointment."

"We're thinking someone killed Eugene and then killed Helga to make it look like she committed suicide because she was afraid of being caught," Mac said.

"Why?" Deborah asked. "I thought Helga killed Eugene because she had some crazy idea that she would become chief trustee."

"Who's chief trustee now?" Mac asked.

"We are seriously looking at Carmine Romano," Deborah said. "But Carmine wouldn't hurt a fly."

Recalling the humane mouse traps that Carmine was buying for the church, Bogie slowly nodded his head. "Or a mouse."

"Okay." Mac clapped both hands down on his knees. "Who else?"

Even though they were looking seriously at Sirrus Thorpe, they wanted the pastor to point the finger at him. No one wanted to be accused of steering suspicion in anyone's direction.

274

"Who else?" Deborah replied.

"No matter how crazy it may sound to you," Mac said, "throw out any names that come to mind when you think about who would want to kill Eugene Newton for any reason. I don't care how nuts it sounds to you."

"I wish Edna was here," Deborah said with a sigh. "She works so much more closely with the members on a daily basis ... some more closely than makes her feel comfortable sometimes. A couple members, especially the lonely men, have become quite attached to her."

Recalling his interview with Eugene's wife, David sat up in his seat. "Marilyn said something similar to that. She told us that one of Eugene's jobs was to run interference for you and Edna when certain people became pests."

Deborah nodded her head with a weak smile. "Yes, Eugene was good about that. He'd come over and say that he needed to talk to us about some church business and then lead us away."

"Marilyn also mentioned something about certain older men occupying too much of Edna's time to the point of becoming nuisances."

The pastor's eyes glazed over. Taking in a deep breath, she covered her mouth with her hand.

"What are you thinking, Deborah?" Archie moved to the edge of her seat.

Gnarly inched in to lay his head on the pastor's hand.

"But he's harmless," Deborah said in a low voice.

"Is it Sirrus Thorpe?" David asked. "Was he the elderly church member who Eugene had to protect Edna from because he had become a pest?"

Abruptly, the glare in Sirrus' eyes when he had stepped into Edna's office the day before flashed in David's mind. *What was it he said? Something about my officers sniffing around their women?*

David's heart began to race.

"Eugene considered it his duty as chief trustee to protect Edna and me," Deborah said slowly, while piecing it together in her mind. "Sirrus Thorpe had never been to church a day in his life until Helga dragged him in after he had a major heart attack last year. He was here one Sunday and dove right in. He became a member and started making donations and coming in everyday—"

"To see Edna," Bogie said.

Archie said, "Sounds to me like it wasn't spiritual enlightening he was seeking."

"If Sirrus is hanging around every day, then he knows how things work around here," Mac said. "Like when Ruth comes in to clean and how she leaves the back door unlocked."

"Yesterday, he walked in when Brewster was helping Edna in her office," David recalled. "He said something about my officers sniffing around the women working at the church. I thought he was angry because we were taking so long to solve the case."

"Oh, he's become very attached to Edna," Deborah said with a quick nod of her head.

"Attached or obsessed?" Mac asked.

"Sirrus would bend Edna's ear all afternoon if we let him," Deborah said. "So Eugene, if he was around, would call her into a meeting or ask her to do something for him, and make an excuse for why Sirrus had to go."

"Then Helga Thorpe started rumors that Eugene and Edna were having an affair," David said. "Could Sirrus have believed them?"

"He's not very bright." Deborah said with a sob.

Mac rose to his feet. "On Wednesday, when the police were searching the Thorpe home, Sirrus came here to the church—"

Deborah stood up. "To fix a leaky toilet in the ladies' restroom."

Mac turned to David. "They didn't find the gun in Helga's car. He must have decided to hang onto it."

Bogie had already thrown open the front door and was running down the steps and along the path leading to the church building. With his long legs, he was far ahead of the group when he reached the back door of the church. Gnarly caught up to rush in ahead of him when he yanked open the door.

"What's going on?" Ruth came out of the ladies' bathroom with a brush in her hand encased in a cleaning glove.

"Which toilet was leaking?" Mac asked her.

She pointed with the brush. "The one in the second stall. Sirrus was supposed to fix it."

Mac pushed his way through the door and lifted the lid from tank on the back.

David squeezed into the stall with him to peer inside. "No gun," he reported to the crowd who filled the restroom.

"But there was something." Mac ripped a piece of duct tape from where it had been stuck to the top and back of the tank. "He brought it here to hide until the coast was clear and then he came back for it."

"Do you mean Sirrus?" Ruth asked. "He was here about a half hour ago to get some measurements on the toilet for some parts."

"Thirty minutes ago?" Deborah asked.

Ruth nodded her head.

"Oh, dear Lord!" the pastor cried out. "Edna! Nate!"

"What about Brewster?" Bogie grabbed Deborah by the elbow.

"He's going to Edna's house today to fix some stuff," Deborah said. "I saw Sirrus watching them at the celebration last night. He brought Edna a plate of food but she turned it down because Nate had already brought her some. I could tell that it broke his heart, so I took the food and led him away and tried to cheer him up, but it just didn't work. He kept watching them. I thought for sure he'd get over it. Now, we're talking about a gun—I really thought he was harmless!"

At a dead run, Bogie was on the radio while running out of the bathroom.

Mac grabbed the pastor by both arms. "Call Edna now! Tell her to make sure her whole family is inside and to lock all of her doors. Don't let anyone in until the police get there."

David was already calling Nate Brewster on his cell phone. "There's no answer. It went straight to voice mail."

278

CHAPTER TWENTY-THREE

"Wow, you're one serious handyman." Edna picked up the nail gun that Brewster was using to tighten the railing on the old deck. "I use a brown, high-heeled pump to drive nails."

"Careful with that." Brewster eased the gun down onto the table on the deck. "It can be dangerous." But then, he thought while observing the railing, the nail gun was not much more perilous than a fall through the loose railing to the rocks below. It was like a rocky cliff going into the lake.

Edna Parker's little ranch-style home consisted of two bedrooms, a country kitchen, living room, and one bathroom. The front yard was almost non-existent with a patch of grass and a hedge in front of the porch, and the back was mostly deck and a minimal yard with an old privacy fence for the three little dogs: Rack, Shack, and Benny. Two sisters and a brother. Their upright ears were almost as big as their heads.

Brother Benny had to be the runt of the litter. For what he lacked in size, he made up for with spunkiness. The little pipsqueak immediately bonded with Brewster, probably the only male he had ever met. While his sisters followed Allison and Kiersten in the kitchen where they helped their mother make a special lunch for their visitor, Benny hung around Brewster like a long lost friend.

Brewster didn't mind one bit. It was much nicer than the little condo he had in Oakland that provided a view of a courtyard that no one used.

Even the noise of the two sisters quarreling was music to his ears. It made him think of the family that he expected him and his ex-wife to have. She had insisted that there was never a right time for children.

Maybe there's hope after all.

"The girls are making cookies for you for dessert," Edna confided. "They couldn't agree on whether to use chocolate or peanut butter chips, so they did both."

"Peanut butter chocolate cookies." Brewster shot two nails into the railing. "My favorite." He tested the rail. It was tight.

Edna cleared her throat. "More like candy," she said. "They *love* the chips more than anything else. It will be extremely rich."

"I love rich." He smiled over his shoulder at her.

They could feel the electricity passing between them while they grinned at each other. The ringing of the phone in the house made Edna cringe. "Oh, I hope that's not Deb. She prepares her sermons on Fridays when I'm off, and always, without fail, she can't find something in the office that she needs."

"Mom," Kiersten called from the kitchen, "It's Pastor Deb."

"See." Edna reached down to pat Benny on the head. "I see you've got a new best bud."

"Watch it," Brewster said. "The way to a man's heart may be through his stomach, but the way to a woman's heart is through her dog. You may find you can't get rid of me." From where he knelt on the deck to work on the next rail, Brewster admired Edna's shapely legs making their way into the kitchen.

Abruptly, Benny exploded into a series of high-pitched barks, scurried across the deck, and leapt from the top step into the yard.

Must have spotted a squirrel. Brewster stood up to set the nail gun down on the table when he saw that he had three missed calls from "Chief David." *Must not have heard it ring over the nail gun.*

"Rats!" He reached for the phone when he became aware of a movement behind him. He turned in time to see the board swung toward his head. He threw up his arm to block the blow and heard his arm break an instant before he felt the pain that went straight to his shoulder and his hand.

"She's mine!" Brewster heard echoing in his ears as he went down.

Beyond Sirrus's cursing, he could hear sirens in the distance. *Oh, God, please protect Edna and her girls.*

"Sirrus answered the phone in his wife's office," David yelled over the sirens while following Bogie's cruiser around the lake to Edna Parker's home. "He found out that Eugene was at the church and assumed Edna was there, too. His jealousy made him go to the church to kill Eugene."

After securing Gnarly in his protective vest, Mac fastened his bullet-proof vest in place. He wasn't taking a chance of wasting time to put on their vests when they reached Edna's house. He doubted if there was time. Sirrus Thorpe had an hour jump on them in going after Edna, her family, and, most likely Officer Nate Brewster, his romantic rival.

The sound of the police sirens had Gnarly on edge. Next to Mac in the back seat, the German shepherd was panting and pacing.

Mac said, "Sirrus must have seen Eugene as intruding on his imagined relationship with Edna and decided to get rid of the competition. Then he killed his own wife to clear the way for him to pursue her."

"Only now Brewster is in the way." David spun the wheel to follow Bogie down a small, side street. Two other Spencer police cruisers fell in behind them. "Please let Brewster have his weapon."

"There are the girls!" Mac pointed to the yard where Edna Parker's two girls, both carrying their little dogs, were running up to Bogie, who had screeched to a halt. His siren was still going when he jumped out of the front seat and took both of them into his arms. He lifted them, dogs and all, from the ground.

"Where's your mother?" Bogie was asking them when he put them down.

Their weapons drawn, officers raced up to the porch.

"She's going after the bad man," Kiersten said. "Mommy was on the phone with Pastor Deb and we heard Officer Brewster yell, and then Benny was barking and he yelped—"

Before any of them could move, several shots rang out simultaneously from behind the house.

Allison screamed, "Mommy!"

With Brewster down, Sirrus tossed down the board and yanked the gun out from the waist of his pants. "I'll teach you to go sniffing around another man's woman."

"Edna! Run!" Brewster fought to raise up and move close enough to kick Sirrus in the knee before he had a chance to cock the gun and pull the trigger.

Click!

Sirrus had cocked the gun.

Benny's high-pitched bark drew closer. The little dog had come running back up onto the deck and was making a bee-line to the intruder.

"Benny!" Brewster gasped out through his pain. "No!"

Brewster rolled over onto his good side to duck behind the table for cover. Swallowing down the pain from his broken arm, he yanked down the table to use as a shield.

Behind the clatter of the falling table, he heard Sirrus scream out in pain before cursing. His outburst was followed by a yelp. "Mutt!"

Way to go, Benny!

"Sirrus!" Brewster heard Edna scream at what had to be the top of her lungs.

"Run, Edna!" With his one good arm, Brewster fought through the pain to rise up onto his knees to see Edna storming across the deck toward Sirrus, who was focused on the officer behind the impromptu barricade. "Get out of here!"

She was too enraged to hear him. *"You* killed Eugene!"

With the gun raised, Sirrus whirled around and aimed it at her. "You're like all of them." He pulled the trigger.

Brewster screamed while he watched the woman who had only just entered his life a few days before run toward the gun aimed at her. As the shots rang out, she dove toward the deck floor. Behind her, the deck doors shattered when the bullets blasted through them. The glass poured down to the floor like a waterfall.

Sirrus was still pulling the trigger when Edna came back up firing the nail gun at point-blank range. Marching toward him, she kept pulling the trigger while Sirrus stumbled back with each nail that struck its target. She didn't stop shooting until he fell back against the railing, which gave way. Her last shot propelled him off the deck and down to the rocks below.

With wide eyes, Brewster stared at her and the spot where the man determined to kill them had stood. Benny's whine broke him out of his stare. At some point the tiny dog had sought refuge between the officer's legs. He patted the trembling dog on the head. "You're okay, Ben."

Nail gun still in her hand, Edna knelt next to him. "Nate, are you okay?"

Weapons drawn, David, Mac, and Brewster's fellow officers charged through the broken deck doors without slowing down to open the empty doorframes.

His nose twitching, Gnarly zigzagged across the deck in search of a suspect to contain for his human teammates.

"Is everybody all right?" David asked once he saw that both Edna and Brewster had apparently survived the shooting—though he was concerned about the bloody arm Brewster was clutching to his chest.

Before anyone could respond, Benny shot out from where he had been cowering between Brewster's legs and made contact with the hundred pound shepherd's back leg.

With a howl, Gnarly whirled around. He seemed to still be in search of whatever was after him when the tiny dog, who was less than a tenth Gnarly's size, went after his front legs. The dog fight that ensued resembled a comical dance between the Chihuahua who was out for blood and the German shepherd trying to defend himself against his opponent's tiny needle-like teeth nipping at his ankles.

In spite of the seriousness of the situation, Mac and some of the other officers, especially Officer Fletcher, couldn't stop laughing at the mismatch and Gnarly's inability to squelch the attack. Benny moved like an annoying gnat that refused to be squashed.

"Mac, stop laughing and help your partner." David reinforced his order with a slight punch to Mac's arm.

"It's good for Gnarly's ego to be on the losing end of a fight for once," Fletcher replied.

"Benny!" Edna snapped in a low forceful tone. "Stop it!"

At the sound of his master's voice, Benny froze. He ceased both barking and growling. He hung motionless by his teeth from the scruff of Gnarly's neck. The tiny dog's eyes rotated as far as they could in the direction of his master.

"Benny, I'm talking to you." Edna's command was not uttered in a loud volume. Rather, the firmness of her order came across in her low, serious tone that made both dogs afraid to move. "Release that police dog and come here."

Benny turned his gaze back at Gnarly's face. He looked almost pleading as if to say it was the first time he had captured such a big dog by himself. How could Edna make him throw him back?

"Now." Her tone was low and commanding.

With a whimper, Benny released Gnarly, dropped to the deck that was a good three inches below where he was hanging, and scurried back to sit in the precise spot where his master had pointed.

His tail between his legs, Gnarly sought refuge behind Mac. The glare in his eyes betrayed his demand for a rematch. It was simply a matter of when and where. No one humiliated this alpha male German shepherd without payback.

"Now that we've identified ourselves as good guys," David said, "is everyone okay and where's Sirrus Thorpe?"

"We've got one injured." Brewster clutched his bleeding arm to his chest. "That psychopath broke my arm!"

Into his radio, Officer Fletcher reported that they needed one ambulance—possibly two.

"Where's Thorpe?" Mac demanded to know.

"He went through the railing." Brewster nodded in the direction of the broken deck rail. "He had to have landed on the rocks below. He should be dead."

Cautious not to fall themselves, Mac and David peered off the deck to the broken body below. Careful not to slip off the wet rocks into the lake, Bogie and two officers were examining the damage.

"That had to hurt," Fletcher said.

From down below, Bogie caught David's attention and communicated with a shake of his head that Sirrus Thorpe was indeed dead. Fletcher called in on his radio for the medical examiner.

"Look at what he did to my doors!" Noticing that her deck doors were now void of glass, Edna stood up.

"We're lucky that's all he shot," Brewster said to her.

Her bedroom eyes were wide with fury while she surveyed the damage. "Look at all this broken glass! Think of all the bugs that'll get in the house—not to mention snakes! I hate snakes!"

"That maniac tried to *kill* you! Three shots! I counted." Brewster tried to sit up, but his injured arm wouldn't let him.

"And she didn't get hit?" David was doubtful. "From how far away did he shoot?"

"Less than eight feet," Brewster said. "From where you're standing to where she is now in front of the doors. I thought for sure she was dead."

Mac stepped over to where Edna glared at her shattered doors. "Thank God he missed you and hit the windows instead. Otherwise, it would be your blood and guts on this floor instead of broken glass."

She clutched the nail gun that she still had in her hand to her chest. Slowly, she turned to Brewster, who Fletcher and David had helped up into a chair. "He shot at me? I …"

"Didn't you hear me yelling to you to get out of here, Edna?" Brewster asked. "Instead of running, you came at him like a momma bear."

"All I could think about was that he killed Eugene and I had to protect you," she said. "I don't remember him shooting at me."

Checking the short distance there had to be between Sirrus and Edna when he was shooting at her, Mac said, "I think someone was looking out for you, Edna."

"I second that," Brewster breathed while lying back to allow Fletcher to examine his broken arm. He glanced up to the blue sky above. "Thank you, God."

Fletcher said, "The bone is broken through the skin. That's one serious break."

"It's my shooting arm," Brewster groaned.

"Desk duty for you, Brewster," David said, "but at least you're alive."

Edna lowered herself down into a chair across from Brewster. "This is all my fault."

Mac eased the nail gun from her hands. "It's not your fault, Edna. You saved Brewster's life. Sirrus would have killed him if you hadn't have thought fast enough to grab the nail gun."

"Poor Eugene … and Marilyn."

"Where was your weapon, Brewster?" David asked him.

"I had left my weapon in the truck. I had no idea how dangerous these church ladies could be," the officer replied with a chuckle, which abruptly turned to worry. "Where are the girls?"

"I sent them to the neighbors when Deborah told me that it was Sirrus." Edna looked up at Mac. "Did—"

"They're safe," Mac assured them both.

Bogie led a couple men up from the yard. "Sirrus Thorpe got nailed but good. I counted three shots to the chest."

"That's how many shots she fired," Brewster said. "She hit him with each one?"

"Square in the chest," Bogie said.

"You were right, David," Mac said. "Never mess with a church lady."

"I told you they scare the hell out of me," David replied.

EPILOGUE

The mild, sunny weather was like a symbol of God's blessing on the bride and groom's wedding. While the church was filled to standing room only, the wedding party consisted only of the bride, groom, maid of honor, and best man. It was all they had time to invite with only eight days to throw the event together.

The reception was as extensive as if they had a year to plan. The groom would not have it any other way.

"A wedding without bringing together the best in food, wine, and friends is like a marriage without love! Eat! Drink! And dance everyone!" After toasting his bride, Carmine Romano wrapped his arms around Ruth and whisked her out onto the dance floor of his restaurant's banquet room.

"I need to put that into my wedding ceremonies," Deborah told David and Chelsea where they were mingling near the dessert table. For officiating the wedding, she was clad in a long white dress with gold trim.

"Things turned out very well for them," Chelsea said. "Ruth and Natalie really did get a whole new beginning when they left New York."

"It was a blessing that she ended up with a good father to show her a truly loving relationship," Deborah said. "Jenny is going to be living with them. She's finally getting her new beginning."

"Well," Chelsea said. "I imagine now is the best time to divorce Reese Fairbanks since he has been charged with assault and assault of a police officer here in Garrett County, and is being charged for bribery and a ton of other federal charges up in New York."

David said, "There's someone else who things have worked out well for."

On the dance floor, Officer Brewster was dancing with both Allison and Kiersten at the same time. Allison clung to his broken arm, which was encased in a cast.

"I've never seen that man so happy," David noted. "He's on desk duty for the next couple of months at least, but he's thrilled."

"That's because he meets Edna for lunch every day," Chelsea said before turning to Deborah. "Is it true she decided to accept the administrator position?"

Nodding her head, Deborah smiled. "After we threw in the guest cottage and assured her a flexible schedule. Allison and Kiersten will be right down the path and Chase has agreed to babysit them while Edna's working."

"I'm sure Benny will be able to protect them," David said. "That's one feisty little watch dog. Gnarly will never live that attack down."

"I'm so glad they aren't going to press charges against Edna for killing Sirrus Thorpe," Deborah said.

"Well, Fleming didn't really see how they could," Chelsea said. "Gnarly found Sirrus' gun down in the rocks, and it proved to be the murder weapon used to kill Eugene."

"Not only that, but forensics found traces of blood in Sirrus' toupee," David said. "DNA connected that blood to

Eugene Newton. Sirrus Thorpe was on the scene at the time he was shot."

"He was obsessed with Edna," Deborah said. "We all saw it, but thought it was totally harmless."

"I'm trained and I saw it, too," David said, "but I disregarded it. On the day of the murder, Sirrus flipped out when he saw you and Edna in the cruiser to take you to the hospital. He was focused then on Edna. I dismissed it because when there's a murder, everyone's emotions get kicked into high gear. I didn't think of it as a clue to the murder."

"He probably would have confessed if you had charged Edna for the murder," Chelsea said.

"Most likely," David agreed. "In thinking about it, I believe killing Eugene was a crime of opportunity. Helga was spreading rumors about him and Edna, which Sirrus had started to believe—"

"Between the rumors and Eugene making excuses for Edna to get away from Sirrus when he would become a nuisance," Deborah said, "he began thinking Eugene was coming between them."

"Then, totally innocent, Helga forgot to sign her check and Eugene called her office," David said, "but Helga wasn't there to pick up because she had a doctor's appointment. Sirrus must have picked up the phone and realized Eugene was at the church. We'll never know if he knew Eugene was alone or if he let himself in with Helga's key or came in through the back door that Ruth had left unlocked. Whatever the case, Sirrus was overtaken by jealousy and went to the church to get rid of Eugene so that he could have Edna to himself." He held up his finger. "But he did have the presence of mind to establish an alibi for himself for the time of Helga's murder."

"What was that?" Deborah said.

"He made a point of telling me that he had caught a twelve-pound bass the morning Helga had disappeared," David said. "Mac told me to check with the taxidermist to see when Sirrus delivered it to be mounted. Turns out he had delivered it to the taxidermist Tuesday morning, not Wednesday."

"So he lied," Chelsea said, "to throw you off the trail."

"Yes, he did," David said. "He had gone fishing on the day of Eugene's murder. The next morning, he drugged his wife and then took her out to Pennsylvania to kill her in order to frame her for killing him. With Helga gone, that left Sirrus free himself to pursue Edna."

"And none of us saw it," Deborah said with a sigh. "I'm almost afraid of being paranoid now. In the church, we deal with so many people who come from such various backgrounds and have so many different needs. How many could, like Sirrus—"

"Or Van Dorn." Bogie slipped into the conversation while passing by with Dr. Dora Washington, his young and vivacious lady. "Look how far he fell."

"Or Helga Thorpe," Deborah said. "How ironic that her husband ended up killing Eugene because he believed a rumor that *she* started—"

"Then her husband ended up murdering her," Chelsea said. "Now that's ironic."

"The root cause of those murders was gossip," Deborah said. "It reminds me of something an Irish writer once said, 'Fire and swords are slow engines of destruction, compared to the tongue of a gossip.' That was certainly the case for poor Eugene."

The band had started another slow dance. Along with the bride and groom, Bogie and Doc Washington took to the floor.

"David, would you like to dance with Deborah?" Chelsea abruptly asked.

After an awkward silence, David led the reverend out onto the dance floor.

"Chelsea needs to work on her subtlety," Deborah said when David took her into his arms.

"Isn't this where you start your sermon?" he asked. "Give me your sales pitch to make me come to church with Chelsea?"

"I don't like sermons. I have found that when you give one to a reluctant audience, it tends to fall on deaf ears."

"You're exactly right," he said in a firm tone.

"But I am willing to talk to you, if you want."

"Talk all you want," he said. "I'll give you to the end of this dance."

"Why are you mad at God, Chief O'Callaghan? Is it because He let your father die of cancer?"

"Dad and I were just getting to the point that we were able to relate to each other as adults—as men," David said. "I know, it's a sin to be mad at God."

"It's okay to be mad at God."

Not expecting such a response, he pulled back until they were arms' length apart. He cocked his head at her. "Really?"

"God and I have fights all the time." She moved in closer. Placing her hands on his upper arms, she resumed their dance. "You should have heard me when I found out my husband had been murdered. Oh, I was mad at God for a good long time. I took a whole year off for sabbatical. How could I possibly preach about a God I was mad at? Just like you, I felt like things were finally perfect in my life. I was pastor of my own church. My husband and I had a beautiful son, and then God took my husband away from me. I felt like God had reached into my life with his giant hand and ripped the very foundation out from under me."

"Exactly." He swallowed. "Even after all that, you came back to being a minister?"

"Yes, I did," she said. "I still get mad at Him, and I still fight with God when things don't go my way, but that's all part of having a relationship with Him. It's just like having a relationship with anyone, Chief O'Callaghan. He doesn't want us to follow Him blindly. You can't get close to God if you don't ask Him questions."

She tapped his chest. "Like that night that I went over to the church because I saw the lights on. Everyone was saying that Helga had killed Eugene and ran off. But you couldn't accept that at face value. Something didn't add up and you had questions. So you continued digging and asking questions until you found the answer … and thank God you did."

"That's what a good detective does in any murder investigation," David said with a shrug of his shoulders.

"Don't you think you should do the same when you have questions about illness and evil and life and death and God?"

Outrageous shrieks caused them to turn to the bar where Marilyn Newton had Edna Parker doubled over in laughter. Marilyn was stunning in a shimmery black dress, while Edna was dressed in a purple cocktail gown.

"No one has a laugh like Marilyn Newton," Deborah smiled. "You can hear it all the way across the lake."

"Senator Fleming pulled strings to get a permit for her to throw Eugene a full Viking funeral," David said, "complete with setting fire to a boat on the lake to sink his ashes. She also got a fireworks permit. That's going to be some memorial service."

"I hear Bill Clark is running scared." Deborah's eyes narrowed. "As he should be."

"It's going to be an interesting election," he chuckled. "Once Marilyn throws her top into the ring, Clark's political career will be over."

"If anyone has a right to be angry with God, it's Marilyn," the pastor said in a low voice. "Her husband was at the church, devoting himself to what he loved and a crazy man came in and blew him away because he believed he was having an affair with her best friend, Edna."

Marilyn Newton was teaching the church's new administrator what resembled a two-step.

Staring at them, David said, "I still can't believe Sirrus fired three shots at Edna from eight feet away and missed her each time."

"I can," Deborah said. "We all prayed for God's protection for Edna and her girls when we realized who had killed Eugene, and He answered our prayers." She added, "Marilyn is taking Edna and the girls on her cruise with her. The girls are so excited." She smiled. "Chase is housesitting Marilyn's place. He'll be taking care of Marilyn's and Edna's dogs. He'll have a dog pack of six."

"You'd think Marilyn would blame Edna for …"

"It's not Edna's fault," Deborah said. "She feels guilty. Sure. How couldn't she? God didn't make it happen. He didn't want it to happen. But it did and somehow God will turn this tragedy around … Somehow, some good will come of it. Just like your father's death. … If it hasn't already." She leaned in to whisper. "Maybe the blessing from his death came in the form of your brother."

"Brother?" David's eyes met hers. "You know that Mac …" Her gaze was already answering his question.

"Your father and I had many conversations while he was dying," she said. "He prayed that Robin Spencer would find their son and that you would have the relationship with him that he never got to have. From what I've seen, God did answer his prayer."

She pulled away from him. "Song's over."

He realized that indeed the song had ended.

"Thank you for the dance, David," she said while walking away. "See you in church tomorrow."

Maybe.

In the middle of the dance floor, David watched the pastor join her son, who took her hand to whirl her back onto the floor.

The music had shifted into high gear and Ruth danced by in her wedding gown with her groom directly behind her.

"Hey, Chief, don't just stand there!" At the end of the Congo line, Marilyn grabbed David forcibly by the arm and placed his hand on her swaying hip. "Join the fun!"

"I love you, Mrs. Faraday."

"That's my name," she purred into his ear, "*do* wear it out." Wrapping his arms around her naked body, she laid her head on his chest and enjoyed the beating of his heart against her ear.

The only other sound in the honeymoon suite of the small ship was that of the ocean off the Alaskan coast.

"Ah, it was a perfect wedding." Archie closed her eyes to take in the warmth of his arms around her. "Just you, me, the pastor, and the whole Spencer police force. Who blabbed?"

"I think it was Gnarly," Mac said, even though he suspected it was Tonya who extracted the information from Bogie.

"That's okay," she said with a dreamy sigh. "The most important man was there." She kissed him. "Everything is just like I imagined—especially this honeymoon."

"Even though someone stole our main course for dinner tonight," he asked.

"Well, now you have a case to work on," she giggled. "The case of the Chilean Sea Bass."

"The captain is swearing up and down that none of his crew would steal the guests' main course of a special order dinner."

"Still, it was perfect ..." She kissed his hand. "My mind has been more focused on something else than the food." She laid back and gazed up at the stars through the skylight. The sky was so clear that she imagined she could see forever into the next galaxy. At least, she felt like she could.

"Alaskan Princess," she sighed. "Even the name of our ship is perfect. I certainly feel like a princess."

They were the lone passengers of the Alaskan Princess, a small cruise ship. Marilyn Newton had given Archie Monday ideas for a ten-day honeymoon cruise off the coast of Alaska. The ship had a crew of sixteen, and a passenger manifest that consisted of two people and one German shepherd. It was only the first day and they had already seen whales swimming off the side of the ship.

"You were so afraid that you'd be bored on this cruise." Archie asked, "Have you been bored yet?"

"It is a honeymoon." A wicked grin crossed Mac's face. "Though, I am curious about what happened to that sea bass. I may not be able to resist questioning witnesses and tracking down suspects." He grabbed her tightly and rolled over to kiss her passionately. "Starting with you, Mrs. Faraday."

She let out a high-pitched squeal while he tickled her ribs.

"What were you doing this afternoon before dinner?" Mac asked with an evil laugh.

Between screams of laughter, she declared, "I was alone ... in bed ... with my husband!"

Their laughter filled the cabin.

The door flew open.

Mac rolled over and dove for his gun in the bed stand.

With a shriek, Archie yanked the blankets up to cover herself.

Gnarly leapt from the middle of the floor to land on top of Mac. Pinning his master down by his shoulders onto the bed, the German shepherd expelled the sum of his stomach contents onto Mac's bare chest—the centerpiece of which was the half-digested, uncooked, Chilean Sea Bass.

Their special order gourmet dinner now resembled road kill.

"Eeeewwwwww!" Archie rolled over to the other side of the bed in an effort to escape the smelly slime that overtook the sweet scent of fresh flowers in their cabin. The discharge smelled like raw fish left outside in the blazing sun for three days.

Gnarly let out a moan before collapsing onto Mac's stomach and gazed imploringly up at him.

"Aw, poor thing. He's seasick." Archie reached over to stroke the sick dog's ears.

Speechless, Mac stared down at the half-digested dog food, biscuits, and seafood that covered his chest and stomach.

Gnarly belched.

"Look, dear," Mac said. "I solved the case of the Chilean Sea Bass. Case closed."

The End

THE GNARLY REHABILITATION PROGRAM

A GNARLY MYSTERY SHORT

By

LAUREN CARR

The bell over the top of the door at the Doggie Hut clang to signal the arrival of a customer; prompting Lizzy, the blonde receptionist, to look up from the business of ordering butter-scotch-scented doggie conditioner from her on-line supplier.

These two guys have to be looking for directions.

Set on the shores of Deep Creek Lake in western Maryland, Spencer's most luxurious pet salon didn't usually have patrons who appeared less groomed than their canine clients. Snapping her spearmint-flavored chewing gum, Lizzy noted that the bald-headed man wasn't in need of a haircut as much as he was in need of deodorant, which became apparent when he stepped up close to the reception desk and flashed her a mouth full of rotten teeth.

"Mac Faraday sent us to pick up his dog."

Lizzy looked him up and down before turning to his companion, who had his gray mop tied back into a loose ponytail. His beard was so matted that it didn't look like a comb could get through it.

At least their clothes are clean. Their khaki slacks and blue button-down shirts still had the factory folds in place.

"Excuse me," the bald man said in a sharp tone and snapped his fingers. "The dog. Mr. Faraday left orders for us to retrieve him as quickly as possible. We don't want to keep the big guy waiting, do we?" He uttered a low chuckle and once more flashed those rotten teeth at her.

"Sure." She popped a bubble in her chewing gum. "We'll get Gnarly for you right away. Today's visit will cost Mr. Faraday three-hundred-fifty-two dollars and thirty-five cents." Drumming her manicured fingertips on the desktop, she smiled at him from behind the reception desk.

He gestured with a wave of his hand. "Put it on Mr. Faraday's account."

Lizzy laughed. Her amusement caused the men's smiles to drop. "Mr. Faraday doesn't have an account." Folding her arms across her chest, she fell back in her seat.

After exchanging stunned expressions, the hairy man found his voice to ask, "What do you mean Mr. Faraday doesn't have an account? All rich guys have accounts. He brings his dog in every month—"

"His fiancée Archie Monday brings Gnarly in every month," Lizzy said. "*She* pays for his grooming. She went to a bridal shower today and told us that Mr. Faraday would be picking Gnarly up. I guess he decided to send you so that he could watch the game. A lot of our clients are being picked up early so that their parents can catch—"

"Put it on his broad—I mean his fiancée's account," the bald man ordered.

"She doesn't have an account either," Lizzy said. "Listen, the only way you're going to get Gnarly is to pay for his grooming which is three-hundred-fifty-two dollars and thity-five cents. We will accept a credit card."

The two men stepped back from the counter.

"What are we doing to do, Ernie?" the hairy man whined. "She won't let us take the dog."

"We can just steal him." Ernie fingered the weapon in his pocket. "I'll show her my gun and order her to turn the dog over."

The two men looked over at Lizzy, who eyed them while chewing her gum. Her eyes were narrowed to thin slits.

"Hey, Bert," Ernie whispered, "do you think she suspects we don't work for Mr. Faraday?"

"She'll know we don't work for him if you pull your gun on her," Bert replied. "How much money do you have?"

"Are you serious? We're crooks. We can't pay our victim's bill. Do you know how wrong that is?"

"We'll tack it onto the ransom," Bert said.

"If I had three hundred and fifty bucks to pay to give a dog a bath, I wouldn't be needing to kidnap rich people's dogs."

"Let's just forget it," Bert said.

"No," Ernie said, "We've put too much into this to just walk away. We got ourselves respectable clothes and did all the casing—following Faraday and that woman around with that dog—"

"Do you really think Faraday is going to pay a hundred thousand dollars to get that dog back?" Bert said. "He doesn't act that crazy about him."

"But his woman completely adores him," Ernie said. "If Faraday ever wants to get laid again, he'll pay up to get his stupid dog back."

"But before we can snatch that stupid dog and hold him for ransom, we need to pay three hundred and fifty bucks," Bert said.

"Not to worry." Ernie ushered his friend out the door.

"What are we going to do, Ernie?"

"We're crooks, aren't we? We're going to do what any self-respecting crook does when he needs money."

A half-hour—and a liquor store robbery later—Bert and Ernie returned to the Doggie Hut with cash to pay for their kidnap victim, who was waiting for them in the reception area.

When they walked through the door, Bert stepped back behind Ernie at the sight of the hundred pounds of newly washed and blown-dry fur, and shiny, white, sharp, teeth—freshly brushed with peanut butter flavored toothpaste. Wearing a bright red bandana around his neck, the black and sable German shepherd sat in the reception area. His majestic ears stood up tall upon his head while Gnarly locked his gaze on the two men and followed their movements around the room.

After taking their cash payment, Lizzy handed them a receipt.

"Leash," Bert whispered to Ernie.

"Where's his leash?" the bald-headed crook asked the receptionist.

Lizzy laughed. Once again seeing their perplexed expressions, she said, "This is *Gnarly.*" She gestured at the German shepherd studying them. "He has no leash."

"Do you have one we can use?" Ernie asked.

"Sure." Lizzy led them over to a rack that had a variety of leashes in lengths, thickness, and colors. "Pick one out."

Eying up the dog, who stared at them unblinkingly, the two men examined the leashes on the rack. "He looks like he needs a really big strong leash," Bert said. "We'll take this one." He picked out the thickest black leather leash he could find and stepped over to Gnarly.

"That will be twenty-seven-fifty," Lizzy called out.

Bert stopped with the leash over Gnarly's head. "Are you serious?"

"Yes." Lizzy held out her hand. "No money. No leash. No Gnarly."

"Pay the woman." Ernie grabbed the leash out of his hairy friend's hand. "I'll get the dog."

Bert dug the handful of bills from his pocket and went up to the counter while his partner in crime reached for Gnarly's collar. He snapped it to the ring and stepped over to the door with the leash in his hand. "Let's go," he called to his companion who was still waiting for his receipt.

"I'm coming."

Hurrying to leave before Mac Faraday arrived to catch them leaving with Archie Monday's beloved dog, the two men threw open the door and ran out into the parking lot of the lakeshore shopping plaza. Leash in hand, Ernie threw open the rear door of their van and gestured for the German shepherd to leap into the back, only to find the leash hanging limp in his hand. The end of the leash was slightly frayed where it had been cut through.

"Where's the dog, Ernie? I thought you got the dog."

"He must have bitten through the leash."

The two men ran back into the Doggie Hut to find Gnarly sitting in the same spot where they had left him. Lizzy was leaning on the reception desk with her chin in her hands. She snapped a bubble in his chewing gum. "Forget something?"

"He bit through the leash." Ernie showed her the frayed end of the now useless leash.

"Of course he did," she said. "Gnarly doesn't like leashes."

"Why didn't you tell me that when I paid twenty-seven bucks for this one?" Bert asked.

"Hey, I told you that Gnarly doesn't use a leash," Lizzy replied.

"But you didn't tell us why," Ernie said.

"You didn't ask," Lizzy noted.

Ernie was about to reach for his gun when his buddy pushed him back with a hand on his chest. "How are we supposed to get him out of here then?"

"You could try telling him to come," Lizzy said.

"And he'll follow us?" Bert asked.

"If he wants to. If not, well ..." Lizzy shrugged.

Bert told Ernie, "Tell him to come."

"I suggest you say please," Lizzy said.

"Gnarly," Bert said in an upbeat tone, "come."

Cocking his head to one side, Gnarly looked at the two men. He narrowed his eyes into a glare.

"Please," Bert added in a pleading tone.

Gnarly stood up and came to him. With a grin, Bert petted the German shepherd.

"Is there anything else you can tell us before we leave?" Ernie asked the receptionist.

"Make sure your health insurance is paid up."

Things were finally looking right for the bad guys when Gnarly followed them out the door.

Lizzy waited until they were gone before picking up the phone and hitting the redial button to call the last number she had spoken to. When Mac Faraday picked up, she announced, "The Gnarly Rehabilitation Program has begun."

Bert and Ernie had rented a small hunting cabin in the woods on the mountain overlooking Deep Creek Lake. It was pricey, but since Gnarly was well-known in the resort town, they needed an out of the way hideout in which to stash him until after Mac Faraday paid the ransom.

Then, they would be on easy street until they ran out of cash and had to move on to their next crime.

Coordinating a dog napping that doesn't work out according to plan can make you hungry. So the bad guys stopped to pick up a pizza from a takeout place on the way up the mountain.

When Gnarly tried to climb up into the front seat to help himself to the pizza, Ernie pushed him back. "You'll eat when we reach the hideout." Thinking about the gross canned food that they had for the dog, he uttered an evil chuckle. "This pizza is much too good for the likes of you, leash-eater."

With a huff, Gnarly fell back into the back seat, uttered a deep sigh, and glared at the criminal who rejoiced in teasing him with the food permeating the van with its delicious scent.

"Ah, the sweet smell of pizza hot from the oven." Ernie turned back to Gnarly. "You probably don't even know that you're a dog. Well, you are. You're a d-o-g, dog. As long as you're with us, you're going to be treated like one. So you better hope your master pays up fast to get you back to your pampered pooch life, dog. Because until we get our money, you're going to be treated like a dog. Got that, dog?"

In silence, Gnarly returned his glare.

Ernie checked his watch. "Step on it, Bert. The game starts in a couple of minutes. We'll tell Faraday to drop off the ransom after the Steelers bury the Redskins." He chuckled. "The Steelers and a big payoff. Can't get any better than this."

"I've got five hundred on the Steelers," Bert grinned. "Yep, this is going to be our big day."

The van turned off the main road and followed a gravel trail back to the cabin. Gingerly carrying the pizza box, Ernie opened the door and slid out. He had only one foot on the ground when a hundred pounds collided with his back to send him and the pizza box flying. Ernie landed face first into the gravel. The pizza box hit the ground and bounced.

The lid flew open and the pizza toppled out to land upside down in the grass.

Bert was running for the food while Ernie wrestled the dog who tore at his clothes before breaking away and running around the corner of the cabin.

"Our pizza!" Bert wailed. "What did you do?"

"The dog got the jump on me. Where'd that mutt go?"

"Really? The dog got the jump on you? Seriously?"

"Seriously," Ernie said with a growl. "That dog isn't going to live long enough to get back to Faraday. First chance I get—" He reached for his gun, but it wasn't in his pocket. "What happened to my gun?"

"Maybe the dog took it," Bert said with a scoff.

"Don't be ridiculous." Ernie searched the inside of the van.

"I don't know, Ernie. Have you seen the way he looks at us?"

The bald-headed crook stopped searching. "What are you saying, Bert?"

"I don't know." Bert shrugged. "He kind of looked at us like the way cops look at you when you see them and you suddenly slow down to below the speed limit. Like they know. He knows, Ernie. He knows we're bad guys and he's just waiting to take us out."

"He's a *dog*, Bert."

"Are you sure about that?" he replied. "Remember what that lady at the groomer's said? She told us to make sure our health insurance was paid up. Why would she say that?"

"Because she's a nut." Unable to find his gun, Ernie slammed the van door shut. "Pick up that pizza and let's go inside. I'm hungry."

"It's got dirt and grass in it."

"What else have we got to eat?"

"Hot dogs," Bert said. "Hot dogs and cheese curls."

"I guess we have to settle for that." Ernie chuckled. "But by the end of the day, after the Steelers kick the Redskins' butts, we'll be feeding on caviar." He slapped his buddy on the back and turned to the cabin.

"I don't like caviar, Ernie."

With a roll of his eyes, the bald-headed dog napper turned back to his partner. "Then you'll be feasting on champagne."

"Champagne gives me gas, Ernie," Bert whined. "You know that."

"Let's find that dog, tie him up, and call Faraday to ruin his day." Seeing that the cabin door was open, Ernie stopped. "Did you leave the door open when we left?"

"No, I shut and locked it," Bert said with a tremble in his voice.

"Who opened it?"

"The dog, Ernie. It was the dog. He must have opened it and went inside. What kind of dog opens doors … locked doors?" He looked around. "Where is he now?" With a gasp, he grabbed his partner in crime's arm. His hand trembled when he pointed toward the doorway.

There in the open doorway, Gnarly sat. His eyes were directed at the two men who had dognapped him. His tall ears stood erect like antenna picking up their very thoughts. After their eyes had all met, Gnarly stood up and turned to go back into the cabin.

"He's waiting for us, Ernie," Bert said in a low voice while backing up until his back was up against the side of the van.

Seeing his fear, Ernie growled. "What's wrong with you? Have you forgotten who we are?" He pound his chest with a fist. "We are the bad guys!" He pointed to the dog in the doorway. "He's our victim! He's afraid of us!"

Bert shook his head. "He doesn't look very scared to me, Ernie."

"Because he's too dumb to be scared." Ernie held up his finger in declaration. "But I promise you, Bert, by the end of the day, someone here is going to be crying in fear and it won't be me!"

"Are you sure about that?"

"It's only for a couple of hours until we collect the ransom from Faraday." Grabbing his partner by the arm, Ernie dragged him to the door. "Let's go. We're missing the game. I'm hungry and I wanna call Faraday with our ransom demand before the kick-off."

When the two men stepped into the cabin, they stood in shock. Taking in the scene that lay before them, they struggled to find their voices. It was Ernie who found it first.

"What the—" he cursed while stepping further into the cabin's great room.

The food that had been resting on the kitchen counter in grocery bags was strewn on the floor. The refrigerator door hung open. Their case of beer had been dragged out and the cans scattered everywhere. The plastic wrappers from the container of hot dogs lay empty.

Any food that had escaped consumption was drenched with dog urine.

The only food that appeared to have survived the siege was the canned dog food, which rested in a neat row on the kitchen table.

Wagging his tail, the culprit eyed them from where he was stretched out on the sofa.

"He did it, Ernie! Notice the cans of dog food? He's trying to send us a message."

Ernie shook him. "Bert, get hold of yourself. He's a *dog*. Dogs rummage for food. He saw the wrappers and he broke in and ate everything." Spying the overturned television, he let go of his partner to inspect the set. "The TV!" The electric cord was bitten into three pieces.

"He heard us talking about the game, Ernie," Bert said. "He did that on purpose to get back at us. You never should have teased him in the van and called him a dog. You got him mad at us."

"Dogs don't do things on purpose."

"Then why'd he wreck the TV and broke into the fridge and stole the hot dogs, Ernie?" Bert said. "And he shook up our beer."

"Only because he couldn't open the cans." Ernie picked up one of the cans of beer. "He's a dog. He's a spoiled mutt that's used to getting his own way. What you gotta do with a dog like that is show him who's boss." He turned to Gnarly. "Off the couch!"

Unfazed, Gnarly sat up on the sofa. His eyes were trained on Ernie and the can of beer that he wielded in his direction.

"I said off the couch!" Ernie pointed at the floor. "Now!"

"He's not doing it, Ernie."

"Because he doesn't know who's boss yet." Ernie said. "This will show him." He hurled the beer can at the large dog.

Without flinching, Gnarly caught the can in his mouth. While the two men stood in disbelief, the German shepherd closed his mouth with his powerful jaws, popping out both ends of the can to send beer flying out in a sudsy explosion. He then went on to crush the can flat in his jaws before spitting it out onto the floor.

With a roar, Gnarly charged at them from across the room to send them up onto the kitchen counter before returning to the sofa and lying down.

"Well," Bert said, "now we know who's boss."

"Give me that phone," Ernie said. "We're calling Faraday right now."

Bert dug the throw away burn phone from his pocket and handed it to Ernie. After dialing the number that he had written down for the multi-millionaire and retired homicide detective, Ernie waited while the phone rang on the other end of the line.

"Mac Faraday here," was the upbeat greeting.

"We have your dog," Ernie said in as menacing a tone as he could muster while trapped on top of the kitchen counter.

"How much?" the multi-millionaire replied.

"One hundred thousand, three-hundred and eighty-six dollars and eighty-five cents," Ernie said.

"Are you sure you can come up with that much cash in one hour?" Mac Faraday replied.

"Me?" Ernie squawked.

"Small used bills," Mac said. "I don't want the IRS asking embarrassing questions."

Ernie was still wrapping his head around the turn of events when Mac interjected, "Oh, I got a call on the other line. What's your phone number?"

"510-555-2948," Ernie replied.

"Who should I ask for?"

"Ernie."

"Okay, Ernie, I'll call you back in one hour and tell you where to bring Gnarly and the money," Mac said. "Oh, and don't call animal control. *They won't help you.*"

Ernie was still sputtering when Mac disconnected the call.

"Did you give Mac Faraday your name and our phone number?" Bert asked.

With a scream, the two men jumped down off the kitchen counter and ran around the room yelling at each other.

"How could you give him our phone number and your name?" Bert asked. "You're supposed to be the brains of this criminal team."

"He asked … it was reflex. Someone asks you for your name and phone number and you give it to them."

Crunch!

They turned back to the sofa.

During the dog nappers' hysteria, their kidnap victim had discovered a monster-sized can of cheese curls, opened it, spilled the cheesy food across the sofa, and proceeded to munch on it—smearing an orange stain from one end of the sofa to the other.

"Ernie?"

"Yeah, Bert?"

"You do realize the rental company will take the cost of cleaning that sofa out of our deposit?"

"We'll cover it up with a blanket and they'll never notice until we're long gone."

Rrripp!

Enraged by a cheese curl that attempted to escape by dropping back behind a cushion, Gnarly grabbed one corner of the back of the sofa and shook violently until he ripped the cover from the back of the sofa to expose the foamy cushion inside the upholstery.

"I don't think we can cover that up, Ernie."

The upholstery flew.

Spencer Manor

Balancing a giant bowl of popcorn and a bottle of beer, Police Chief David O'Callaghan hurried into the home theater in time to hear Mac Faraday disconnect the call from the kidnappers before turning his attention back to the football game between the Washington Redskins and the Pittsburgh Steelers. "What was that about animal control? What's Gnarly gotten into now?" Plopping down into the seat next to Mac, he offered him the bowl of popcorn.

"Oh, Gnarly's gotten picked up by a couple of dog nappers."

"Again?" David sat up. "Seriously?"

"We've just kicked-off." He gestured for the police chief to sit back and enjoy the game. "I'll check in with Gnarly at half-time."

"Are you sure they have that long?"

"That all depends on them." Mac took a drink from his bottle of beer. "Gnarly likes to play with his food first. Once they cease to amuse him, then they're in trouble."

"Now what are we going to do?" Bert asked. "Mac Faraday is going to call the police and give them our phone number and then they'll track the GPS and—those satellites see things!"

"That means we need to get out of here," Ernie said. "We need to make a run for it." He started gathering their belongings.

"What about the dog?" Bert looked over at the German shepherd who was still digging up the gutted sofa in search of escaped cheese curls.

"We'll shoot the dog," Ernie said. "He's been nothing but trouble since the beginning."

"You lost the gun. Remember? Once he's done eating the sofa, he may decide to start on us!" Spotting Gnarly, Bert let out a squawk. "Ernie, I don't think he wants us to leave."

Ernie looked up to see that Gnarly had abandoned the sofa and was now sitting at attention in front of the door leading out of the cabin. "He's just sitting there. What are you afraid of?" He waved his arm at Gnarly. "Git out of here! Back up on the couch!"

When he moved in closer to the dog, Gnarly charged to send both men running back into the kitchen and up onto the counter. Once they were in place, the dog returned to lay down in front of the door to block their escape.

312

"I don't think he wants us to leave, Ernie," Bert said.

"You think so, Bert?"

The dog nappers lost the feeling in their butts by the time the burn phone rang. Seeing the caller ID read Mac Faraday, Ernie snapped up the phone. "It's about time." He could hear the half-time of the football game he was missing playing in the background.

"Hey, Ernie, how's this life of crime working for you?" Mac asked.

"I'm going to kill your dog!"

"Good luck with that. Have you got the money?"

"He's got us trapped on the kitchen counter."

"I guess that means no," Mac said. "Too bad. I was looking forward to buying something pretty for my fiancée with this ransom. Well, maybe next time."

Ernie let loose with a string of cursing.

"Now, Ernie, that's no way to talk to your victim," Mac said. "Gotta go. Kick-off for the second half is about to start."

"Who's winning?" Ernie sputtered out.

"Who do you think?"

Ernie spewed out another round of cursing.

"I'll check in again at the end of the game. You're missing a great game."

With another curse, Ernie threw the phone down onto the floor. It broke into pieces.

"What did he say?" Bert asked.

"Redskins are winning."

"Damn! I've got five hundred on Pittsburgh. This day sucks, Ernie. It's all because we kidnapped that dog."

"That's right. It's that dog's fault!" Ernie yelled. "He's cost us close to four hundred dollars."

"Not to mention the security deposit on this cabin since he tore up the furniture."

"Forget the security deposit!"

"We might as well!"

"He's making us miss the game," Ernie screamed. "Hell! I wouldn't be surprised if it wasn't his fault the Steelers were losing! I'm going to kill him!"

"How?"

Ernie realized the small bathroom, with a tiny window over the back of the toilet, was the perfect cell in which to place their captive. With an evil laugh, he picked up one of the cans of beer and shook it in Gnarly's direction. The glint of the sunlight made the silver can sparkle.

Gnarly cocked his head.

"Want to play catch?" Ernie moved over to the bathroom door and opened it.

Gnarly stood up and moved in closer.

Ernie continued to shake the can to hold the dog's attention. "Come and get it. Come on, boy. Let's play. Fetch the can." He tossed the can so that it rolled into the bathroom.

Gnarly gave chase. As soon as he was inside the room, Ernie slammed the door shut on him.

Gnarly let out a low bark.

"Now who's the boss?" Ernie said with a loud cocky tone. He continued to laugh. "Let's see what Mac Faraday has to say about paying up now." He grabbed the phone and pieced it together to make the call.

The Steelers had just scored a touchdown to tie up the game when the phone rang in the home theater at Spencer Manor.

"I take it you got off the kitchen counter," Mac said.

"We have your dog under control now," Ernie said.

"Very good," Mac said. "Only fifty percent of the dog nappers have ever gotten that far. I hope you didn't lock him in the bathroom."

Ernie was silent.

"Of course, you're a smart man, Ernie. You wouldn't lock Gnarly in your only bathroom. ... Or would you?" After receiving no response, Mac said, "That's okay. Forty percent of the dog nappers who decide to lock him in the bathroom don't think about that either. Now, what are you going to do if you have to go?"

Ernie started sputtering.

"Listen, Ernie, you sound like a nice guy," Mac said. "I like you and don't want to see anything bad happen to you. So, I'm going to give you this piece of advice. Now, I don't do this for all of the dog nappers, but like I said, I like you. Whatever you do, don't go outside and drop your pants."

"Say what?" Ernie said with a squawk.

"I said don't turn your back on Gnarly and drop your pants."

"Why?"

"The last dog napper who did that is still in the hospital."

On the television, a Redskin player intercepted the ball from the Steelers. The crowd cheered.

Ernie was still translating Mac's warning when he said, "Gotta go. The Redskins are going all the way for a touchdown!"

Click!

His gaze locked on the player running down the length of the field with the football, the police chief, carrying a platter of Buffalo wings, plopped down in his seat. "Is Gnarly locked in the bathroom?"

"Not for long." Mac snatched a drummette from the platter and jumped out of his seat to cheer for the Redskin touchdown. After bumping fists with David, he dropped down onto the sofa and took a bite from the snack. "I hope Gnarly is kind and doesn't finish them off until after the game."

Ernie was alternating between pacing and stopping to cross his legs.

"I wouldn't go in there if I was you, Ernie," Bert said with a shake of his head.

"He's quiet," Ernie said. "Maybe he's asleep."

"I don't think he sleeps," Bert said. "What did Mr. Faraday mean about not going outside and dropping your pants?"

"He's trying to psyche me out," Ernie said with a growl. "Well, I refuse to be psyched out."

"The lady at the Doggie Hut warned us about keeping our health insurance paid up," Bert said. "And now Mr. Faraday said the other dognapper is still in the hospital. I think there's something weird about that dog, Ernie."

"He's a dog!" Grabbing his crotch, Ernie danced.

"Wasn't there a dog on the SEAL team that took out Osama Bin Laden?" Bert said. "Dogs can be pretty smart."

Ernie squeezed his legs together and crossed them at the knees. "I refuse to let a dog make me pee my pants!"

"In case you haven't noticed, Ernie, this dog ain't like other dogs." He lowered his voice. "I think he's a demon dog from hell."

Unable to stand it any longer, certainly not long enough to talk about it, Ernie tore out of the cabin and ran around to the woods behind the cabin. Leaping over a fallen tree, he barely made it to the tree line before stopping and unzipping his fly to relieve himself.

The feeling of relief washed over him.

Then, in the stillness of the quiet of nature, he heard a familiar click. It was not the type of click that you hear when someone steps on a tree branch to break it. It was a metal click, like that of someone cocking a gun.

Leaning against the tree, Ernie turned his head to look over his shoulder.

What's he doing outside? How—Ernie looked beyond where Gnarly was perched with his front paws on top of the fallen tree to the open bathroom window.

With his long tongue hanging out of the side of his open mouth, Gnarly looked like he was laughing at him—as he should with one paw placed on top of what Ernie recognized as his gun. Gnarly placed his other paw on top of gun at the trigger.

He wouldn't. He couldn't—

He saw Gnarly wink before jerking a claw to pull the trigger.

The football game was down to the two minute warning when the phone rang.

"That dog," Mac said with a curse. "Why couldn't he wait until the end of the game?"

"Maybe they can't get the game at the dog napper's place," David suggested while offering Mac a brownie.

Mac snatched up the phone and placed it to his ear. "What do you want?"

"Your dog made Ernie cry."

"How's that my problem?"

"Mr. Faraday," Bert sobbed, "come get your dog."

"Do you have my money?" Mac asked.

"No, but … pul-eze," Bert begged in a choked voice. "What kind of man are you? We're only a couple of small-time criminals trying to redistribute the wealth of the rich who have it to the poor who are motivationally challenged when it comes to working for a living. It's the American way! Pul-eeze! We'll do anything you want!"

"Hey, your buddy Ernie set the terms," Mac said with a small grin. "Where is Ernie?"

"He's up a tree with his pants around his ankles," Bert said. "Your dog shot him in the butt while he was taking a leak."

"Caught him with his pants down, huh?"

"That dog is vicious! He doesn't play by the rules."

"That's not true," Mac said. "When burglars come to our house to play hide-n-seek, Gnarly always counts to one hundred before going after them."

"Your dog chased me inside when I went out to help Ernie," Bert said. "I had to leave Ernie up in the tree. I had no choice but to save myself. I thought he was going to kill me. What kind of dog is he? He's supposed to be scared of us!"

"Where is he now?"

"I told you," Bert said. "He's up in a tree with his pants down."

"I meant Gnarly," Mac said.

"He's got a gun," Bert said. "He's crazy!"

"Of course he is," Mac replied. "I warned Ernie about turning his back on Gnarly and dropping his trousers."

"I'm not talking about Ernie being crazy," Bert said. "Your dog! He's got me trapped in the cabin! He shot Ernie in the butt! What kind of dog shoots guns? You have to help us."

"No, I don't," Mac said.

"Have you no compassion for your fellow man?" Bert said. "Due to our amoral psyche we are incapable of obeying the law. We deserve your understanding. Maybe if people like you offered mercy to people like Ernie and me for our social deficiencies instead of judging us when we threaten, rob, and steal from you, then we'd all get along more peaceably."

"You really do believe that, don't you?" Mac replied with a chuckle. "You and Ernie can think about that worldview while spending the night with your kidnap victim. See you in the morning."

"Wait! Don't hang up!" Bert blurted out. "We'll rob a bank tomorrow and pay you anything you want!" He sobbed. "Please, Mr. Faraday! I'm begging!"

Mac glanced over at the television. The Washington Redskins were ahead by two touchdowns and David was finishing his second brownie.

The police chief shrugged his shoulders. "Is Gnarly done playing with his new friends?"

"I guess so," Mac said before turning back to the phone. "Okay, Bert, here's what you need do. Do you know how to say, 'I confess …'"

The Washington Redskins won the game against the Pittsburgh Steelers: 36-20.

Bert and Ernie were waiting on the doorstep of the cabin when the police arrived ten minutes after the end of the game. Bert was sitting. Ernie was bent of the porch rail. Both men were sobbing.

Gnarly gave up his weapon after Mac gave him a bone stuffed with peanut butter.

Mac and Gnarly beat Archie home by five minutes.

"Don't say anything," Mac warned Gnarly after he climbed up onto his loveseat with his new bone. "You know how she is. She'll never let you out of her sight again if she finds out you got dognapped again." He paused. "On second thought, it would save her several thousands of dollars a year if she stopped taking you to the groomer."

Gnarly cocked his head at him.

"But then you'd stink and I'd have to give you a bath."

With a growl, Gnarly dropped his head.

Dressed in a flowery lilac dress, Archie swept through the door. "Ah, it was a lovely shower." She kissed Mac on the cheek on her way to greet Gnarly. "How was the game?"

"Great," Mac said. "Redskins won."

"Good." She bent over to give Gnarly a kiss on the top of the head. "Did you have fun at the groomers, Gnarls?" A frown crossed her face.

"They gave him the works," Mac said.

"What's that smell?"

"Huh?"

"He smells like beer." She brought her nose close to the dog's snout. "His breath smells like hot dogs and cheese curls. I ordered peanut butter." She whirled around to Mac. "What did you and David do to him?"

"Nothing," Mac said. "It's a new scented shampoo the groomer used. It's called the pub scent."

"Well, I don't like it," she said. "Take him back." With a wave of her hand, she ordered the two of them out the door. "I want a redo."

A smile crept to the corners of Mac's lips. "Back to the groomer, Gnarly."

The End

ATTENTION BOOK CLUB-BERS!

Want to add some excitement to your next book club meeting? Are you curious about this mystery author's theme regarding the dark side of perfection? Do you wonder where she picks up her inspiration for such interesting characters? What does she have planned next for J.J. and Poppy? Well, now is your chance to ask this international best-selling mystery writer, in person, you and your book club.

That's right. Lauren Carr is available to personally meet with your book club to discuss *Murder by Perfection* or any of her best-selling mystery novels. Discussion questions can be found and downloaded directly from the book pages on her website.

Don't worry if your club is meeting on the other side of the continent. Lauren can pop in to answer your questions via webcam. But, if your club is close enough, Lauren would love to personally meet with your group. Who know! She may even bring her muse Sterling along!

To invite Lauren Carr to your next book club meeting, visit www.mysterylady.net and fill out a request form with your club's details.

About the Author

Lauren Carr

Lauren Carr is the international best-selling author of the Thorny Rose, Lovers in Crime, Mac Faraday, and Chris Matheson Cold Case Mysteries—over twenty titles across four fast-paced mystery series filled with twists and turns!

Book reviewers and readers alike rave about how Lauren Carr seamlessly crosses genres to include mystery, suspense, crime fiction, police procedurals, romance, and humor.

Lauren is a popular speaker who has made appearances at schools, youth groups, and on author panels at conventions. She lives with her husband and two German Shepherds, including the real Sterling, on a mountain in Harpers Ferry, WV.

Visit Lauren Carr's website at www.mysterylady.net to learn more about Lauren and her upcoming mysteries.

CHECK OUT
LAUREN CARR'S MYSTERIES!

All of Lauren Carr's books are stand alone. However for those readers wanting to start at the beginning, here is the list of Lauren Carr's mysteries. The number next to the book title is the actual order in which the book was released.

Joshua Thornton Mysteries

Fans of the *Lovers in Crime Mysteries* may wish to read these two books which feature Joshua Thornton years before meeting Detective Cameron Gates. Also in these mysteries, readers will meet Joshua Thornton's five children before they had flown the nest.

1) A Small Case of Murder
2) A Reunion to Die For

Mac Faraday Mysteries

3) It's Murder, My Son
4) Old Loves Die Hard
5) Shades of Murder
    (introduces the Lovers in Crime: Joshua Thornton
    & Cameron Gates)
7) Blast from the Past
8) The Murders at Astaire Castle
9) The Lady Who Cried Murder
    (The Lovers in Crime make a guest appearance
    in this Mac Faraday Mystery)
10) Twelve to Murder
12) A Wedding and a Killing
13) Three Days to Forever

Lovers in Crime Mysteries

Thorny Rose Mysteries

Chris Matheson Cold Case Mysteries

A Lauren Carr Novel

CRIMES PAST

A Mac Faraday Mystery

It's a bittersweet reunion for Mac Faraday when members of his former homicide squad arrive at the Spencer Inn. While it is sweet to attend the wedding of a late colleague's daughter, it is a bitter reminder that the mother of the bride had been the victim of a double homicide.

The brutal slaying weighing heavy on his mind, Mac is anxious to explore every avenue for a break in the cold case—even a suggestion from disgraced former detective Louis Gannon that one of their former friends is the killer.

When the investigator is brutally slain, Mac Faraday rips open the cold case with a ruthless determination to reveal which of his friends is a cold-blooded murderer.

Coming Fall 2018!

Pre-Order Your Copy Today!